Gerry looked up through the branches of the maple tree at the clear autumn-blue sky.

He let his eyes follow the line of the soon-to-be crimson maple and dogwood trees down Stoneybridge's Main Street toward the clock tower, now sending out nine chimes over the town. People of all ages were walking along the road, going in and out of shops, carrying parcels, and warmly greeting one another. Gerry felt as if he'd stepped into a painting of a bygone era.

But he hadn't.

This was modern America.

He let out a deep breath of contentment. For all that it was a normal Monday morning, there seemed to be a celebratory feeling in the air. It was the same feeling he remembered from Main Street in his hometown when he was a kid.

He looked back up at the cat. "What a nice town you live in," he said. "It really does feel just like home."

Saving Main Street

THE STORE NEXT DOOR

A Heartwarming Contemporary Romance

Melanie Ann

Sara B. Bentley

ISBN: 9798657375954

All Scripture taken from the Authorized Version of the King James Bible

Disclaimer: Any and all errors are purely unintentional. With the exception of PJ KABOS Extra Virgin Olive Oil that is a real company (pjkabos.com)—this is a work of pure fiction. The characters and events portrayed in this book are fictitious. Any similarity to real persons, living or dead, is coincidental and not intended by the author.

Cover design by: Sara Bianca Bentley
(sarabiancabentley.com for more of her work)
Edited by: Paula Eykelhof/Helen Salter
Library of Congress Control Number: 2020910511
Printed in the United States of America

Reviews

THE STORE NEXT DOOR

"A sweet delight; as light and enjoyable as one of protagonist Aimee's
palmier biscuits."

Helen Salter, Librarian
Guildford, England

"Entering into the lives of Aimee and Gerry as they fall into a pure, authentic love is a rare and welcomed journey.
It is a delightfully entertaining romance novel."

Brenda Sansom, RMR, CRR, CMRS,ret.
Shalimar, Florida

"This book is absolutely fantastic!
The plot is interesting and gripping, the dialogues flow naturally, the language is rich, and the descriptions are fascinating.
I didn't want to put it down!"

Melita Vangelatou, Photographer/Author
Casablanca, Morocco
(Books: *India Through My Lens*; *Casablanca*; etc.)

Main Street, USA is America at the turn of the century—
the crossroads of an era.
The gas lamps and the electric lamp—the horse-drawn car
and auto car.

Main Street is everyone's hometown—
the heart line of America.

WALT DISNEY

Trivia from the Authors…

While reading the story, when you come upon mention of PJ Kabos Extra Virgin Olive Oil shop on Stoneybridge's Main Street, know that it *is* a real company. If you are an olive oil connoisseur and want to try a fabulous product—an extra virgin olive oil that you can trust to be the real deal (and which our characters like, too!)—check out PJ Kabos' website.

Website: pjkabos.com

As for now, welcome to Aimee and Gerry's world and to that of all the amazing characters living in the fictitious town—but one that is like so many real ones across America and the world—of Stoneybridge, Connecticut.
Happy reading!

Contact information:

For Melanie: MelanieAnnAuthor@gmail.com
For Sara: SaraBiancaBentley.com

Contents

1—The Patisserie

"See you tomorrow morning, Mayor." Aimee Hart waved good-bye to Mayor Brown—a sixty-something, retired NASCAR driver from South Carolina—as he opened the Patisserie's front door.

"Save me my usual," he said in his soft Southern drawl.

"As always." Aimee could count on her regular morning customers, all dear neighbors and friends. Just like the ten or so still seated at "their" tables staring expectantly over at Aimee for her answer. An answer she was reluctant to give.

"So, what shall I put you down for?" Mrs. Fonteyn repeated. Her pen was at the ready to jot Aimee's reply. Mrs. Fonteyn was a big woman with a big voice and a heart to match. She'd been an opera star at the Lincoln Center in New York City until retiring six years ago to Stoneybridge in Connecticut, which was more than a dozen train stops away from Grand Central Station in NYC. She was one of Aimee's favorite people.

But Aimee didn't feel that way about her question.

The whole town of Stoneybridge was taking bets as to what the new store next door would be. The unveiling was in two days and Mrs. Fonteyn was leading the guessing "committee."

Aimee forced a smile. After six months of noisy renovations to what used to be Mr. Wong's Dry Cleaning, the dreaded day of her bashed dreams was at hand.

"Honestly, as long as it isn't a pastry store or a bakery, I don't care what it is."

None of the townspeople, with the exception of her best friend and part-time employee, Becky—who was sworn to secrecy—knew that she'd been prepared to buy the store next door when it had come up for sale late last year. But the same week it was listed, that freak storm hit Stoneybridge, and the damage it caused to her Main Street store, then by the Coronavirus and the ensuing lockdown, not only killed her dream to purchase the property next door, but left her with a financial mess. The news that Mr. Wong's old dry cleaning store had been bought by someone from out of town had been excruciatingly hard for her to hear. She had coveted the space for as long as she could remember in order to expand the Patisserie.

But her answer wasn't good enough for Mrs. Fonteyn or for any of the ladies at her table. Aimee's gaze scanned each of them. She smiled.

Miss Maggie, a lady of Mrs. Fonteyn's age who owned the Treasure Trove where Becky worked in the mornings, was seated to her right in her garment of choice, one of her many gloriously colored muumuus. Dr. Lovejoy, an elegant thirty-something woman who never had a hair out of place and was one of the town's leading cardiologists, sat across from her. Forever jovial and ever optimistic, Penny sat to her left. A year or two younger than Aimee's thirty-one, Penny owned Sound Waves, the music store located three doors down. She taught piano there, too, and had become like a daughter to Mrs. Fonteyn. The four were enjoying their morning escargots—a French word for "snail" because of the pastry's spiral shape—and a cup of hot chocolate. Same table, same ladies, same order. Aimee loved the familiarity.

"Really, dear," encouraged Miss Maggie to the echoes of everyone at her table. "The betting is for fun. You must have some thoughts on the matter."

Aimee had thoughts, all right. They pretty much resembled the agitated ones of old-fashioned comic strip characters, featuring lots of stars, numbers, hashtags and percentage signs. They certainly weren't thoughts anyone enjoying breakfast in the Patisserie this morning would want to hear.

"Remember," Mrs. Fonteyn added. "The winner of the bet gets free tickets to the Lincoln Center and Puccini's opera, *La Bohème,* which is currently playing at The Met. Mr. and Mrs. Fitzgerald are even going to give the lucky winner a lift in their helicopter to the city and back again."

"Well, I wouldn't mind going to the Lincoln Center with or without the helicopter ride." Sheriff Jones spoke as he put down the newspaper he'd been reading at "his" armchair in the corner by the window. The women at Mrs. Fonteyn's table were momentarily distracted from Aimee.

Aimee sent Bob a smile of thanks. Everyone knew that the sheriff was an opera lover.

"I think..." He tapped the table with his fingertips. "The new place is going to be a bike shop," he declared with certainty. Lifting his big frame from what he called the most comfortable chair in town—a vintage, brushed-velvet, upholstered *fauteuil*—he placed the money for his café au lait on the table.

"Bob, no," Aimee objected. Same as she did every morning. "Knowing that you and your deputies are around keeping a watchful eye on all the shops, City Hall, churches, apartments, restaurants, parks and everything else on Main Street is payment enough."

"Aimee, I've told you. I'm a public servant. I can't accept your offering—"

"Bob Jones! I've known you since we were five-year-old children, when I first came to live with Grand-mère. You used to come and drink your morning milk with me at this very counter." She indicated the ornate, old oak counter. The scuff marks from where their shoes had kicked against it could still be seen. Bob's family had lived on the town's fringes. Aimee's French grandmother had become like his grandmother, too, and it was because of Grand-mère's love and encouragement that Bob was a sheriff today and not an inmate in a jail. "None of that nonsense," Aimee instructed with the same inflection her grandmother had used.

He smiled. Aimee knew he was remembering Grand-mère and her words. Exactly what she'd intended.

"Now go. I'll see you tomorrow. I have a patisserie to run." She spoke the way a sister might and put the money back in his hand. Everyone knew they were like brother and sister, so no one minded that Aimee always offered him his café au lait for free.

"And I've recorded your bet, Bob," Penny said, looking at him with the sweetest doe eyes. Everyone, except the sheriff himself, knew that Penny was in love with him.

Aimee wished they'd get their act together. They both loved music, Stoneybridge's historical society and children. But she knew better than to do any pushing about something as important as that. Two years ago, Aimee had been jilted at the altar by Professor Timothy Bainbridge. All the unwanted attention it had brought from her friends and neighbors had instilled in her a fear of involving people in her personal business—both romantic and professional. Likewise, she vowed never to intrude in the affairs of others. Certainly not Bob's.

"Thanks, Penny," he said. He could have been talking to Mrs. Fonteyn for all the emotion he put into it.

"I think you might win, Bob," Penny persisted. Aimee silently gave her kudos for trying. "Ever since the storm last year blew Mike's Bike Shop away, we haven't had one in town. You might just be taking that trip to the Lincoln Center." Everyone in the Patisserie—except for Bob—knew that Penny would go with him if he invited her.

"What's the *Incon Sester*?" little Tommy Floyd looked up and quietly asked Aimee. He was sitting at the counter with his mom, Valery, dunking *palmier* biscuits in a supersized mug of warm milk. Aimee had bought the huge mug expressly for the little boy. He'd been a very finicky eater even before his father passed away from complications caused by Thalassemia Anemia, an inherited blood disease which thankfully, Tommy didn't have. Now, coming to the Patisserie every morning and letting him eat those light, puff-pastry sugar cookies was the only way his mother—a high school friend of Aimee's—could get milk into her three-year-old son. Aimee smiled over at Valery. She felt sad for her friend. Valery had been so happily married to Nick. She had loved being a fulltime wife and mother. Thankfully, Nick had left her financially secure so she was still a fulltime mother to their child. She only helped out at her mother's florist shop whenever she was needed.

Aimee ruffled Tommy's red hair and stooped down to his level. "The *Lin-coln Cen-ter,*" she said, carefully pronouncing the words for him, "is a place in New York City that's something like our civic center, Tommy. Where talented people like Mrs.

Fonteyn sing and dance and play musical instruments to make people happy."

"Oh…" Tommy said and took a big gulp of his milk. Valery and Aimee exchanged a smile.

"So, Aimee," Miss Maggie persisted. "What do you honestly think the new store will be? You must've given it some thought, what with being its next-door neighbor."

Valery exchanged a commiserating glance with Aimee as Aimee stood and turned back to Miss Maggie. "As I said, as long as it's not a pastry store, I don't care what it is."

***

"Good girl," Gerry Mitchell said to his big dog, Cynthia. He'd tied her to the dog house under the maple tree outside the Patisserie. "Look at this nice place the owner of the shop fixed up for you."

The sign on the dog house made Gerry chuckle. He read it to Cynthia. "Welcome all dogs. Please make yourselves at home while your friend is inside the Patisserie. I will be out to take your order soon."

But Gerry's curly-haired, light brown dog wasn't looking or listening to him. Cynthia had her head turned upward in the direction of the cat-size treehouse about eight feet above.

Likewise, the orange-and-white feline proprietor of the house had his green eyes trained on Cynthia. Gerry really didn't understand how Cynthia could see anything through the long and scraggly hair that covered her eyes.

He brushed the hair back.

Her nose was wriggling and twitching.

Gerry had his answer.

Her tail started waving back and forth in a friendly wag. Cynthia liked cats, almost more than she liked dogs.

Gerry stretched his arm up to the cat, not needing to stand on the brick at the base of the tree, which he figured was there in order to reach the cat. "You're not going to take my dog's eyes out, are you, fella?" he asked. When the cat sniffed his hand, rubbed his cheek up against his thumb, and then went in a circle to find his favorite position in the sun, Gerry knew he wouldn't be a problem.

"Good boy, catch some Zs and your vitamin D for the day." Gerry looked up through the branches of the maple tree at the clear autumn-blue sky. He let his eyes follow the line of the soon-to-be crimson maple and dogwood trees down Stoneybridge's Main Street toward the clock tower, now sending out nine chimes over the town. People of all ages were walking along the road, going in and out of shops, carrying parcels, and warmly greeting one another. Gerry felt as if he'd stepped into a painting of a bygone era.

But he hadn't.

This was modern America.

He let out a deep breath of contentment. For all that it was a normal Monday morning, there seemed to be a celebratory feeling in the air. It was the same feeling he remembered from Main Street in his hometown when he was a kid. He looked back up at the cat. "What a nice town you live in," he said. "It really does feel just like home."

Gerry's rumbling stomach reminded him that he hadn't eaten anything since yesterday. He gave Cynthia a quick pat on her head, and then turned to the Patisserie. With its pink and white striped awnings and lavish window display, it would easily fit in Paris's Le Marais district. So would the offerings on the other side of the glass. Only a true professional pastry chef with years of study and experience in French pastry-making could create such exquisite sugar confections. Gerry had a huge appreciation for that kind of talent.

The *Chocolate Fraisier,* a sponge cake with airy Mousseline cream, a thin layer of marzipan, the perfect amount of chocolate shavings and a token strawberry on top looked superb. As did the hard-to-get-right French *macarons,* in at least ten different flavors and all the colors of the rainbow, stacked beside it. But it was *La Gourmandise,* a beautifully crafted pastry with chocolate slivers and fresh cream wrapped in layers of puff pastry that he thought he'd treat himself to this morning. He ran four miles every night just so he could enjoy such sugary, buttery sweets.

But when the town's sheriff opened the door of the Patisserie and brought with him the scent of freshly baked croissants, that decided it for Gerry.

A warm croissant—or maybe two—with fresh Connecticut blueberry jam. That was exactly what he wanted.

The sheriff tipped his peaked cap in greeting. Gerry returned the salutation with his ever-present Stetson.

"Good morning," he replied to the sheriff's welcoming nod and, taking the open door from him, stepped in.

***

Aimee looked up as a new customer entered—a tall man in a blue plaid shirt, jeans, a cowboy hat and boots. Aimee glanced away but as the "something" in a woman that likes the look of a certain man kicked in, her gaze immediately returned to him.

Aimee hadn't wasted a second glance on a man since being jilted by Timothy. But this man had that elusive quality that she liked. Although as tall as Bob, he was nothing like blond, blue-eyed Bob Jones. Rawboned and lean with dark hair and deep-set eyes, with the Stetson on his head and western boots covering his feet, he definitely fit Aimee's impression of a cowboy. He carried his six-foot-plus frame with the agility of a man who was at ease and accustomed to using his body.

She was intrigued.

But not for *her*, she quickly told herself. She was too busy for frivolities like dating. She was intrigued on behalf of her friend Becky. Too bad this man had shown up during the hours Becky was working at the Treasure Trove. The guy would definitely have set off Becky's "man alert."

"I don't blame Aimee for not wanting a bakery of any kind opening in the store next door," she heard Ruth Lovejoy declare and turned to her. "Besides, only a fool would open a pastry store or a bakery beside a lovely establishment like the Patisserie."

"Thank you, Ruth." Aimee deeply appreciated the doctor's words. "That gives me hope."

"Your Patisserie is a very special place. Not just for us but for all the people on Main Street and in Stoneybridge and the surrounding area."

Aimee smiled her thanks and let it encompass all her morning regulars, who murmured their agreement, before she went forward to greet the newcomer.

The assessment in his sharp, dark eyes—presumably at the conversation of praise for her shop that he'd walked in on—was one of respect, but with an enigmatic glimmer she couldn't quite decipher. Regardless, her own smile broadened.

She had to admit to herself that pre-Timothy, she would've done a wedding band search. But not the current Aimee, the injured her. "Hi, would you like to take a seat?" she asked. "Or would you prefer something for the road?" She suspected he was just passing through. As Becky might have said, "*This* kind of man is always just passing through."

"No, I'm staying." His gaze was direct and sure and oh, so male. Aimee felt more feminine than she had in the last two years. She kind of wished he wasn't staying. Serving up a croissant or a box of *macarons* to go would have been easier. She wiped the smile from her face at the same moment a movement outside the door caught her attention.

She saw a scruffy brown dog trying to peer inside through its hair-hidden eyes. Aimee smiled again. Dogs always made her smile. "Is that your dog?" she asked the man even though she knew it must be.

He nodded. "Cynthia." Glowing warmth radiated from the man's eyes as he looked at his dog.

Aimee removed her apron and reached for the small cookie jar she kept on a stand by the door. "Is it okay if I give her a doggie treat? I make them myself and I use only the finest ingredients." She was careful to ask dog owners before offering their animals a treat. Some dogs had health issues and were on stringent diets.

"Of course. I'm sure she's waiting." He nodded toward the dog house. "The sign did say you'd be out soon to take her order."

"Absolutely. Would you like to introduce me?"

"Well, now," he drawled. Not the soft southern sound of Mayor Brown, but more like the cowboy from out west she imagined him to be. "I'd like that very much." He sent her a lazy grin. "But in order to do that, I need to know your name, don't I?"

Was he flirting with her? She held his gaze for a second and reminded herself that he wasn't from around here; at least, she'd never seen him before. She could indulge herself for a few minutes. "Aimee."

"I'm Gerry."

One of her favorite names. "Spelled with a J or a G?"

"G. My mother was very cognizant of the fact that it's a diminutive of, among other names, George. And your name? A-M-Y?"

She shook her head. "No. Actually, it's A-I-M-E-E. My grandmother—Grand-mère—was French and insisted on my parents spelling it the old French way," she explained as she walked out the door. But she cringed as she heard the tongues of her customers start to wag just as quickly as the dog's tail.

Ever since Timothy, most of her friends were forever trying to urge Aimee into a new relationship. But she had no interest in that after Timothy made her the town's fool. Within a week of leaving her standing at the altar, he'd transferred to another university. She'd been left all alone to deal with everyone's sympathy and pity. Enduring a year and a half of it had become demoralizing. It was only six months ago that people had finally stopped telling her how sorry they were about the whole mess. As much as she loved living and working on Main Street, she felt a bit like a goldfish swimming around a bowl. Aimee never wanted to give people reason to talk about any aspect of her life again. She might not be able to keep them from observing and commenting, but she'd vowed never to let anyone see her "swimming" in romantic circles or to know too much about her private life. That most definitely included the financial mess she was currently in, too.

Cynthia started prancing around bringing Aimee's attention back to her. "Oh, my! You *are* a sweetheart," Aimee cooed as she rubbed Cynthia behind the long, curly hair of her ears and let the dog lick her hand.

"Cynthia. Sit!" Gerry held his hand up high. The dog immediately sat.

"That's impressive," Aimee said. "It's hard to get excited dogs to pay attention so well."

"Cynthia's good at paying attention." He grimaced as he tried over and over to move the long hair away from his dog's eyes, only to have it immediately fall back. "Just not at being groomed."

Aimee had already noticed how long and wild her hair was. But that didn't extend to her hygiene. "She smells nice and clean." She sniffed again. "Like cherries?"

The man named Gerry grinned sheepishly and shrugged his broad shoulders. "What can I say? She likes cherry-scented baths. Just runs a mile when she hears the sound of shears being brought out. I think she must've had a traumatic time being clipped when she was younger."

"You haven't had her since she was a puppy, then?"

"No." He knelt down to Cynthia's level. "About a year. I adopted her from an animal shelter." Cynthia put her front legs on his shoulders. There was complete adoration in her stance. And in Gerry's. "It was love at first sight." He gave Cynthia's nose a quick kiss and stood. "I can't imagine my life without her now."

Aimee got that. She glanced up at Louis and smiled. Her cat was keeping careful watch over them all from his perch in the tree. Kneeling down, Aimee brought the cookie jar to the dog's level. The *macarons* had to come out of the oven soon so she had to be quick about it. "Which would you like, Cynthia? The red ones are meat, and the yellow ones are cheese. Whoa!" The dog jumped forward and pushed her backward. Aimee lost her balance and her bottom bounced on the pavement. "Ouch!"

"Cynthia, down!" Gerry commanded. "I'm so sorry." He wrapped his hands around Aimee's arms and pulled her up as if she weighed no more than a single sheet of puff pastry. Aimee wondered what exactly he was apologizing for. His dog pushing her over or the way her heart started pounding at the touch of his hands. "I should have warned you. C-h-e-e-s-e," he spelled, "is her favorite food in the world. Are you okay?" he asked as he continued to keep his hands around her upper arms.

They were only about two inches apart, both standing in the shade of his Stetson's wide brim. Aimee wasn't thinking about cheese or meat or dogs or cats or her throbbing rump or even the *macarons* that had to come out of the oven soon. She was thinking how nice this man smelled, like cedar chips and Mexican hot chocolate. She was thinking what an attractive chin he had, angular but kind. She was thinking about his lips, how very pleasant they were. She was thinking… She stopped thinking.

She looked up. Mistake.

That got her thinking again.

This time about his eyes. Their corners reminded her of phyllo dough when it's baked—softly, perfectly crinkled. While his irises… She stopped. *No more thinking!*

"I'm fine," she heard herself say and quickly stepped back. "Really." She was glad he'd let go of her arms. The awareness in his gaze and the touch of his hands were unnerving.

He chuckled but she heard the same question in it that she was feeling herself. *What just happened between us?* So he'd been *thinking,* too! "I guess you know Cynthia's preference now."

"*Yellow—*" she was careful not to say the word cheese "—it is." Aimee opened the jar and gave Cynthia her treat. The large dog gobbled it in an eighth of a second.

"I'd say you've made a friend for life. So if my dog ever goes missing, I'll come here to find her. At your Patisserie," he said and reached up toward Louis.

"I don't think..." She tried to warn him not to touch Louis, who didn't normally let many adults get that close. But Aimee was left with her mouth hanging open when not only did Louis *not* swipe a claw at Gerry, or hightail it farther up the tree, but actually allowed him to rub his ears. Louis hadn't liked his ears touched since he'd had an infection in them when he was a kitten. If animals were good judges of character—and Louis had proven himself to be a very good judge—she knew this man had to be a decent person. Louis had given Gerry permission to do something *she* could hardly do.

"Your cat, I presume?"

She nodded. "Louis."

"Great name. Louis and I are already friends," Gerry said. He had no idea how impressive that was. Or how much it meant to Aimee.

She pointed to the door. "I've got an oven full of fresh *macarons* I've got to go take care of."

"I thought I smelled croissants earlier?"

"They came out fifteen minutes ago." She slanted him a smile. "Still fresh."

"Just what I'd like for breakfast. Two, please," he said and followed her inside.

***

Aimee couldn't believe it. "Come on, people!" she exclaimed when they walked back in and heard someone betting that a computer shop was moving in next door to her. "Are you still taking bets about what the new store might be? Seriously?"

While placing his hat on the shelf above the antique coat rack, Gerry joined in the fun and asked, "Well, if I may…?" At Miss Maggie's nod he said, "I think it's going to be a pet-grooming salon." He made no effort to hide his amusement.

"Write that down," Miss Maggie directed Penny. "The stranger named Gerry thinks it's going to be a pet-grooming salon," she said, and Aimee noticed that Miss Maggie's bespectacled eyes kept darting between Gerry and her.

"Got it!" Penny said. "Although I don't think Colin would be very pleased."

"Unless he's the one opening it," Valery softly pointed out as she wiped a milk mustache from Tommy's upper lip.

"Now there's a thought." Aimee had to admit it was a possibility. Except, unlike her, Colin was an open book. He shared his dreams with everyone. They all knew it was his ambition to someday open a pet-grooming salon on Main Street. A brick-and-mortar place to go along with his grooming van. "But wouldn't he tell us?"

"And miss all this hype?" Mrs. Fonteyn sounded positively incredulous. "It's worth a small fortune in free publicity."

"True," Aimee conceded. "Well, I guess we'll all find out in two days," she said, directing Gerry to the *fauteuil* by the window. "Now enough betting already." She was happy to see that Lucy, the college student who helped out five days a week, had cleaned the table.

"It's not every day that a new store opens, Aimee," Lucy reminded her from behind the counter. "Let them have their fun."

What was fun to her patrons was akin to having salt poured in a wound for Aimee. But, as Becky always reminded her, no one knew why the new store bothered her so much. Nobody realized that she'd been one storm away from buying that space—which was two times the size of her own—to merge with the Patisserie. She had to stop being so sensitive about it.

"Would you like something to drink to go with your croissants?" she asked Gerry as he sat in the large chair recently vacated by Bob. She couldn't help noticing how good he looked seated on its old velvet fabric. Funny how she'd never noticed that about Bob. But then Bob was more like a brother to her than…than what? That wasn't something she wanted to even *try* to answer.

"Yes, thanks, I'd like a coffee. A café au lait. Okay, *this* is very comfortable," Gerry said. He leaned his head back and stretched out his legs. They seemed to define long, longer and longest. His pointy cowboy boots settled out on the other side, and a great sigh of contentment escaped him. "I rarely find chairs in cafés that fit me. How thoughtful of you to provide one," he said.

"My grandmother, actually." Aimee felt the need to explain. "She bought this chair and its matching one—" she indicated the other chair by the fireplace "—in Paris just after the Second World War." She walked behind the counter and started washing her hands before filling Gerry's order.

He sat up, and she watched as he studied the chair. Most of the gilt on the wood was buffed to a dull sheen from use, but other than that, it was in good condition. "So it's at least an early twentieth-century *fauteuil*," he stated, making Aimee pause as she rubbed the soap thoroughly around her hands.

"You speak French?" She'd learned bits and pieces from her grand-mère and had also taken high-school French. She'd been promising herself for years that she'd become a serious student one day. It was her dream to live in Paris—while studying at Le Cordon Bleu. But there hadn't been the time. And with trying to repay the money she'd reluctantly been forced to borrow from her uncle, there wouldn't be the time, or the money, for quite a while.

He nodded. "I learned the basics in high school and then, after living in Paris for a couple of years, picked up a pretty good knowledge of comfortable everyday French."

"To live in Paris…that's always been *your* dream, Aimee, hasn't it?" Miss Maggie commented, echoing Aimee's own thought.

Aimee turned to her and was about to agree. But she saw Miss Maggie glance between her and Gerry with twitching lips. Aimee knew that, thanks to her momentary negligence, Miss Maggie would make her the romantic talk of Main Street by lunchtime. As the ladies at her table all stood to go, the bright look in their eyes and knowing smiles spoke of the same thing. Aimee knew the best course of action was none at all.

"Please put it on my tab." Miss Maggie indicated the entire table. "It's my turn today."

Aimee nodded her appreciation. The ladies always took turns paying to make her life easier.

"One bill instead of four," Mrs. Fonteyn twittered just as she did every morning.

"I'll send Becky over in an hour," Miss Maggie warned, "to pick up my fresh strawberry *macarons*."

"*Macarons*!" Aimee had forgotten the *macarons* in the oven. She grabbed a towel to dry her hands and dashed toward the kitchen.

"Don't you dare burn my lovely cookies," Miss Maggie called out good-naturedly.

"I was about to come get you." Mark—another college student who worked part-time—said as Aimee burst through the door into the kitchen. He was boxing up the croissants for the student union coffee shops at the town's two colleges. It was his job to deliver them before the eleven o'clock rush. Aimee always delivered an earlier batch at quarter past seven.

She looked in the oven. "Perfect," she breathed. Tossing the hand towel into the bin, she reached for her oven mitts and removed the strawberry *macarons*. The strawberry-and-almond aroma that wafted out from the thin meringue wafers always made Aimee think of Grand-mère. She didn't need any other reminders of her beloved grandmother. These signature cookies personified the dear, sweet lady who had given Aimee a home after her mother, Cleo—Grand-mère's daughter—died in a boating accident shortly after Aimee's father, a decorated Coast Guard officer, was killed in a drug raid that went wrong.

Putting them on the rack to cool, Aimee sent Mark an encouraging smile. "Only another hundred croissants to box," she sang out as he sent her a "give me a break" look in response. She shrugged her shoulders and returned to the front of the café. She knew Mark really didn't mind boxing.

She was happy to see that Lucy was finishing Gerry's order. "I'll take it," she said. She loved serving her customers, loved watching their expressions as they got the first glimpse of what they'd ordered. And since Miss Maggie and company were now gone, she figured why not see what else he might be able to tell her about his time in Paris? Aimee loved travelling vicariously through other people's stories. She would make it to the City of Lights herself. Someday...

But for the moment—she was quick to convince herself—hearing Gerry's stories about Paris was the only reason she wanted to spend any more time with him. Picking up the tray, she walked over to his table.

2—Difficult Relatives

"So you want to live in Paris?" Gerry asked Aimee as she brought his order. It was as if there'd been no break in their conversation. He hadn't yet looked at his tray; he was only looking at her with those deep, dark eyes.

She gave a nervous laugh. "A pie-in-the-sky dream," she said. She didn't add that she seemed to have lots of those.

He grinned. "The perfect pun in a pastry shop," he said. "It's a good dream to have. Few places in the world, except wherever home is, compare," Gerry said and finally looked at his plate. He tilted his head to the right. Aimee couldn't tell what he was thinking until he took a bite of his croissant. Then she didn't have to guess. "Whoa! This is great!" he exclaimed and she felt fingers of pride walk up her spine as he went on to seriously critique it. "Buttery and flaky, the right texture and color. I'd say it's even more buttery and flakier than the ones I ate in Paris. And the presentation—" he pointed to the tastefully decorated enamel tray, complete with an iris sitting with old-world Parisian charm in a cut-crystal vase "—is *exquis*."

She had to shake the impulse to giggle. "Exquisite. Now there's a compliment."

"This croissant is the *pièce de résistance*. Truly fabulous." People had told her that before but she didn't mind hearing it again.

"Thanks." The extra time she spent rolling out the dough by hand and spreading the butter between the layers made such a difference. Plus Grand-mère's old ovens. There was something special about them; they made everything taste extra-good.

"A well-deserved compliment." He took another bite, then a sip of his café au lait.

"Did you eat your way around Paris?" she asked.

"Well, let's put it like this. I gained twenty pounds in the two years I was there."

Her brows rose as she quickly scanned his body. He didn't look as if he had an extra ounce on him.

"I've lost it all."

She felt the blood rush to her cheeks. "I'm sorry. I— "

"It's okay," he said as he glanced freely down her body, too. She had it coming. She stopped breathing for a moment. When his gaze met hers again, she could tell from the way his eyes brightened that he liked what he saw. "Only fair."

She smiled and started breathing again. "Only fair," She agreed. Still, she was glad she'd worn her dark blue jeans today. The confidence they gave her probably kept her from bolting.

But she honestly didn't want to bolt. She wanted to find out more about his years in Paris. Not even her reaction to him would keep her from asking. He would be leaving soon, after all, wouldn't he?

"What would you say you liked most about Paris?" To Aimee's own surprise, her voice sounded just about normal.

"The cafés, the bread, the language, the music, the way the Seine flows through the city. The countryside around Paris. And the antiques." He patted the arm of the chair. "Do you have any idea where this came from?"

"Grand-mère said from a chateau."

"I thought so. Only the very wealthy had this kind of upholstered armchair in older days." He ran his hand over the seam where the material was connected to the wood. "The workmanship is superb."

"Do you know about furniture?" Aimee asked. A cowboy who'd lived in Paris and knew about fine old French furniture? Now there was an interesting combination. Although, she realized that thinking he was a cowboy was based purely on his wearing a Stetson, cowboy boots and his body type. He was probably as far removed from being a real cowboy as she was. She thought to ask him where he was from, but decided against it. *Did she really want to know?* she asked herself. *No, not really.*

"Just from watching reruns of the *Antiques Roadshow* on TV."

She laughed. "And here I thought it was something you studied in France."

That brief glimmer she'd seen when he first walked into her café was back. She now thought it might mean that he wanted to say something, explain something. He opened his mouth to speak but closed it and left the words unsaid. Shaking his head, he gave his attention back to the croissants on his plate. "No."

In a town with two colleges, the next logical question from her might have been, "Did you study anything while you were there, and if so what?" But for some reason Aimee got the impression that he didn't want those questions asked.

She was glad.

She really didn't want to know either.

Why? Because he was too interesting to her, made too many warning bells go off in her head and made her knees go weak in a way they hadn't…well, ever. No. She assumed Gerry was just passing through town and she was happy about that. Weak knees were the prelude to turning her into a pathetic woman. She didn't need that. Not ever *ever* again. "Well, enjoy your breakfast," she said and with Lucy taking care of the front of the store, Aimee escaped to the back.

She told herself she had some chocolate *macarons* she had to get to baking and then fill the cooling strawberry wafers for Miss Maggie's ten o'clock "fix." But she knew she was really hiding out from a man she could've fallen for if their paths had crossed longer than half an hour one Monday morning on Main Street in Stoneybridge, Connecticut.

She only hoped the next time a guy Becky might label "hot" came around, Becky would be around, too. Becky had a very carefree attitude to dating. She either broke up with a guy every month or he broke up with her. She dated for the fun of it. Aimee wasn't like that. She didn't do casual. It was all or nothing and so far, it had been all…then, nothing.

Aimee took the farm-fresh, free-range eggs out of the fridge and started cracking them, separating the yolks from the whites to make the meringue. She knew that she definitely didn't need man complications in her life. She'd cracked as easily as an eggshell two years ago; she couldn't go through that again. Half an hour of flirting was enough to last her another two years.

***

Fifteen minutes later, Gerry walked out of the Patisserie. As he paused to untie Cynthia, several of the townsfolk were trying to peer through the soaped-over window of the new store...

His new store—Uncle Gerry's Cakerie.

He could feel his smile widening as he watched them turn their heads this way and that, as they futilely rubbed at the window that was soaped from the inside. Their antics, and their curiosity, made him happy. Gerry's philosophy in life was to bring as much joy, delight and whimsy into people's lives as he could. He tried not to take life too seriously; the few times he had, it'd backfired on him.

Since he'd needed to be on hand to close down his Los Angeles store, he'd given the designing and refurbishing of the Connecticut Cakerie over to Industrial Interior Designs, Inc. Consequently, no one in Stoneybridge knew he was the proprietor of Main Street's newest establishment. Other than early this morning when he'd hung out the sign announcing the "Grand Opening" of the store in two days and taken photos of Main Street for the cake he was designing for the great event, the only time he'd visited had been the evening he'd bought the old dry-cleaning store six months ago. Even though he realized that his absence during the renovations would result in some extra kinks to work out, Gerry liked the way keeping the Cakerie a secret from the people of Stoneybridge had turned out. It was amusing hearing them try to figure out what the new store might be. Kind of like guessing what Santa Claus might leave them on Christmas Eve.

It wasn't about free publicity, despite what the lady in the Patisserie had said. The very idea made a shiver run down Gerry's spine. Soaping over the windows and not revealing what type of store it was until the grand opening might seem to be a marketing scheme—and from the standpoint of letting people in the area know about the store, he supposed that in an old-fashioned way, it probably was—but it really had nothing to do with hard sell. It was just about fun; being friendly and hospitable.

He would advertise, for sure. He'd already started to do that in area newspapers, and with appropriate bloggers and vloggers, inviting one and all to the Grand Opening and the physical uncovering of the store.

But with Stoneybridge's townsfolk it was different. This was about presenting the people of his new town with the gift of a cake shop on *their* Main Street and personally inviting and welcoming them to it. From the oldest "kid"—who remembered when car dealerships soaped over their windows each fall to conceal the new models before the "grand reveal"—to the youngest, no one could wait to find out exactly what the new place would be.

Gerry looked back at the *macaron* display in the Patisserie window.

Well, maybe one person could do without the news.

A pretty woman with the most charming dimple to the left of her perfect mouth. A woman named Aimee.

Gerry knelt down and rubbed Cynthia behind her ears. "What's the beautiful owner of the Patisserie going to do, girl, when she finds out the store next door is going to be a cake shop? Our very own Uncle Gerry's Cakerie?"

Cynthia pranced around. Putting her nose in his hand, she gave a great big whine.

"Yeah, that's what I think, too," Gerry said as a new group of people tried to see through the few deliberately left cracks in the soap that hid what was behind it. They couldn't see anything, really. From what they could make out, the store could be a hobby shop, a bookstore or even a beauty salon.

Their anticipation and expectations, their betting and wondering made Gerry smile. Not even his trepidation of what Aimee would think when a bakery—well, cakerie actually—opened next to her French pastry shop and café could diminish his hopes for his new store.

Gerry had a lot riding on the success of his shop. Moving the financially stressed company from Los Angeles to his home state of Connecticut was a huge monetary and emotional strain in a long list of worrying things. If it hadn't been for his nationwide online sales, his business wouldn't have survived the events of the last year. Other than wanting to move back to Connecticut in order to be close to his sister and her children—which was his primary reason—he'd taken the plunge because of a great opportunity that had landed on his proverbial plate.

Last year, the CEO of Northeast Supermarket Chain had been vacationing in Los Angeles with his family when he'd come into Uncle Gerry's Cakerie. He'd immediately loved the over-the-top, celebratory cakes. He thought Gerry's creations would be perfect for the in-house "Main Street Bakery" he was pushing his supermarket chain to inaugurate and he told Gerry he would personally support Gerry's bid.

The only thing was...Gerry had to move his bakery to Connecticut—or any New England state—to qualify as a candidate for the contract. Not just that, he had to open his flagship store on an actual Main Street.

With his personal life in California in shambles—and likewise his sister's in Connecticut—the timing couldn't have been better. Gerry's romantic problems had even carried over to his business. All these things combined to motivate him to go for it and transfer his life from LA to New England.

But not just any New England state.

Home.

Gerry would have liked to find a storefront property in his hometown of Nazareth—located about forty minutes away from Stoneybridge—since his sister, Sabrina, still lived there. But Nazareth was several train stops closer to New York City;

the price for the one and only Main Street property available there was out of his range. However, a feasibility study performed by one of the best marketing agencies on the East Coast showed that Stoneybridge was within driving range of a good fifty million people and a very wise investment for his company, regardless of whether he won the supermarket bid or not.

He looked at the Patisserie again.

In truth, he would've preferred being at the other end of Stoneybridge's Main Street. That would have put some distance between him and the Patisserie. But nothing else was available. It was either this or nothing.

And yet, the same aspect of Gerry's personality that saw the bright side of almost every situation refused to let him feel too concerned. For one thing, his target audience was very different from the Patisserie's. Where the Patisserie sold classic pastries based on recipes that went back decades and sometimes hundreds of years, Gerry offered big, over-the-counter cakes and cookies and even larger bespoke ones. He often described Uncle Gerry's Cakerie products as "edible fantasy" and a surefire way to bring smiles to people of all ages. If someone wanted a huge cake in the shape of a castle, he would make it; if someone wanted a cake in the shape of a golf course, he would ask which one; if someone wanted a favorite computer game turned into an edible fantasy, Gerry would do it. The only recipe he followed was that his cakes had to make people happy.

After untying Cynthia, he reached up to the cat staring down at them. The cat started purring, making Cynthia bark and Gerry laugh. "You don't mind us coming in next door, do you, boy?" he asked as he rubbed the cat's chin.

Louis purred even more loudly.

Gerry stretched up and whispered, "Would you put in a good word for us with your mistress?"

The orange-and-white cat blinked his handsome green eyes.

"Thank you."

But as Cynthia and Gerry walked away, a nagging feeling persisted—that the young Patisserie owner would be very upset when she found out that the only shop she *didn't* want opening next door was the very one moving in.

As always, Cynthia picked up on his mood and pranced around him. "Everything will be all right, girl," Gerry assured her. "You'll see."

If nothing else, Gerry liked his next-door neighbor. He didn't mind answering her questions about Paris as long as it kept her expressive brown eyes sparkling and trained on him. He was especially intrigued because, unlike a lot of women, she'd been genuinely interested in what he had to say. It wasn't just an excuse to talk to him.

But what sealed the deal for Gerry was that cookie jar filled with homemade doggie treats. Cynthia had even given Aimee's hand her lick of approval.

Not that he was interested in Aimee *that* way. "Been there, done that, don't want to do it again," he told his dog as she raised her head to look at him. At least Gerry supposed Cynthia was looking at him. "Besides, she'll probably hate me when she sees our shop."

As he and Cynthia walked down Main Street toward the Cape Cod-style cottage he'd rented on a parallel road—only a five minute walk from his store—Gerry didn't try to figure out why that bothered him so much.

***

"So tell me! Tell me all!" Becky buzzed over to Aimee that afternoon at the start of her shift, tying her apron around her super-slender waist. Becky could eat anything without gaining weight and had more energy than anyone Aimee knew. And that was with sleeping only five hours a night.

"Tell you what?" Aimee asked as she continued to pipe icing onto the pistachio *macarons'* halves. But she knew what Becky was asking. Aimee had no doubt that Miss Maggie had gone back to the Treasure Trove and told her all about the stranger in the Patisserie that morning.

"About 'hot guy'!"

Aimee wasn't surprised that was how Becky would describe Gerry. "There's nothing to tell."

"There is, according to Miss Maggie. She was raving about him," Becky said and carefully pieced the two halves of the *macarons* together. She was extremely gentle with the delicate wafers and held the Patisserie's record for breaking the fewest. She even beat Aimee. Becky somehow managed to have a petit woman's delicacy in a five foot, nine inch frame. There wasn't a clumsy bone in her body. "And I saw him with his dog after he left the shop. The guy is *so* hot. If anyone was going to get through your 'man alarm,' it would definitely be a striking guy like him."

Aimee laughed. "Appearances can be deceiving."

"True. But not this time. Miss Maggie said he reminded her of the old Marlboro Man advertisements. She said he had the classic American cowboy look about him."

So I'm not the only one who thought he could be a cowboy! It somehow pleased Aimee.

"Miss Maggie raved about him," Becky repeated and pointed to the *macarons*. "She said the inside of him had to be as good as the outside."

Aimee raised her eyebrows. "Please. It's fine to think a man looks like a cowboy but comparing him to a *macaron*?"

"Well! What's the sense of him looking good on the outside if he isn't just as good on the inside?"

"Becky!" Aimee held up her hand. "Stop while you're ahead!"

Becky laughed. "Miss Maggie said he joined in the fun. That he bet the new store would be a pet-grooming salon. But most important—" Becky wiggled her thick, dark eyebrows "—she told me about the chemistry she saw bouncing between you two."

Aimee huffed and went back to piping the filling. "Miss Maggie needs to get her glasses checked. There was absolutely no chemistry in the Patisserie this morning, other than that which turns raw ingredients into edible delicacies."

"But you asked his name," Becky stated.

"Only so he could introduce me to his dog."

"And it's…"

"Cynthia."

Becky bumped her hip against Aimee's. "Not the dog's name, bozo!"

"Oh," Aimee hedged. "Can't remember." Of course, she remembered but she wasn't going to tell Becky. It was Gerry. Gerry with a G.

"You're hopeless!" Becky wailed and wagged her finger. "If you don't jump headfirst out of your comfort zone, Aimee Hart, and get back in the dating game, you're going to turn into an old pastry maid."

Aimee placed the pastry bag on the counter and faced Becky. It wasn't that she didn't *want* to date. "What would be the point, Becky? You know I don't have time right now. I've got to get that supermarket contract if I have any hope of keeping the store. If Uncle Cain and his wife have their way, they'll be part-owners by Thanksgiving." After the hundred-year-old dead elm had crashed through the back wall of the kitchen during that microburst that hit Stoneybridge the previous year, Aimee had discovered an unknown clause in her grandmother's insurance policy. The damage caused by the *dead* tree, which included flooding, wasn't covered. Not even the hefty deposit she'd been prepared to pay for the property next door was enough to repair and renovate the Patisserie. And with the Patisserie so badly damaged, Aimee couldn't get a loan to complete the untimely renovations.

In desperation, Aimee had done the worst possible thing. She'd borrowed a great deal of money from her wealthy but very stingy Uncle Cain and his overbearing wife Gertrude—"Grasping Gertrude" was how Aimee often described her. In hindsight, there might have been other options, but at the time she couldn't think of any. And now, if Aimee didn't have the funds to repay him by the due date, she was certain he and Grasping Gertrude would demand a stake in the Patisserie. She shuddered at the thought.

Ironically, the repayment deadline this year happened to fall on what had been Aimee's favorite day of the year ever since she was a little girl—the day before Thanksgiving. The start of the holiday season! She's always loved the preparations for the holidays as much, if not more, than the actual days. Now, her only hope was in scoring a big contract with Northeast Supermarket Chain for the in-house Main Street

Bakery they were inaugurating. She was hoping the age and reputation of the Patisserie would be a major selling point. With no helpful connections, Aimee knew the supermarket contract was a long shot but one she felt she had to try for—especially since there was no way her Uncle Cain—or more likely, Aunt Gertrude—would grant her an extension on the loan.

Becky paused in piecing *macarons* together; a really unusual occurrence for Becky who was never still. "Aimee, there's always going to be an excuse not to date." She lowered her voice. "Not all men are like the Prof."

Aimee gave a little smile. Becky always referred to Professor Timothy Bainbridge as the "Prof." She drew in a deep breath before answering her friend. "I know, Becky. But I just don't think I could stand it still if things were to turn sour with another man. To risk putting myself in the position of being the talk of the town again, well, that's not something I can even begin to contemplate."

Becky pursed her lips. Aimee could tell she wanted to say something other than what she said. "It was ages ago, Aimee."

"Doesn't feel that long ago."

"Two years."

Aimee nodded. "Grand-mère had just died."

"Bad timing. The Prof was a bad apple. Maybe 'hot guy' isn't."

"He was just passing through." At least, she assumed so.

"Fair enough. But promise me that if another hot guy like him isn't just 'passing through' you'll at least give him, and yourself, a chance."

Aimee sighed. "I'll try." She didn't think she actually would. But she knew her best friend. Becky wouldn't leave the subject alone if she didn't make *some* concession. To say she'd make an effort was better than saying nothing or saying never. And it would placate Becky. For a while.

"Good." Becky went back to piecing the *macaron* halves together. "Besides, what's wrong with a little harmless flirtation when a handsome stranger walks through your door? The good Lord knows that since you spend every waking moment either in the café—" she motioned to the front of the store "—or here in the kitchen, the only way a man could meet you would be to walk through the Patisserie door."

"Boss," Mark interrupted from the doorway. "Your uncle's here."

Aimee's startled gaze flew to Becky's. Becky grimaced. "Not the man I had in mind," she said.

"What could bring him here from his lair in Manhattan?" Aimee asked. "He normally avoids venturing this way."

"Yeah. He never used to visit his mom. Ever."

"Not even at Christmas," Aimee agreed while untying her apron. "He and his wife preferred skiing in Aspen with her family and their friends to spending Christmas with us. What could he want?"

"Boss, you better do something." Mark glanced out the front window before turning back to the kitchen. "Louis isn't too happy he's here." He giggled. "He's sitting in his treehouse growling. It's entertaining to everyone except your uncle, who's refusing to walk under him to come in." Mark held up the store's phone—his hand was covering the mouth piece—and giggled again. "He called for an escort past the cat."

"That cat definitely has a sixth sense about people," murmured Becky.

The admiration in her voice for their feline guard made Aimee smile. "And just think…it's Uncle Cain's wife who Louis really hates." Turning to Mark, Aimee said, "Please escort my uncle past Louis into the Patisserie and ask him to come to my office."

Mark clicked his tongue. "Got it, boss."

Alone with Becky again, Aimee said, "I still have a month and a half before the loan is due."

Becky removed her gloves and gave Aimee's shoulder a little squeeze. "Be strong, my friend. I'll go handle the front and give you some privacy."

***

As she waited for her uncle in her small, tastefully decorated office, Aimee took Louis's warning to heart. Uncle Cain never brought good news. He was up to something. She reached for her ever-present glass of water. Took a sip. It helped calm the nasty black flies that seemed to be racing around her stomach.

She looked over at Grand-mère's cookbooks. All twenty leather-bound volumes were kept behind lock and key in the antique French armoire to the right of her desk. She breathed out yet another prayer of thanksgiving that they hadn't been damaged by the storm's wrath. Completely handwritten and illustrated by Grand-mère, and comprising both Grand-mère's recipes as well as her mother's from over one hundred years of French pastry-making, they were probably Aimee's most prized possession.

Having those precious volumes there was a little like having Grand-mère standing beside her. Grand-mère said it had taken many years, but she'd finally learned to take her son's mean-spirited ways in stride. She'd done her best by him, had reared him exactly as she had his older sister, Aimee's mother.

But whereas Aimee's mother was always thoughtful, kind, loving, Uncle Cain was...well, he wasn't. Grand-mère said it had to be DNA. Sometimes there was no accounting for the egotism of certain people; it was a trait that slipped into otherwise nice families and upset the whole balance of things. Add to that Uncle Cain's nasty wife, who accentuated and encouraged his worst qualities, and Aimee was left with an uncle in name only.

"So this is where you're hiding out." Her uncle's sardonic voice reached her before his mocking eyes invaded her office, her sanctuary. He sauntered in and plopped down on the tufted-back chair opposite her desk before Aimee even had a chance to welcome him. "I never did understand why my mother didn't make a proper office in this place," he commented and looked around with a proprietary air. It set alarms sounding in Aimee's head.

"Uncle Cain." What could she say? *Nice to see you?* That would be a lie. "This is a surprise." At least that was the truth. "May I offer you a cup of coffee or a pastry?"

He waved off her offer. "I bought a coffee at a drive-through on my way here."

Silence. Aimee heard the clock in the kitchen ticking. She heard the town hall clock chime the hour. It was three o'clock. The four pastors would soon be coming in for their afternoon coffee. Why did she think of them right now? Maybe because of the peace that always accompanied those dear men who were churchmen from four different Christian backgrounds—Greek Orthodox, Roman Catholic, Presbyterian and Evangelical—and yet were best friends and truly as brothers to one another. Thoughts of their friendship, faith and love always edified her.

"Is there a reason you came out this afternoon?" she asked after a moment.

"Of course. I wouldn't come all this way without a good reason."

Seeing your niece isn't reason enough? she wanted to ask. But of course she didn't. He didn't like her any more than she liked him. They were the only living blood relatives either of them had. It was such a shame. She wished she wasn't an only child, wished she had brothers and sisters. Unless they were like Uncle Cain. No, maybe it was better being an only child.

She watched as he opened his briefcase and brought out the loan contract he'd had her sign. "Your loan is due in exactly six weeks and two days."

"Yes, I know."

"I just want to remind you that if you don't repay it in full by five o'clock in the afternoon of November 27, according to paragraph 5, clause 10, the Patisserie will be mine. Lock, stock and barrel."

Aimee flew out of her seat. "What?!" She bumped her knees on her desk, but hardly felt the pain.

"Of course." He looked around at everything as if, Aimee thought, he couldn't wait to get his hands on it and throw it all away. "You can take whatever you want from the place. I'm going to gut it anyway," he said, confirming the sour expression on his face.

"What are you talking about?"

"My dear, didn't you have your lawyer read the contract?"

"Lawyer? *You're* a lawyer!" To have another lawyer read the contract hadn't even crossed her mind. "You're my uncle. I didn't think I had to worry about underhanded dealings."

"Darling girl." He spoke expansively as if he were a great benevolent creature. "Why would I lend you so much money without there being anything in it for me?"

Aimee's mind was reeling. "I thought...at the most...you'd want a stake in the business—"

"Business!" He spat out the word as if she had no idea what she was talking about. "Is that what you call the Patisserie?" His lips turned up in what was almost a sneer. "A business?"

Something, a combination of hurt and gumption, rose up in Aimee. The business her grand-mère had built after her first husband—Aimee's grandfather—had died was being smeared by her Uncle Cain. His father, Harry Bell—Grand-mère's second husband—had loved the Patisserie and been very proud of it during the decade and a half they had together before he died when his son—the man Aimee was now confronting, her Uncle Cain—was a teenager. "You bet I do!" she returned. He might try to take the store but he couldn't take Grand-mère's good name or everything the Patisserie had offered the community during the last seventy years. "The Patisserie is a business as businesses in America were meant to be, an establishment that supports families. *This* business supported Grand-mère and her little girl—my mother—after her first husband died and she was left alone to support herself and my young mother. This business put clothes on your back after her second husband died—your father—and Grand-mère had a teenage age boy to feed and clothe. *This* business paid for your very expensive university education. *This* business—"

"Should have been mine after *my* mother died. *My* mother. Not yours."

Aimee sat back down. "So that's what this is all about."

"She was my mother. Not yours," he repeated. His eyes were icy. Aimee didn't realize brown eyes could look so hard.

"Funny you only remember that now that she's gone and there's a profit to be made. How many times did you see her during the last ten years of her life? Oh, yes, I remember." Aimee held up two fingers. "And that was when she went to Manhattan to see you. Oh, no." Aimee lightly smacked her head with the palm of her hand. "I'm wrong. You saw her only once. The last time your ninety-year-old mother went into the city to see you, your secretary said you had an appointment."

"I did." There was defiance in his tone.

Aimee lowered her voice and finally spoke the words she had wanted to say for the past five years. "Grand-mère saw you leaving the building, Uncle Cain. She was walking right behind you." That had hurt Grand-mère terribly. For days afterward, she hadn't been her normal, bright self. Until finally, she decided that the young man, whose given name was Ebenezer, was no longer the son she'd borne and brought up. She at last accepted that the man who'd given himself the name Cain when he went off to college, the man who loved business more than he loved his mother and orphaned niece, had taken his place. Marrying Gertrude—and being further changed by her avaricious ways—made it final. Her son was gone.

"This *business* will be mine in exactly forty-four days unless you pay me back. In full." Aimee wanted to tell him to get out. But she didn't. She just sat there trying to understand how one family member could be so hurtful to another.

"Don't worry." He spoke as if he were her benevolent uncle again. "I'm not going to sell the shop. That wouldn't be smart business, either. These old Connecticut Main Street storefronts are too hard to come by. No," he said, glancing around, a shrewd glint in his eyes. "No," he repeated. "I'm going to turn it into a Play Ball Sports Bar," he said, naming a well-known franchise, "for the university students. I'll make a fortune getting them to spend mommy and daddy's money here. I tried to tell my mother. But she had some sentimental attachment to French pastry. She couldn't even do something American. Had to be French."

"That's enough," Aimee heard herself say. Both Grand-mère's first husband and her son-in-law—Aimee's father—had died in service to the United States, in serving their beloved country.

His cold gaze hit hers. "What?"

"I will not have you slurring Grand-mère's good name and reputation."

"She was *my* mother. Not yours," he repeated, like it was some sort of litany.

"Funny. You never seemed to remember that, Uncle *Cain*." She put emphasis on his self-chosen name. "You didn't even keep the beautiful name she gave you."

"I hated Ebenezer. What's an Ebenezer?" he said. But something flickered in his eyes. Aimee wondered if it was regret for what he might have been. Or perhaps remorse for the bad son he'd turned out to be? Aimee doubted it. Regardless, by the time he stood, that brief look was gone. "Forty-four days."

She stood. "Don't count on the Patisserie dying that easily, Uncle. I'll pay you back in full by 1700 hours on November the 27, the day before Thanksgiving."

"And just how do you plan on doing that?" he asked with that sardonic twist to his lips she hated so much. "Bake the cash in Mom's ancient oven?"

"I'll have the money," she answered with a conviction that surprised her.

"Well, then, niece, you better get cooking."

3—Grand Opening

"Are you letting HurriCain strike again?" Becky wailed two days later when she walked into the Patisserie. She was on her fresh-from-the-oven strawberry *macarons* run for Miss Maggie and had caught Aimee looking as down in the dumps as Aimee, in fact, felt. The café was empty, unusual for that hour of the day. It allowed Aimee the unwanted time to relive her latest encounter with her uncle. She sent Becky a guilty look.

"Come on, friend." Becky went around the counter. Putting her slender arm around Aimee's shoulders, she gave her a friendly little shake. "You weathered that real storm last year admirably. You're not going to let Uncle HurriCain blow you away now. Are you?"

Aimee stepped back and smiled weakly at her friend. She loved how expressive Becky was. "HurriCain," she said with a feeble laugh. "That pretty much describes him. When he does blow into my life, it's with the force of a ferocious hurricane."

"Then why are you giving him a second thought?"

"I'm just so tired, Becky. And angry with myself." She wiped vigorously at a nonexistent spot on the counter. "Why didn't I read the fine print?"

"That's simple," Becky said and took the dishcloth out of Aimee's hand. She started wiping down the counter where it actually needed wiping. "There's something in normal people that has to believe their relatives have their backs. It's as simple—and as complicated—as that."

"Hey." Aimee tried to take the cloth from her. "You're not supposed to be working now."

Becky wouldn't relinquish it. "I like working here. Working here isn't working at all. It is home. It's where I want to spend every afternoon. And, hey!" She bent her knees and bumped her hip against Aimee's. "The owner pays me for it, too."

Aimee smiled at her again and then glanced around the café. "It *is* home. To so many of us," she agreed. Aimee knew that when Becky was a child, she'd been passed from one foster home to another. Until landing in a nice foster family in Stoneybridge, she'd had no real home. That family had since moved away, but Becky remained here, even though she was still in close contact with them.

"That's why we can't let it go without a fight. The world doesn't need another Play Ball Sports Bar. It needs to keep its privately owned, old and established feel-good places. Win that supermarket contract, girl. Win it and save the Patisserie from Uncle Cain! I'll taste every sample you make until we're sure you'll wow them into awarding you that contract!" Becky was the best taster in the world. Aimee always told her she should be a restaurant critic. Her palate was spot on, distinguishing between and appreciating different flavors. Plus, she never gained weight, something Aimee had to watch.

Aimee could feel strength flow into her system at Becky's encouraging words. A happy wave of possibilities, a can-do attitude, coursed through her. "You're right, Becky!" Where Aimee had felt downtrodden and all alone a few minutes ago, she now felt as if she could capture that supermarket contract. She threw her arms around her friend in a great big hug. "I can do it!"

"You bet you can! Grand-mère left you twenty volumes of recipes." She pointed in the direction of the office. "You've only used ten percent of them. If that."

"I'm going through them and I'll find the best—"

"And win that contract!" she repeated.

"Can't you see Uncle HurriCain's face when I present him with the money?"

Becky screwed up her own face. "Like Ebenezer Scrooge—at the beginning of *A Christmas Carol*!"

"Exactly." But that, of course, reminded Aimee. "Did you know that Ebenezer is Uncle Cain's real name?"

"You're kidding!" Becky's dark blue eyes opened wide, then narrowed the way they did when she was perplexed. "Why in the world would your grand-mère give her son that name? Didn't she realize she was asking for trouble, for him to turn into a man like the character, Ebenezer Scrooge?"

"Actually, it was my step-grandfather, Harry Bell's, idea. He was a Bible scholar—a professor at Stoneybridge College—and other than being an old family name, he knew that it's actually a Biblical one with a great meaning."

"Really…? I have only heard about Charles Dickens's character. What does it mean?"

"Rock or stone of help."

"You've got to be kidding," Becky groaned. "That's the *last* thing your uncle's been to you—or was to your grand-mère."

"I know. Grand-mère told me Grandpa Bell gave him that name hoping their son would always be a "rock or stone of help" to his mother should something ever happen to him. That he'd grow into a man Grand-mère could rely on."

Becky was oddly silent a moment before saying, "The truth is, oh, friend of mine, that at the end of Charles Dickens's book,

Ebenezer Scrooge *did* become a great help to everyone around him. He became a very fine man."

Aimee shrugged. She held out no such hope for her uncle. But a memory of the flicker in his eyes the other day while he was in her office, one of regret or remorse, sped through her mind. But in the nature of any brief and sudden memory, it was soon gone. There was no way Uncle Cain would ever change. Maybe if he hadn't married Grasping Gertrude... But with Gertrude in the wings, always pushing him to torment his family in new ways, forget it. After all, Charles Dickens's character didn't have a dreadful wife. "Well, his name isn't Ebenezer anymore. He changed it to Cain ages ago."

"The man in the Bible who committed the first murder," Becky stated and then giggled with the high-pitched hysteria that meant she wouldn't be stopping soon.

"That's hardly funny," Aimee said. Sometimes she didn't get her friend's humor.

"It's...hilarious!" Becky said between giggles. "Here...your uncle thinks he's so smart...and he spurned a beautiful family name with a great meaning...for the name of—"

"—a murderer," Aimee finished. "Yeah, you're right. It really is comical, in a sad sort of way. Poor man."

"*Poor* man... I think saying he's a 'poor' man...must be the most—"

"—insulting thing someone could say about him," Aimee said, and joined her friend in laughing at the absurdity of it all. It felt good to release some of the tension she'd been feeling since her uncle's visit. By the time the door opened and Miss Maggie waltzed in, they were practically doubled over.

"What are you two still doing here?" From the way her eyes danced, she was obviously happy to see them enjoying themselves, but equally aghast that they were still inside. "The big moment is at hand!"

That got them going again. "You're...right...about...that, Miss Maggie," Aimee said between breaths. Of course, she and Becky were thinking about the repayment of the loan and her future run-in with Uncle Cain as "the big moment." But that was their secret.

"Then why aren't you outside with everyone else watching?"

"Watching?" Becky looked at Aimee. Aimee looked at Becky. Then they both glanced through the window. While Becky had been inside, Main Street had filled up with people. Traffic was at a near standstill.

"The grand opening of the new store! The soap's been cleaned away and only a huge sheet on the outside of the storefront hides what's behind the window!" Miss Maggie sang out, giving Mrs. Fonteyn and her operatic voice a run for her money. "Get a move on, you two! Now!" She shooed them toward the door. "It's good that Louis is upstairs or he'd be terribly upset."

Aimee had remembered the Grand Opening earlier and had left Louis upstairs for that very reason. Removing her apron, she said to Miss Maggie, "The last thing I care about right now is what the new store will be."

"Now that's a *bah, humbug* attitude if ever I heard one," the older woman said, which got Aimee and Becky going on yet another laughing spree.

"Ebenezer Scrooge...strikes...again!" Becky said.

"Girls!" Miss Maggie sounded appalled. "Where's your community spirit?"

That question was like a punch in the stomach. It forced the laughter right out of Aimee and sobered Becky almost as quickly. Putting her arm through Miss Maggie's, Aimee sent a wistful look at Becky, and then assured the older, well-meaning woman, "It's here, dear lady. We promise." If only Miss Maggie knew. To continue being part of the Main Street community was all Aimee desired.

Miss Maggie patted her hand as they followed Becky outside. "I know it is, dear. I know. Now let's go see what this new store's all about." Her mission done, she left them in a whirl of fabric and joyful busyness the second they stepped onto the sidewalk.

That grey feeling began to descend on Aimee again. She hated how volatile her emotions had become since her uncle's visit. As she and Becky crossed the street, she forced herself to look at the beloved buildings on either side of the road. With their arched-head windows, storefront cornices, transoms, display windows, recessed entryways and awnings, the buildings were a steady and much-needed constant in her life.

She considered how privileged she was to have grown up here. The town and its people were as much a part of the land as the Connecticut granite that held it secure. Its history stretched all the way back to Colonial days, to the Mohegans and beyond. Some even said that shipwrecked Romans had crossed the ocean in Late Antiquity and built the enigmatic stone bridge over the river—the bridge that gave the town its name.

Aimee felt a part of that history. She knew that all the residents of Stoneybridge did. Every day was history in the making. And today was a gorgeous fall day, the kind New England was famous for giving the world in mid-October.

Aimee loved every crimson and gold leaf hanging on the trees, every brick in the sidewalk and every person gathered on this street.

Her eyes stopped moving when they landed on a certain man. It was Gerry from Monday morning. At the exact same moment, Becky nudged her.

"It's the 'hot guy'," she whispered. "Over there."

"I see him." Aimee was astonished by how her mood changed again when she saw Gerry. So he hadn't just been passing through town... He was still here. *Still here!* She didn't want to question why that made her feel happy. This morning he was dressed in stone-washed jeans, a white T-shirt, a jean jacket, cowboy boots with a Stetson—a different one—riding low on his head. "I wonder if he really is a cowboy or only looks like my image of one?"

"He sure looks like mine, too," Becky said, and Aimee was startled that she'd spoken her thought out loud. "One who isn't passing through, either, since...there he is!" Becky pointed out. "That means, the promise I got you to agree to—"

Aimee grabbed Becky's arm, cutting her off in mid-sentence. Taking a quick look through the crowd, she'd noticed something, something that if she was seeing correctly around the heads of the people, sent a chill, a heart-throbbing coldness, running through her. "Becky?" She nodded carefully toward the new store. "What's he doing?"

Becky stretched up. She could easily see over everyone. "He's..." She paused and glanced down at Aimee. "He's about to pull the sheet off the window."

"He's the new store's *owner*?" Aimee was incredulous. "No wonder he knew it was going to be a pet-grooming salon!" she exclaimed. "But how can he have a pet-grooming salon when he can't even groom his own dog?" What she was really wondering was why he hadn't told her on Monday that he was the new proprietor. What was the big secret? Men! *Can never trust 'em.*

"Ah, Aimee... It gets worse." Becky nodded toward the shop as the sheet fell to the ground. "Look at the sign."

Aimee craned her head upward. She stood on her tiptoes in order to see over Maude Campbell's full 1980s-styled hair.

She read the blue-and-yellow sign on the now unveiled window. "Uncle Gerry's Cakerie."

Aimee dropped back down. Her heart seemed to miss a beat at the realization of what she'd just read. "*Cakerie*! A cake shop is opening up right next to the Patisserie?" she exclaimed. As she did, that feeling of once again being made a fool of returned with a vengeance. She felt the blood rush to her face. The man had come into her Patisserie on Monday morning to scope it out! She'd been nearly flirting with him, asking him all about Paris, thinking he was just passing through, when all the time he was *spying* on her. Aimee felt as if a ten-pound sack of flour had come crashing down on her head. She almost couldn't breathe.

"Uncle Gerry's Cakerie? I've heard that name..." Becky tapped her foot.

Aimee groaned. *Uncle Gerry's Cakerie!* Memory swooped in. "Oh, no! Becky... It's that...that...place...that cake bakery—" she muttered the words in disgust "—from California that makes huge...stadium-sized...*monstrosities* and dares to call them cakes."

"The one you read about in one of your baking magazines? That place you hated?"

Aimee nodded. "Big, brash and crass. The total antithesis of the refinement and elegance of classic cakes."

"Then...maybe he's not direct competition?" Becky, always positive, suggested.

"It's a *bakery*, Becky," Aimee couldn't help wailing but smiled sweetly at Maude when the other woman glanced back at her in question. Aimee lowered her voice as she continued speaking to Becky, even when the townspeople started to applaud as Gerry stood up on a small podium. "That fact alone makes it—*him*—competition. What's he doing here? According to the article, Uncle Gerry's Cakerie was based in Los Angeles and was supposedly doing very well."

"The article was written last year, wasn't it?"

"Yes."

"A lot can happen in a year, Aimee."

Aimee sighed. "Don't I know it. Last year I still felt sorry for myself about being the unrequited love story of the town. That makes this year's problems seem like..."

"A piece of cake," Becky suggested and grimaced.

"Ladies and Gentlemen, boys and girls." Gerry started to speak and everyone on Main Street, including Aimee and Becky, quieted down. "I'm Gerry Mitchell and I'd like to welcome you to the grand opening of Uncle Gerry's Cakerie on Main Street in Stoneybridge, Connecticut!"

There were cheers all around. Aimee and Becky looked at each other and then at the crowd. Everyone seemed thrilled with the new arrival in town.

"The concept behind Uncle Gerry's Cakerie, which by the way—" he interrupted himself "—was named by my niece and nephew, Pattie and Benji, whom you'll see with me on our company's logo," he pointed to the window. Above the store's name there was the image of a man wearing a cowboy hat—obviously Gerry—while on either side of him was a child. The boy and girl were in profile looking up at their uncle, who faced forward. "And who also join me here today." He indicated two broadly smiling children who were obviously siblings.

The kids waved proudly and everyone waved back at them. They were standing on either side of a huge table that had been set up under the dogwood tree by the Cakerie's door. The tabletop was covered with a large white sheet. Aimee assumed that it concealed one of those obscenely enormous cakes.

"The concept behind Uncle Gerry's Cakerie is simple," Gerry repeated. "It's all about fun. It's about edible whimsy and fantasy. Whatever you might imagine as your perfect birthday cake…" Aimee took Becky's hand and squeezed it. "Or wedding cake…" She squeezed Becky's hand even tighter. "Or anniversary cake…" Another squeeze. "Or graduation cake…" Becky quickly placed her other hand over Aimee's, stopping her. Aimee only then realized she'd almost hurt her friend. She released her grip. But with every word Gerry spoke, she felt as if a vise was being tightened more firmly around her head. *He was taking Stoneybridge's cake-making business away from her!* "Uncle Gerry's Cakerie will make *any* cake for *any* occasion in *any* size you want it. The only criterion is that it has to make you, or the person it's intended for, very happy."

Once again, enthusiastic, welcoming cheers erupted all around. Aimee felt like sinking into the ground in defeat. How was she ever going to pay back Uncle Cain now? *Her* Main Street was turning on her. *Her* town was leaving its tried and true Patisserie behind.

"I'll bet he used to make cakes for Hollywood royalty," Becky snorted softly in Aimee's ear. For a reason Becky had never disclosed, she had an unreasonable dislike for anything to do with Hollywood.

Aimee nodded. "According to the article I read, that's exactly what he used to do. And made a fortune at it, too."

"So what's he doing here?"

"You might wonder why I've left California," Gerry's voice rang out over Main Street, seeming to answer Becky's question, "and relocated to Stoneybridge. There are many reasons but two major ones." He indicated a young woman, clearly related to him. "First of all, my sister and her great kids live in our hometown which is located close by and..." He gestured to Benji and Pattie to remove the cover from the cake that was the size of a ping pong table. They did, and everyone gasped as Gerry shouted out, "...and secondly, your Main Street!"

Wonderment over how perfectly the cake represented Stoneybridge's Main Street sounded all around.

"Beautiful!"

"Awesome!"

"Yummy!"

Gerry continued when the oohs and aahs quieted, "I felt it was time to return to my roots and build my business in my home state—beautiful Connecticut!"

Connecticut pride made the crowd erupt in loud applause once again. Even the drivers of the few cars that had been trapped by the temporary closing of Main Street honked their horns as they joined in on the fun.

"It's exactly where we are right now, Mommy!" Aimee heard Tommy Floyd say to his mother as she and Becky walked up to take a closer look at the so-called cake.

Tommy was right. It was identical, down to the last detail. Sugar-sculpted people of all ages walking along the sidewalks, the maple trees, the dogwood trees, even Louis's treehouse were there. Her quick gaze registered more; Hale's Hardware Store, PJ Kabos Extra Virgin Olive Oil Shop, the barbershop, the bricks on the sidewalk, Joe's Diner, Maple Tree Bed & Breakfast, Paige St. James's Bridal Designs, the train station, Second Presbyterian Church with its distinctive steeple on the hill, the Georgian Town Hall with its clock tower, Miss Maggie's Treasure Trove, Uncle Gerry's Cakerie...and the Patisserie. With a sugar sculpture of Aimee outside the front door giving a sugar sculpture of Cynthia a doggie treat. Complete with a sugar-sculpted Gerry standing beside them.

"That's unbelievable," she heard Becky say.

Aimee felt eyes trained on her. But she knew almost everyone was looking at this cake. If it could really be classified as such? And yet, she could feel someone watching her. She turned away from the baked likeness of Main Street and glanced around.

Gerry, still on the podium, was staring at her. Everyone else was oohing and aahing over the workmanship that had gone into making the humongous cake, but Gerry had his gaze on her.

Not just that, he was smiling.

She squinted at him. On Monday morning, he'd voted that it would be a dog salon moving next door to her pastry store—all along knowing it was a cake shop. *His* cake shop. Had he been mocking her? Was he now?

Why did he keep it a secret and even more, why did he have to open a bakery right next to her Patisserie?

She looked back at the creation in front of her.

It was a fabulous model made out of sugar and flour and all the ingredients that go into making a cake. That Gerry Mitchell was a master craftsman; Aimee had no doubt.

But it *wasn't* a cake.

It was a gimmick.

It was a passing fancy.

But it—and other creations like it—were going to take her clientele away...

Uncle Gerry's Cakerie coming to Stoneybridge was a disaster for her.

The cake started to swim before her eyes, becoming as elusive as her hope of keeping the Patisserie from being turned into a money-grubbing Play Ball Sports Bar. Her eyes filled with tears.

The people of Stoneybridge obviously loved the Cakerie already. Aimee could feel their excitement, could feel their egos being stroked by the so-called cake that depicted their town, her town.

Gerry Mitchell sure did know how to reel people in. He'd reeled her in on Monday and now he was reeling in her friends and neighbors. Her customers...

Turning away from him, Aimee moved toward the back of the crowd. She wanted to disappear. She *had* to disappear. It was too much for her.

"Aimee." Becky wrapped one hand around her wrist. "It's going to be okay."

Aimee shook her head, knowing she had to get away before the tears fell. She glanced toward the Patisserie's entrance. Because of the crowd around the table, it was blocked. Mrs. Fonteyn and Dr. Lovejoy were standing beside her outdoor stairs—the only way into her apartment. Aimee couldn't go home. She couldn't face their comments.

Following Aimee's gaze, Becky reached into her pocket and held out the blue baby-sneaker keychain from which dangled her apartment key. Her building was located on the far side of the street, which fortunately wasn't blocked. "Go. Compose yourself. I'll be up soon."

Sending her best friend a grateful nod, Aimee grabbed the baby-sneaker. To the sound of plates being brought out and Gerry saying, "Now, it's time for everyone to find out if this cake tastes as good as it looks. Who wants a slice?!"

Cheers erupted even more loudly.

Aimee felt as if she'd fallen into her worst nightmare. A cake shop was moving in right next to the Patisserie! A cake shop!

She ran. Her heart felt as if it were about to explode.

After meeting Gerry, she'd thought she'd like him.

Now she knew differently.

He'd tricked her.

Tricked her with his Stetson, cowboy boots and lazy manner into assuming he was from out west and just passing through. Tricked her into enjoying his company. Tricked her into…

As she pushed opened Becky's apartment door, she didn't even know.

Men. They could never be trusted. Not one.

***

"What we need is a plan of action," Becky said later that night as they sat at the Patisserie's counter, each nursing a cup of herbal tea. They'd just closed the store that, not surprisingly, had been relatively empty all afternoon and evening. The college kids—a staple during the evening hours—had gone next door to the Cakerie rather than the Patisserie. Only the four pastors made a point of coming in at their normal time.

"Plan of action? About what?" Aimee asked.

Becky nodded toward the Cakerie. "We've got to go on a reconnaissance mission."

Aimee groaned. "Becky. It's right next door."

"Nah. To my mind, Mr. Wong's Dry Cleaning is still next door. Uncle Gerry's Cakerie is a whole different story. We have to see exactly what he's selling."

"Other than his football-stadium cakes the size of ping pong tables, cornucopia cakes the size of a small dresser and princess-tiara cakes the size of a dollhouse that you saw through the window? Not to mention the Main Street mega-cake that turned everybody's head today."

"Who cares about those things?"

"I do!" Aimee protested.

"Those cakes aren't your direct competition. You'll lose a bit of business to them in the beginning—"

"During a time I can ill afford to lose a single dollar's worth," Aimee cut in.

"But in the long run—"

"Will I even be here for the long run?"

"Of course, you will! Don't lose faith, Aimee." Aimee knew that if anyone understood living by faith, Becky was the one. That faith had sustained her, from the time she was just a little girl when she'd steadfastly believed that someday her friend, Jesus, would direct her to a good family in a good town, a place to call home. And that was exactly what had happened.

Aimee smiled at Becky. "I guess I could go over there and see." She *was* curious to find out what Gerry sold over the counter. She knew that he had to have consultations with people concerning their visions for their "super" cakes. But what did he sell on a day-to-day basis? Was the Cakerie a café too? Did he sell croissants and *macarons*? Could college kids go there and study all evening, as they could at the Patisserie?

"Where's the fun in that?" Becky huffed.

"I don't find the situation fun at all," Aimee huffed back.

"That's why we have to *make* it fun."

In spite of the dread that had settled in her stomach since the grand opening of the store next door, Aimee was intrigued. "Okay, dear friend, what do you have in mind?"

"Well, by coming in here, sitting on that chair—" Becky motioned to the *fauteuil* by the window "—and not telling you he was your new neighbor and confectionary colleague, Gerry Mitchell came into your store undercover." She held up the *red* baby-sneaker keychain that Aimee knew was the keeper of the Treasure Trove's key. Becky was notorious for losing her keys so she kept them on different keychains. "Why don't we do the same thing?"

Aimee looked from Becky to the key. "You mean, play dress-up with Miss Maggie's stuff?"

"She's always telling me I can."

Aimee could feel herself grin. Becky was right. "Payback time!" she exclaimed and lightly pounded her fist on the counter. "Let's do it!"

4—Reconnaissance

When Gerry flipped the Cakerie's "Closed" sign to "Open" at 8:00 a.m. on Thursday morning, people had already formed a line along the brick sidewalk in front of his shop. It extended halfway past Hale's Hardware, a good forty feet. Wearing his white chef's hat and coat, Gerry went up and down the line shaking hands and welcoming everyone.

It was exactly what he'd hoped for.

Three hours later, he had five appointments scheduled for consultations concerning made-to-order cakes and he'd taken four orders for his football-stadium cake, two for the princess-tiara and one for the cornucopia…

But right now an older woman asked for, "A slice of five-layer Black Forest Cake, please."

"Our one-hundredth slice of five-layer Black Forest Cake!" Gerry shouted, and reaching over to the wall, he rang the bell that hung there, startling everyone in the store. While dishing up the cake, Gerry did his signature, hundredth-slice jig—a gyration of hips, shoulders and twists. He handed the cake to the very pleased customer. "Free of charge, ma'am," he drawled with a lift of his hat, and then grabbing his jar of Uncle Gerry's homemade lollipops, he danced his way around the store, handing them out to everyone. People were laughing and clapping and joining in the fun.

"Hey! You're just like Tom Cruise in that 1980s film, *Cocktail,*" a college girl said, and holding her phone up, she took Gerry's photo and immediately sent it out into the world. She wasn't the only one. Lots of people were taking his picture and videoing him as he danced from person to person.

"Service with a routine! I like it," another girl said, and putting her own head close to Gerry's, she took a selfie.

Even the few people not snapping the shutter buttons on their phones went wild. Gerry had started this tradition in his Los Angeles store. He hadn't been sure whether to continue it in Connecticut. But habits are hard to break and when he'd sold the hundredth slice of cake, his body simply took over. He was glad it did. More and more people were coming in from Main Street to see what all the fuss was about.

Two hours later, he'd just finished his second hundredth-slice jig of the day. He was ringing up a large order of supersize blueberry cupcakes, and having fun deflecting the flirting airs of the latest wave of college girls who'd come into the shop to scope him out, when an oddly dressed young woman caught his eye. Standing near the ten-by-ten foot mural of him with his niece and nephew—the one that had inspired the logo that was on his jackets, boxes, website, bags, and vans—something about her movement, the tilt of her head, the curve of her spine was familiar.

He frowned. Other than his local employees, whom he'd interviewed and hired via video conference calls during the past month, he didn't really know anyone in town.

She was wearing a mini mini-skirt, thigh-high boots with four-inch heels and a jean jacket that covered a shirt like the one Julia Roberts wore in the opening scenes of *Pretty Woman*. She was very attractive in that fake blond way but her style of dress wasn't one he liked. He'd never warmed to that skimpy 1980s look that was so popular among certain young women today. He glanced away from her for a moment to answer a question about the state-of-the-art cash register asked by one of the college students—a very pretty girl of about twenty. When he looked back, the woman in the thigh-high boots had turned enough for him to see the dimple that appeared on her left cheek when she smiled at her supermodel-tall friend.

"Aimee?" he called.

When her body twitched, as if she had to stop herself from answering, Gerry knew it was her.

She started clumping across the blue-and-yellow checkered linoleum toward the door, in that tottering way of women who don't normally wear towering shoes. He knew she was aiming for escape, so he jumped out from behind the counter, slamming his thigh on the corner for the twentieth time that day—one of those minor kinks in the design of his shop that he had to work out. He clamped his mouth on the moan while dodging the persistent college girls in his path.

"Aimee?" he called out to her quickly retreating back. "Are you spying on me?" The idea amused him. He heard the twittering giggles of the college pack behind him but tuned them out.

Aimee paused. Her tall friend gave her a nudge. Two more steps and she'd be out the door and in the clear. He wouldn't run after her; that would be ridiculous.

At the last second, Aimee did the unexpected.

Reaching up, she grabbed the blond wig from her head, pulled her Jackie O sunglasses from her face, shook out her rich, dark hair and, turning, looked him square in the eye. Well, kind of. Even with those ridiculous high-heeled boots she was still several inches shorter than his six feet, two inches. Gerry liked that. It answered some primitive male call in him. He couldn't help stretching his vertebrae just a little more.

"The way you spied on me, you mean?" Although she spoke softly, there was a steely edge to her voice. "Don't you think it might have been a professional courtesy to tell me on Monday—" she waved her hand "—or actually at some point during the many months since you bought this space, that you were moving a *cake shop* next door to my *pastry shop*?"

He stepped back. He'd just been verbally slapped. His former fiancée, Scarlett, had done it often enough for him to immediately recognize the tactic. Not giving himself a chance to consider that perhaps this time he deserved it—it *would* have been an act of professional courtesy, one he should have offered long ago and one he'd planned to last Monday when he went into her shop. But hearing that she didn't want a bakery of any sort next door to her store, he'd set that idea aside, especially since he'd had such fun talking to her. But he didn't say that; instead he met her gaze and using words he might have spoken to Scarlett said, "I didn't think it was pertinent."

"Not pertinent?" she retorted. Her right foot tapped against the linoleum with the agitated cadence of a hornet trapped against a windowpane.

This Aimee was a totally different woman from the engaging one he'd met on Monday. He made a feature-by-feature study of her face. The same full mouth, the same delicate nose, the same sculpted ears and dark brown eyes were looking back at him. But in place of Monday's vibrancy was suspicion. Instead of Monday's service with a smile, he saw skepticism and firm, unforgiving lips.

Today she reminded him too much of his ex-fiancée—even minus the blond wig—for his own peace of mind. Like Scarlett, today she was a businesswoman who wanted answers. No, one who *demanded* answers.

Whether his next-door neighbor was right or wrong made no difference to him. Not at the moment, anyway. Being put under such scrutiny—and in his own store, with an audience listening closely—annoyed him. Annoyed him a lot. "Not at all pertinent," he stubbornly insisted. "Your approval, or the location of the Patisserie next door to this property, had no bearing on my buying the store." It hadn't.

"How can you justify that?" *Tap, tap, tap* went her foot.

"Easy. I needed to relocate here. This property was available at the right price. I bought it." He shrugged. "It's just business."

Did this woman, who was showing herself to be the consummate capitalist, flinch? He wasn't sure. He was gearing himself for the next assault when suddenly the teeny-tiny electrons that were charging the air around them seemed to abruptly settle down. He was further surprised when she let out a slight breath, one that carried the sound of truce.

"I guess I have no choice but to accept that," she said quietly. Gerry was totally taken aback. Scarlett would never have capitulated so quickly. Scarlett wouldn't have capitulated, period. Maybe, just maybe, unlike Scarlett, it wasn't all about business with Aimee. "I only wish you'd told me on Monday," she qualified.

Even though she was still looking at him with hooded eyes, as if she wasn't sure she could trust him, she didn't sound angry anymore.

Just weary. And resigned. Like he was a problem she could have done without.

She stood straight but her shoulders were slightly rounded, as if she were carrying the weight of the world on them, or at least the weight of her store. Her eyelids seemed heavy, too.

Like they wanted to close and stay closed for a week. He'd noticed the same thing yesterday after he'd unveiled the Main Street cake. He wondered what was going on in her life. *Would telling her that he was opening his Cakerie next to her Patisserie have helped her in any way?* It prompted him to offer, "I'm truly sorry. I almost did." He'd been about to tell her when she'd asked if he had studied old furniture when he was in France. He'd opted not to tell her the truth—that he'd studied at Le Cordon Bleu and was opening a Cakerie next door to her Patisserie—for no reason other than his purely male reaction to her. He'd liked their easy banter and didn't want to change the mood between them with business talk. They'd had a connection. Not that he wanted another relationship with a woman any time soon, but it had been there. It had been fun.

After a tense moment, her eyelids softened, then widened in appreciation of the apology. He was glad. He meant it. In hindsight, he knew he should have introduced himself and told her immediately, as he'd planned to do when he'd gone over there on Monday morning. But it hadn't occurred to him that the owner of the Patisserie would be so averse to his Cakerie's arrival. At least not until he heard the woman named Ruth say that "only a fool would open a pastry store or a bakery beside a lovely establishment like the Patisserie" and he saw how Aimee liked that assessment. It was another reason he didn't tell her then. He'd been exhausted and wanted to enjoy his breakfast. Besides, similar stores often existed in the same parts of cities—the so called clothing district, candy district, bookstore district, theater district, bakery district, and so on. But now he could see that not telling her who he was had given her every reason to believe he'd been spying.

He watched her look around his shop. Who was he kidding? She was on a reconnaissance mission of his store right now. Seeing it through her eyes, as her glance landed on the model of the princess tiara cake, the display case filled with supersize edibles, and the huge football-stadium cake that took up ten feet along the plate glass window, he knew that his Cakerie was the direct opposite of her old-world Patisserie, with its antiques and dainty pastries that would've been perfectly at home on Paris's Rue St. Honoré.

It was because he was watching as her gaze settled on his cupcakes the size of Frisbees that he saw the exact moment resignation that his bakery was indeed next to her pastry store became a different look altogether. It was an attitude he'd come up against several times in his career—a grim, cold objection to his type of baking. It was in the intolerant lift of her left brow, in the distasteful wave of her slender hands, in the silence of her now-still foot. She was the judge, dismissing the Cakerie as a fad. From the quicksilver flash of her dimple—not attached to a smile—he knew she was going to be sarcastic even before she spoke.

"I guess these enormous cakes you make—" she motioned toward his samples and then nodded at the college girls milling around the shop "—must be some sort of deep-seated need to be the center of attention."

He ignored the jab. He got what she was really saying; she was attacking his product. He glanced at his football-stadium cake, knowing that the best defense was always an offense. "You're a cake snob," he returned. "You're one of those people who take cake-making too seriously."

When her shoulders became a rigid line he knew he'd hit the mark. "Cake-making is an art," she declared. "There are classic standards that must be adhered to."

"Your attitude doesn't match your clothes, lady. You should be wearing a high-necked, eighteenth-century school teacher's dress instead of this eighties' skimpy look." He was glad when a mixture of embarrassment and twenty-first century ire sprang into her eyes, replacing the self-righteousness. Her right hand reached up to button the middle part of her jean jacket.

"It's just pastry, Aimee." He sighed when she remained quiet. "It's not rocket science." Gerry had come up against cake snobs several times in his career. The position that cake-making had to follow certain rules and cakes had to be small and elegant to be truly labeled "cake" was one of the reasons he'd left France and, forswearing small-town life, had gone to freethinking Los Angeles. Like he told the townsfolk at his Grand Opening, to him, cake-making was all about joy and fun, whimsy and imagination. And great-tasting cakes.

The people out west got it. He was hoping New England was ready for it, too. James Monroe, the CEO of Northeast Supermarket Chain seemed to think they were. Gerry nodded at Doug—the fifty-something chef who believed so greatly in Uncle Gerry's Cakerie that he and his wife had relocated from California in order to continue working with Gerry—and Hank, who'd also moved to Connecticut with him, as they refilled the display case with giant pumpkin muffins. The quantity of goods Uncle Gerry's Cakerie had sold that morning and the special orders he'd received seemed to indicate New England *was* ready. Only "Neighbor Lady" seemed stuck back in time. Not the people of small-town Stoneybridge, Connecticut.

"There's a decorum and grace involved in pastry presentation," she persisted and looked pointedly at the football-stadium display cake.

He did, too. Moving closer, he righted a leaning linebacker made of edible sugar that had been compromised by too many curious hands touching it. Gerry was especially proud of this cake. It was his personal whimsy escape. It reminded him of good times out on the gridiron on Friday nights, back in his high-school days. "Don't you know, Aimee, it's football season? I've already got four orders for this exact cake. That, and the two orders I've received this morning for the princess-tiara cake, will pay my full-time employees this month."

Her eyes widened and he knew he'd impressed her. "Just six cakes?" she whispered.

He laughed. "Well, they are rather big and take many hours to construct."

Her lips opened as if she wanted to say something. But with a confused shake of her head, she seemed to think better of it and turned away to leave.

Reaching out, he caught her arm. He didn't want her going like this.

Her arm felt nothing like the soft, pliable one he'd touched on Monday after Cynthia had knocked her down. Today she was stiff, resistant, erecting a wall of reserve between them. It seemed much stronger than the plaster wall—with the mural of him, his niece and nephew—that separated their stores. "Aimee," he said, speaking to her back, "there's more than enough room on Main Street for us to be happy neighbors."

She swiveled to face him and her gaze swiftly met his. She had eyes that could look right into the heart of a man. He wasn't sure he wanted her looking at his, not with that combination of outrage and uncertainty in her expression. Not with guilt over not introducing himself as the new store owner last Monday morning edging his own. Just before she shook off his arm and opened the door to exit his shop, she sent him another tight, little smile. *How could she make such full lips go so narrow and thin?* She must have practiced, maybe as a way of warding off unwanted male attention at her Patisserie?

He frowned. Did she see *him* as unwanted attention? He dismissed the thought because the look on her face revealed something else—something he recognized from recent personal experience. Pain and trepidation; it disturbed him with its intensity.

Her supermodel friend, whom he realized had been beside her the whole time, leaned near him—she was his height in those ridiculously high 1970s platform shoes she wore—and whispered through the feathers of her purple boa. "Don't you know that having your bread buttered on both sides makes for…an oily mess?"

He wasn't quite sure how to answer that and was glad when the sound of Cynthia jumping up on seeing Aimee exit the store relieved him from having to respond at all. Gerry had tied Cynthia to the Kousa dogwood tree. Aimee immediately went to greet the dog and, as if they were long-lost friends, Cynthia frolicked all around her.

"Cynthia really likes you." He spoke to Aimee above Cynthia's joyful tapping. He'd followed her outside since she stopped to say hi to his dog. Besides, he wanted to be neighborly and build some semblance of cooperation between them.

Aimee rubbed Cynthia behind her ears. Garry watched as she tried unsuccessfully to push the dog's hair out of her eyes.

He could have told her it was hopeless. "I like her, too." She stood and glanced back at him. "Too bad her owner can't seem to find a way to groom her. Is it a tell-tale sign of a lack of trust on the part of a dog?" She held up her hand to stay the quick retort on his lips.

Fine. She had more to say. He'd wait.

Looking him directly in the eyes, she volleyed back to his previous comment. "For us to be happy—" she put the word *happy* in air quotes "—neighbors on Main Street, Gerry Mitchell, there has to be trust." Bending, she gave the dog another hug before turning and clumping down the brick-paved sidewalk toward the outdoor stairs that Gerry had learned, from the talkative Miss Maggie, led to her apartment above the Patisserie.

"That accusation came out of left field," he murmured.

Her tall friend sent him an "are you serious?" glare and followed Aimee.

"Women," Gerry said, looking down at Cynthia. "Present company excluded, of course."

Shaking his head, he went back into the store and planted a big smile on his face as no fewer than four college girls started flirting with him. As he bantered with them, and filled their numerous orders, he knew that this was the only sort of female entanglement he wanted in his life.

Because of what Scarlett had done... She'd chewed him up and spat him out. As if that hadn't been enough, because of the high profile nature of her PR work, she'd tried to ruin his business, too, claiming his Cakerie was successful only because of her connections. She had definitely helped him, but his product was what had made the Cakerie a success.

He breathed out deeply. He might have wanted a wife and children last year.

He paused and looked out the window in the direction Aimee had gone.

Not this year.

This year he only wanted to make a success of his Cakerie in his home state, be a good uncle to his niece and nephew, brother to his sister, neighbor to the people of Stoneybridge—and win that supermarket contract.

Still, as the day wore on, Gerry couldn't shake the image of Aimee and that wacky blond wig and those gorgeous legs. He chuckled as he sliced another piece of five-layer Black Forest Cake. At least Aimee, as the owner of the store next door, definitely eradicated the one nagging worry left over from when he'd fled small-town life. There was no way Stoneybridge would be boring.

But then he recalled that deep pain in her eyes, and he couldn't shake that away, either. Had he put it there by moving to *her* Main Street, and even more, by not telling her about his store? He hardly wanted to consider that, because hurting another person went against his honey-coated philosophy in life: Just as a spoonful of actual honey can turn a sour recipe into something sweet, likewise, figurative honey—speaking well, being considerate and helpful of others—can change an unpleasant situation and turn it into something nice.

He'd started off on the wrong foot with his neighbor. As she'd pointed out, he should've introduced himself when he bought the store or, at the very least, last Monday. He acknowledged that now.

He glanced out the window at his scraggly dog.

Aimee was right.

It really was about trust.

He needed to find a way to persuade Cynthia to let him groom her, to trust him enough to do so. His inept clipping attempts while she slept weren't enough.

Likewise, he had to earn the trust of his neighbor. He wasn't sure how he was going to do that, since she blamed him for moving in on what she considered her territory. But it was essential to gain it if they were going to coexist peacefully on Main Street.

If her problem was with competition in direct sales, that would end after he was awarded the supermarket contract. Then he could refrain from having a large array of over-the-counter cakes and concentrate on supermarket orders, bespoke orders and his ample, nationwide internet business, which the size of this property, and having Hank, Doug and Doug's wife, Joanne, transfer to Connecticut with him, still made possible.

But until he got that contract, it was all about making as much money and generating as much interest in his business as he could. He would just have to find a way to do it while being considerate of his new neighbor.

***

Aimee's alarm clock—the Town Hall's clock tower at the western end of Main Street—chimed the hour. It was four o'clock Friday morning.

Aimee opened her eyes and scooting onto her knees, pushed her grand-mère's hundred-year-old Chantilly lace curtains aside and peeked out the window above her bed. This was how she always got an idea of what kind of day it would be. Some people watched the weather report on TV. Aimee watched the early-morning sky and listened to the wind. In the late spring, summer, and early fall the birds and the insects, whose ancestors had made Stoneybridge their home long before humans had ever come, gave her clues about the weather to come that day, too.

The morning star twinkled above the church steeple with all its celestial neighbors shimmering around it in the predawn sky. The backdrop wasn't black as people often thought; it was a deep, cobalt blue and as clear and stunning in its own way as the sunlit noon sky would be on this eighteenth day of October. It was going to be a glorious fall day in Stoneybridge. She was certain of it.

After a quick prayer, Aimee hopped out of bed and padded into the bathroom she and Grand-mère had remodeled the year before the dear lady's death. Since Aimee ended each day with a long, rejuvenating soak in the large tub, it only took her a few minutes to get ready in the morning—a brush of her teeth, a little foundation under her eyes, sunrise-red gloss over her lips, a comb through her hair, a scarf across her brow and tied behind her neck, and she was ready to go.

Aimee loved this time of the morning when the whole day with its many possibilities, most depending on her attitude and choices, stretched before her. She could never wait to start baking the *croissants* for the student centers at the universities. The buttery crescent rolls filled the Patisserie with their own special Parisian perfume as she set up the café for her morning crowd. It felt like welcoming people into the dining room of her home.

Sometime during the night, between tossing and turning—and totally disrupting poor Louis's sleep so that at about 2:30 he gave a mighty meow and leaped from Aimee's bed into his own paw-print one—Aimee decided that being at odds with her new neighbor wasn't something she either wanted or had the energy for. He'd been insensitive about opening a bakery right next to hers, that was true. But what was his real crime? Not telling her? Would it really have made a difference if he had? And what was the sense in being angry? Was it going to make him leave?

And did she even want him to leave? a nagging voice asked over and over again. It was *that* question more than the other that had kept her from sleeping. When she finally allowed herself to think about it, she had to admit she'd liked him, *really* liked him, last Monday. But then came Wednesday and Thursday. She hated how those days had intruded on their delightful first meeting. She'd liked bantering with the cowboy she'd imagined he might be on Monday. She'd liked knowing that a hot guy passing through town had awakened a part of her she'd thought as deeply asleep as Perrault's heroine who'd slept for a hundred years. But she disliked the part of her that had fought with him on Thursday.

She'd finally decided that thinking about Gerry Mitchell in either the Monday way or the Thursday way just consumed too much time and effort that was better spent on baking some of her grand-mère's more difficult recipes in order to wow the supermarket people at her preliminary meeting. She'd found out by text message late yesterday that it would be in exactly one week. She also decided she couldn't let her problems with her new neighbor or with her uncle and Grasping Gertrude disrupt the lives of those who came to the Patisserie.

Uncle Cain and his audacious wife might have their always-looking-for-a-profit eye on her Patisserie to turn it into a money-grubbing sports bar, but until November 27th it was hers.

Grand-mère used to say that people came to the Patisserie because it had an innate "pinkish glow," like all things French seemed to have. It was cheerful and happy, a place where people could forget their problems for a little while and dream their big dreams. Aimee had to keep it that way in spite of her own troubles.

As she pulled a fresh pair of her favorite jeans from her closet—she had seven in the exact same style and size but all in a slightly different wash—she knew that no matter what, the Patisserie had to be her focus. Not Uncle Gerry's Cakerie and definitely not her uncle and his nasty wife.

She paused as she only now remembered how happy Gerry's niece and nephew had been at the grand opening of his Cakerie on Wednesday. He seemed to be a good uncle. He'd even let them name his business.

And that mural... She'd noticed yesterday that its likeness was embroidered on the pockets of the uniforms his staff wore and on the chefs' coats too.

The painting showed Gerry in the middle, holding his nephew's hand with his left and his niece's hand with his right as the three walked towards a bright and shining future. The kids were in profile, looking at their uncle as if they could always trust him to be there for them.

Gerry seemed to be exactly the kind of uncle she wished Uncle Cain had been, the kind Grand-mère always maintained he might have become if not for the woman he'd married. Grand-mère had often said that had her son married a woman with a soft and caring heart, his own would have mellowed toward them. He had been moderately hard-hearted and emotionally distant from his family before marrying Gertrude, but he'd become much more so afterward. Since her uncle's last visit though, Aimee wasn't so sure.

But to Louis she said, "I have to admit, the fact that my new neighbor is a good uncle makes even Thursday Gerry seem fine."

Louis opened one eye and blinked up at her.

"I know. You like him."

Louis stretched out his front paws and blinked both eyes.

"A lot. Got it." She poured food in a clean bowl and gave him fresh water. "I'll be back for you in a few hours. Catch up on your sleep, little guy. Sorry I kept you awake last night."

Louis yawned and curled in a tight little ball, sound asleep again by the time she closed the door behind her.

5—Tryst

Two hours later, with the croissants baking in the oven, her accounting books all up to date, the kitchen organized for the day, and the Patisserie just waiting for its first patrons—always the young Wall Street crowd who ran in for their café au lait to give them strength for the hour-plus train ride into New York City—Aimee donned her light jacket. Taking her new, orange broom from the utility closet, she unlocked the café's front door and walked out onto the sidewalk.

Next to baking, this was her favorite part of the pre-opening hours of the day. She loved sweeping the twenty feet of space between her building and the street and the thirty-two feet of storefront that made up "her" part of the sidewalk. Or maybe it wasn't the sweeping so much as being out on Main Street at the start of the day. Regardless of the weather, everything was fresh and clean. Apart from sharing it with her almost-brother, Bob, to whom she waved as he cruised by in his police car, Main Street was all hers before the clock in the tower struck six. Most of the stores would be without any activity for at least another hour, with many of them not opening until nine. Only Joe's Diner and the Maple Tree B&B were getting set up at this time of day. But they were quite a distance away at the opposite ends of Main Street.

The sound of keys rattling behind the glass door of the neighboring shop startled her. She swiveled to look but continued to move the broom back and forth, the ancient movement somehow comforting. It was such a strange feeling to hear the next-door shop being opened. Mr. Wong never opened his dry-cleaning store a second before eight o'clock. Was her middle-of-the-night resolve concerning Gerry Mitchell about to be tested?

When Gerry walked out holding an identical broom—he must have gotten it from Hale's Hardware, too—Aimee froze.

When he saw her, Gerry paused.

They were looking directly at each other, and they were speaking volumes without communicating in words.

Let's be friends, his gaze seemed to say.

I want to, she responded hesitantly.

Then let's, he encouraged.

Vaguely Aimee shook her head.

She wanted to get along with her neighbor, but being friends? She'd been good friends with Mr. Wong.

The soft breeze blew through the dogwood tree, making its leaves sing a romantic song reminding her that this man was not grandfatherly Mr. Wong. The man in front of her now was Gerry, and so far, she'd seen different sides of him every day this week. Or at least that was how it felt…

But today was Friday. Maybe she could find a Friday way to like him. Becoming friends was a slow, unfolding process. Sometimes people had qualities you didn't like but others you did.

Liking the man who ran the store next to hers really wasn't a choice. Last night, she'd decided to get along with him; she had to act on that. Poor Louis couldn't take another miserable night of her tossing and turning. Neither could she. Grand-mère always said that the strength you gained from a good night's sleep is mighty. One of Grand-mère's other sayings, though, was that a smile could lead to a million things. Did she want it to lead to even a hundred with Gerry Mitchell?

A lone leaf slowly fluttered to the ground. It landed on the red-brick sidewalk equidistant between Gerry's space and hers.

That lazy grin she'd liked so much on Monday spread across his face. "Good morning," he finally drawled, tipped his Stetson and leaned nonchalantly on his broom handle, still looking every bit a cowboy to her.

She smiled back. She couldn't help it. Her facial muscles just moved that way and…she didn't *want* to stop them. He was her neighbor, she told herself again. She had to get along with him. She could let her smile lead if not to a hundred things at least to one. Being neighborly. "Good morning," she returned.

The town's clock rang out six times. He breathed in deeply and glancing up the street toward the Georgian Town Hall and its timepiece, said, "Looks like it's going to be a glorious fall day."

Aimee nodded. It was as cool and crisp and golden a day as Aimee had expected it to be.

"One of the many reasons I love Connecticut," he continued.

"Everyone loves Connecticut in the fall," she said. "You have to love it during the bitter winters, stormy springs and humid summers too."

"Trying to scare me off? Get me to go back to warm LA?" he asked with a crooked curve to his mouth. She heard amusement in his lazy drawl.

With a smile tugging at her lips, she said, "Of course."

He grinned, obviously at ease. "Don't believe you."

"That, Gerry Mitchell, is up to you," she said and as she saw the first of her Wall Street café au lait drinkers rushing across the street toward her, his tie flapping behind him, she opened the door of the Patisserie and went inside. Wall Street café au lait drinkers weren't to be kept waiting, not on any day of the week but particularly not on Fridays.

***

Her Wall Street crowd might not have had an early-morning date with the train on Saturday or Sunday mornings, but it was as if she and Gerry Mitchell had a 6:00 a.m. tryst. Each holding their identical brooms, first Gerry would smile, tip his hat and say, "Good morning," and then Aimee would reply.

She wanted to be neighborly, but every single day at six o'clock, her favorite time? She just couldn't seem to *not* say, "Good morning." She didn't want to be labeled the town Grinch, after all. Green was so not her color.

But by Monday morning—exactly one week after meeting Gerry—even if she didn't look it, she felt like a Grinch as those nagging feelings that her neighbor had everything to gain and she had everything to lose started to play again in her head. She tried to tune them out, but over the weekend more college students—granted, mostly young women who probably saw Gerry's resemblance to a virile all-American cowboy, too—went to the Cakerie for cupcakes and cookies than into the Patisserie for croissants and *macarons*. Out-of-towners, too—at least fifty—had driven into Stoneybridge specifically to go to Uncle Gerry's. They'd left with huge cake boxes that barely fit in the back of their SUVs. The idea that she was losing clientele began to slowly prey on her again. But still, this Monday morning, she'd stupidly smiled at him just as broadly as she had on Friday, Saturday and Sunday mornings.

She pounded the cookie dough she was working on for a batch of *sablés* that she would fill with apricot jam.

She blamed her smiling on reflex. A dangerous one. Like an unwanted knee jerk that resulted in kicking a table with a crystal wine glass full of red wine and spilling it all over a brand new silk carpet—white, of course—and, worst of all, in another person's home. She wouldn't have minded their just nodding at each other. But he was so totally keen on saying "Good morning." And smiling. And why shouldn't he? He was the one who'd moved in on her territory, who didn't have the decency to tell her Uncle Gerry's Cakerie was coming to *her* Main Street and was going to start devouring all her customers. She'd done nothing wrong.

She shook her head.

She had to stop thinking this way. *She thought she had!*

She had to remember her resolve to get along with her neighbor.

She pounded the dough.

She paused.

She had to stop pounding the dough or she'd be serving the hardest *sablés* anyone in Stoneybridge had ever tasted.

***

As Gerry poured a fifty-pound bag of flour into his Hobart mixer, he was thinking about Aimee's Monday-morning smile. It had hit him with the force of *two* fifty-pound bags of flour. When her lips turned up, the dimple to the left of her mouth flared like a shooting star. He'd found himself looking forward to seeing that elusive hollow on her smooth cheek every morning. He was a sucker for dimples, and particularly on women whose entire package was so perfect. He hadn't planned on sweeping the sidewalk in front of his store every morning at 6:00—it was normally a job he allocated—but ever since their unplanned meeting on Friday, as soon as he got to the store at 5:00 a.m. he'd set his phone's alarm to go off fifty-five minutes later. Hearing it, no matter what he was in the middle of preparing in the kitchen, he'd wash his hands, grab his broom, keys and hat, and dash out onto Main Street.

Dared he believe that her super-size smile—and Gerry liked super-size things as his cakes proved—was a sign that Aimee was getting past the whole competition issue?

To say that he *hoped* so would be an understatement. "Get over yourself, man," he muttered as he pushed trays full of giant cupcakes, a huge favorite with the high school and college crowd, into the oven. Aimee was only being polite in smiling at him.

Or was she?

He set the timer for thirty minutes and paused as he gazed in at the blueberry cake batter that the oven's heat turned from liquid into one of the most delicious solid sugar confections in the world.

He and Aimee had shared one of those quick and true, nearly magical attractions the previous Monday, the day they met. That was before she'd found out he was her next-door neighbor and that he came complete with a Cakerie. It had changed everything.

But all the ingredients for turning smiles into something more were still there. It couldn't be denied—even with events interfering—that some kind of feeling was growing naturally and surely between them.

As the cupcakes started to rise before his eyes, Gerry smiled. If Aimee's smile was anything to go by, he knew she still felt that way, too.

"Boss." Hank, the young man who had a real knack for sculpting things out of any medium, called to him from behind.

Gerry shook himself.

Correct ingredients or not, he knew that the situation could become too complicated.

It was better to keep his last-Monday relationship with Aimee as "batter" and not mix it with "heat"—the volatile, emotional kind—that might make it grow. Flirting with her had been fun.

But now, he didn't want anything other than to be a good neighbor to Aimee Hart. Anything else would complicate his life in a way he had no desire to do. He'd left complications like that behind in California. He didn't want a new one arising in Connecticut.

"What's up?" he asked Hank and threw himself into his workday full force.

***

"There is absolutely no possibility of us ever defecting to the bakery next door," Miss Maggie assured Aimee the next morning as Aimee placed her standing order of hot chocolate and *escargot* in front of her. "I just couldn't believe it when the store was unveiled and it was a *bakery*," she huffed.

"And owned by none other than the good-looking man who bet it was going to be a pet-grooming salon," Penny said. She hadn't held back how annoyed she'd felt over the way he'd duped them all.

"He wishes," Ruth muttered. "Have you seen how unkempt his dog is? And she's a standard poodle."

"Standard poodle!" Aimee exclaimed. She'd had no idea.

"Probably with a pedigree, too," Ruth added.

"I thought she was a gorgeous mutt like Louis, but a canine version."

"No, definitely a poodle." It was well-known that Ruth Lovejoy could have been an animal doctor as easily as she was a people doctor. "A poodle who needs her hair trimmed on a regular basis." Ruth loved animals and hated to see them neglected or abused in any fashion.

"She has some sort of issue with having it trimmed," Aimee offered, but when she registered the same, wide-eyed look cast her way by all four ladies, she wished she'd kept her mouth shut.

"Really," Mrs. Fonteyn said and arching her eyebrows, she asked with interest, "What else do you know about your new neighbor, dear?"

Aimee was determined to keep her cool, even with her heart rate picking up at her blunder. Otherwise, she'd leave herself wide open to gossip. She shrugged. "Not a thing. Just that he moved a bakery next to my store."

"The one type of store you didn't want it to be," Mrs. Fonteyn reminded her, breathing out a great operatic breath.

Aimee was more than a little relieved that she'd managed to change the focus of the conversation. "Exactly."

"You would've thought he'd tell you beforehand," Penny said. "I'd sure want to know if another music store was moving to town." Unlike Aimee with the Patisserie, Penny's music store, Sound Waves, wasn't even her real passion. Teaching people to play the piano—and to love it as much as she did—

was. She even offered free tutorials at the civic center for anyone who wanted to learn but couldn't afford private lessons.

Aimee smiled at Penny. It made her feel good to hear another Main Street store-owner think the same way she did.

"Well, we—" Miss Maggie nodded to the others at her table "—will never set foot in his shop."

"I've heard whispers around town," Bob interjected, "that everyone's talking about boycotting it." They all turned to him. It didn't surprise anybody that he'd been listening to what the locals had to say. That ability of his to stay on the alert was what made him such a talented sheriff. He always knew what was going on in Stoneybridge. Carefully folding today's paper so the next person would find it in perfect condition, he stood. "But, of course, that's not something I can condone."

"Of course not, Bob." Aimee smiled over at him as she waved off his attempt to pay for his café au lait. "Still, I must admit, it's good to hear that my town is on my side."

"That doesn't mean the college girls will stay away," Valery pointed out and nodded encouragingly at Tommy as he took another swallow of milk.

Penny guffawed. "Well, the fact that he's nice-looking certainly can't be denied."

"As our dear Sleeping Beauty here seemed to wake up and notice before finding out he was enemy-pastry-chef-number-one," Miss Maggie said and winked at Aimee.

Aimee groaned to herself. Her vow never to be the subject of town gossip again—especially over a man—was in danger of being breached. This had to be stopped before it got out of hand. "I just welcomed his dog, Miss Maggie."

Miss Maggie exchanged a glance with Mrs. Fonteyn.

"Whatever you say, dear," Mrs. Fonteyn answered for both of them.

Aimee took a deep breath and picking up the cup left behind by Bob, said, "Well, I thank you all for your support of the Patisserie. But it sure seemed busy at the Cakerie over the weekend."

"Right now it's just a gimmick, Aimee," Bob said as he checked his phone for messages and walked toward the door. "It's a new store. After a bit of time, his business will slow down to a more normal rate."

Penny nodded in agreement. "When I went to give a piano lesson in Stamford, I saw it advertised in their town paper."

"Seriously?" Aimee had never suspected that Gerry might have taken out ads.

"And in the *News Times,* too," Mrs. Fonteyn said.

Aimee shook her head. "Extraordinary. Grand-mère never advertised the Patisserie, and it never crossed my mind, either."

"Well, maybe you should," Becky said. She walked in on the conversation just as Bob walked out.

"Becky!" Miss Maggie seemed concerned to see her manager enter the Patisserie. "Who's minding *our* store?"

Becky motioned vaguely in the direction of the vintage Rolls Royce parked in front of the Treasure Trove. "'Carole Lombard' just came in. I thought you might've seen her car—"

Miss Maggie's eyes nearly popped out of her head. She jumped up, making the antique table shake and almost toppled the four cups of hot chocolate. "Oh, my, Becky! Good girl! You did right to come and get me." Miss Maggie didn't like phones, neither mobile nor landlines. She was a people person and preferred to speak face-to-face.

All heads swiveled to catch a glimpse of the gorgeous Rolls Royce that was parked across the street. Aimee bent down and noticed through the window that even Louis was gazing at it from his treehouse. She knew that its gleaming chrome, which picked up the morning sunrays and sent their reflection dancing on the street, was what had caught his attention. The car took up almost two parking spaces and its driver was dressed in a whipcord coat, a chauffeur's cap and gloves. Everyone's idea of how a chauffeur should look.

"What's she doing in town so late in the month? And…so early in the morning?" Miss Maggie mused about the eccentric woman everyone in town referred to as "Carole Lombard." She wasn't, of course. They just thought she looked how the Hollywood star would've had she lived to be an older woman. Married to Clark Gable, the forever-young Carole Lombard had unfortunately died at the age of thirty-three in a plane crash, nearly eighty years ago.

Becky shrugged in a nonchalant manner. True to form, she was never impressed by anything remotely suggesting so-called Hollywood royalty. And she had mention to Aimee several times before that she was certain this lady had to have some connection to Tinseltown. "She said something about having an unexpected soiree during which her friends will put on a private performance—"

"A private performance! Oh! Wonderful!" Miss Maggie broke in. "Just like in English manor homes in bygone days when the members of the house and their guests would stage plays…just for themselves. She normally hosts a soiree only once a month, during the first weekend. But every now and then, she arranges an extra one." She paused to think for a moment. "Or else, maybe she won't be able to host it the first weekend of November. Whatever. They need my mood-setting clothes now! Wonderful! Wonderful! I must go! I must go!" she said to the entire café. Then to Becky, "You bring the *macarons* and the Belgian Drinking Chocolate, dear. Aimee knows how to make it just the way she likes it," she instructed before turning to Aimee. "Do you have blueberry, coffee and pistachio *macarons*? Fresh ones? Those three are her favorites. But they *have* to be fresh."

Aimee pointed over her shoulder toward the kitchen. "I just finished the blueberry *macarons*. The coffee *macarons* have cooled enough to be filled, and I'll whip up a batch of pistachio now." She sought to calm Miss Maggie as she headed toward the kitchen. "The pistachio will be ready and boxed for her to take home in about two hours."

"Thank you, dear," Miss Maggie breathed in relief. "Give me about twenty minutes alone with her," she instructed Becky. "Then bring the blueberry *macarons* and hot chocolate over using Grand-mère's—Aimee's," she corrected, "Victorian china tea service." She paused. "You'll come back for the coffee *macarons* in an hour. She likes things brought out in increments."

"Will do, Miss M." Becky called her by her personal pet name—something Miss Maggie didn't mind at all—and smiled with genuine fondness at the older woman as Miss Maggie ran out the door, her long muumuu flowing behind her. Everyone in the shop knew that "Carole Lombard"—no one knew her real name—single-handedly supported Miss Maggie's Treasure Trove. She left her estate in the hills above Stoneybridge once a month—sometimes twice as she had this month—and bought half of Miss Maggie's inventory. Becky watched her employer leave. Then, giving a push on the wooden easy-swing kitchen door with its peek-a-boo window, she followed Aimee into the kitchen.

Aimee pulled three dozen eggs out of the fridge to start on the pistachio *macarons*.

Becky washed her hands and after donning gloves, checked to see if the coffee meringue had cooled enough to pipe onto the mocha filling Aimee had already prepared. "They need another ten minutes."

"Okay," Aimee said as she separated egg whites from their yolks. She used only free-range eggs from farms in the area and nothing mass-marketed. Except for her massive and very old ovens, the Patisserie kitchen was basically the same as a well appointed kitchen in someone's home. She knew she'd have to do things a little differently when she landed the Main Street Bakery contract, but she'd deal with that when the time came.

Becky leaned against the counter. "Aimee, you should think about advertising the Patisserie."

Aimee glanced up at her. "Where did that come from?"

Becky nodded toward the wall that separated Aimee's kitchen from the one next door. Many different sounds—sounds Aimee and her employees couldn't yet identify—could be heard coming through it. "Since your neighbor does, why don't you? You need to fight fire with fire, not fire with sugar." She pointed to the canister containing powdered sugar.

"I've decided not to fight the pastry man next door at all." She knew she was always flip-flopping on that issue. But…he was her neighbor and her colleague. She *had* to get along with him.

"Really?"

Aimee could tell that wasn't what Becky wanted to hear, and she appreciated the control it took her friend not to say anything more concerning it. Aimee liked being in this detached frame of mind, not being upset with Gerry Mitchell. It had been hard to achieve, even harder to maintain, and it would've been impossible without her faith. That morning, while reading the Twenty-Third Psalm, Aimee had immersed herself in the beautiful words and the peace they brought her. They were still sustaining her.

"In that case," Becky said, continuing but in another direction, "you should at least be honest with the townspeople and let them know *why* it's so important that they keep on supporting the Patisserie. Tell them about the loan you have to repay your Uncle Cain and his *darling wife*." Aimee knew that Becky blamed the "darling wife" more than her uncle for everything. "Just the way Miss Maggie let you know she needed your support with 'Carole Lombard,' you have to let people know about your need, too."

"It's different," Aimee said and with all the egg whites in the bowl, she set the whisk timer on the mixer and turned it on.

"How do you figure?"

Aimee gave Becky her full attention. "Miss Maggie doesn't care if people talk about her. I do." She took a deep breath and admitted to Becky her deepest fear, one she'd finally acknowledged to herself while soaking in her tub the previous night. "Grand-mère ran this Patisserie for nearly seventy *successful* years. I don't want people to think that within two years of her passing, I can't do it."

Becky's dark-blue eyes opened wide. "Aimee Hart, if that's the reason for not telling your neighbors and friends about your current situation, I'm sorry, but I don't think it's a very good one. That storm—the real one, not your Uncle Cain—is to blame. As well as the pandemic that kept the stores on Main

Street, including yours, closed for months. Your entrepreneurial skills are *not* to blame."

"Regardless, Becky, the idea of being the center of town gossip for *any* reason—" she shuddered "—makes my skin crawl. Especially if it got around that I might lose the Patisserie." Aimee smiled over at her friend, hoping she was portraying determination—even if she only felt it slightly. "I trust the loyalty of my customers. They aren't going to desert the Patisserie or me."

"I think they'd be even more inclined not to if you told them what's at stake," she insisted. "You're doing them a disservice by not being totally forthcoming." She shrugged her shoulders in a way that meant she wasn't going to overstep the bounds of friendship. Becky always knew when to leave a subject alone. "But it's your business." She flashed a smile. "No pun intended. I won't break your confidence."

"Thank you."

Aimee could see that Becky still had more she wanted to say, but she merely nodded as she picked up one of the coffee wafers. "Cooled to perfection," she said. She took a nibble. "Mmm. Delish! I'll get to work piping the mocha filling."

Nodding, Aimee checked the egg whites. They were being whisked to the glossy, fluffy meringue that was so important to the success of a "just right" French *macaron*. Another four minutes and the peaks would form.

"Are you ready for your preliminary presentation Friday morning?" Becky asked.

"My contact with the chain says they need three samples. I'm going with raspberry *macarons,* chocolate *éclairs* and *St. Honoré* cakes."

"Don't see how you can go wrong with those classics."

Aimee groaned. "A million ways."

"That's not being positive!" Becky admonished.

"And a positive mind is a 'sure –"

"—recipe for success'!'" Becky finished Grand-mère's saying and they both laughed. "What a smart lady…"

"A tough act to follow, that's for certain."

"But you're doing it, Aimee. Grand-mère would be proud of you."

"Let's hope so."

Aimee was reaching for the ground-almond-and-sugar mixture to sift into the meringue, the most delicate part of the process, when…the power went out.

"Oh, no! Not again!" Aimee wailed as she heard her clients in the café start the "no power" murmur over their cups of coffee and pastries. "This is the third time in as many days!" She looked with horror at the egg whites that had been prematurely stilled. Running over to a far drawer, she pulled out an ancient, hand-held whisk.

"Grand-mère's old whisk!" Becky exclaimed. "I haven't seen that in years."

"After this happened yesterday, and I lost yet another three dozen egg whites, I went looking for it so I'd be prepared. Just in case. I have no choice but to finishing whipping these eggs the old-fashioned way." She quickly started whisking by hand. "I don't understand what's going on with the electricity in this town," she muttered.

Becky frowned in confusion. "What do you mean? The power hasn't gone out across the street at all. Nowhere else in town from what I know, either."

"What?" That she was the only one with this problem wasn't something she'd considered. "Then why—?" She tilted her head, listening. Nothing. No hum of a mixer or buzz of a freezer or any sound whatsoever coming from the store next door. The quiet was almost deafening. Then it hit her. "I don't believe it!" she thundered. She handed the vintage whisk to Becky and said, "It probably needs another minute or so. Just keep the strokes even." When Becky had taken over the whisking, Aimee untied her apron, threw it in the bin and stomped toward the back door.

Becky was totally confused. "What gives?" she asked without losing the whisking rhythm.

"It's all his big equipment!" Aimee pointed at the plaster wall that separated her kitchen from Gerry's. "We're on the same grid, and his large-scale equipment is draining all the power!"

Becky's eyes opened wide. She motioned to the meringue. "I've got this covered. You go get him, girl!"

Aimee was ready. Having her power cut off every day was asking too much of her tentative neighborly spirit. As she ran out the back door into the alley, she heard Becky loudly humming the "Battle Hymn of the Republic."

It was exactly how Aimee felt.

Battle lines had been drawn.

Whether she wanted it or not, a pastry war with her next-door neighbor was at hand.

6—Baker Man

Gerry turned on the revolution oven for the Harley-motorbike cake he was making for his window display when "click," the power went down.

He groaned.

"When did you say that new generator was coming in, boss?" Doug asked as he watched the Hobart mixer grind to a rotating halt around the nearly hundred and forty pounds of vanilla cake batter he'd been preparing. Doug was a whiz in the kitchen. Unflappable and ever calm, he had retired two years ago after thirty-five years with the LA fire department, where his cooking experience consisted of doing all the baking for his unit—as well as performing his duties as chief. He'd been known as "Chief Chef" to his crew. For the millionth time, Gerry reminded himself that it was because Doug and his wife, Joanne, as well as his master craftsman, Hank, had agreed to move east with him that he could even have attempted such a drastic change.

"This afternoon," Gerry said. "Hang on." He flipped off the revolution oven and a couple of other energy-draining appliances. He strode over to the utility room where the fuse box was located. He reprimanded himself. If he hadn't been thinking about sales, he wouldn't have turned on the oven while the mixer, proofing cabinet and sheeter were all on, too.

But he was concerned.

A week minus one day had passed since the grand opening last Wednesday and, despite his initial success, he sensed that there was some sort of loyalty thing going on that kept the people of Stonebridge out of his shop and *in* the store next door. He could understand their being dedicated to Aimee, but it was beginning to disturb him seeing one person after another walk into her Patisserie while sending covert glances—as if he were the enemy—his way.

He could tell they were curious and wanted to see what Uncle Gerry's offered, but not even the policemen in town had stopped by. Policemen were notorious across America for always being the first to try out a new bakery. He'd gotten to the point where he avoided being in the front of the shop—except during the time of day when the college girls came in—because being ignored by the townspeople bothered him more than he'd ever imagined it would. Gerry wasn't the type of man most overlooked.

As he had told Aimee, he truly believed there was more than enough room on Main Street for the Patisserie and Uncle Gerry's to exist side by side. They could work as a team, learn to complement each other.

Although the supermarket deal seemed to be on the right track—he had a preliminary meeting on Friday afternoon—Gerry wasn't one to trust anything until he'd signed on the dotted line. In spite of great nationwide online sales, his relocation to the East Coast and the remodeling of the store had left his finances in desperate need of a boost. The support he'd received the previous weekend from his sister's friends and their friends, who had come out in droves, was nice but not enough.

He was making a massive cake in the shape of a Harley Davidson motorbike hoping to draw in more college men. So far, the college women were his main patrons for over-the-counter goods. To increase his current bank balance he needed to attract the people of the area, at least for now, and—

"You're draining all the power!" Aimee's angry voice broke into his thoughts. He poked his head around the utility door. Sure enough, there she was in all her vengeful glory.

"Beg your pardon?" Doug asked calmly as he turned to face her.

"Oh, sorry." Gerry saw Aimee take a step back. "I thought you were Gerry." *So she reserved her wrath for him. Wonderful.*

Gerry watched as Chief Chef's brows rose and a nostalgic smile spread across his face. "It's been a while since I've been mistaken for a thirty-something man. Thank you, Ms. Hart." He nodded in Gerry's direction. "The man you want is over there, looking into getting our power going again." He frowned. "Your power's down, too?"

Gerry switched on the fuse, and the humming and buzzing of the refrigerator and freezer started up. He was glad that was all it took this time. The previous two days it had taken a couple of hours of painstaking wire cutting and splicing by Doug and him. A wary tension strung his senses to a high pitch of awareness as he approached Aimee. He hated women being angry with him. "Aimee? Your power went out?" He repeated Doug's question.

"Yes." She swiveled to face him, and Gerry was once again hit by the knowledge that, even with her face stormy, he was very attracted to her. He couldn't understand the logic of that. What was wrong with him? The woman was fuming. And at him. So why did he still like her the way a man likes a woman? Perhaps if they'd met another time, another place...before Scarlett...before he'd opened a bakery next door to hers...before her power had gone out… He shook his head over his pointless thoughts.

"I'm sorry. I didn't know," he offered, hoping she'd accept his apology and let bygones be bygones. He didn't like conflict on the best of days, and today wasn't one of those. "I assumed it only affected this property."

She waved her hand toward her side of the wall. "It's happened *three* times. We've lost nine dozen eggs. I never had this problem with Mr. Wong," she snapped, nothing like the smiling woman who'd greeted him that morning at six. The flip side to the smile coin, Gerry thought.

"Sorry," he repeated. He was determined to keep his cool. He was uncharacteristically down in the dumps today and didn't want to be drawn into a pastry battle with his pretty neighbor. "After today you won't have it with me, either. A generator's being installed." He reached for the slice of cake he'd planned to eat. "Carrot cake?" He held it out to her. Cake always boosted his mood, and none more than carrot.

But perhaps not Aimee's. She scowled as if the slice were poison. "I'm not hungry."

"Excuse me," Doug interrupted. "It concerns me that the power problem's affected your shop, too," he said. Ten years of being a fire chief and having dealt with such issues was reflected in his knowledgeable eyes.

Aimee shrugged. "Once upon a time, long ago, before my grandmother even bought the store, our properties were connected. Maybe that has something to do with it."

"That would be it," Doug agreed, and with the electrical mystery solved, he went back to his batter.

So the properties had been connected at one time. Gerry found that bit of trivia anything but trivial. "It would be nice if we could connect our properties again," he ventured and at the look of horror that filled her face, he quickly explained. "I mean in some sort of complementary way, a way that might help both our businesses." He voiced his thought of a few minutes earlier.

She glanced at him with what seemed to be amused tolerance. "My business is doing fine."

Gerry studied her.

Self-assured with just a touch of arrogance in the angle of her chin, the lift of her brow and the tilt of her neck. It seemed to him that Aimee had everything he was hoping to achieve.

She had a secure, well-established store that she owned outright. He had a crippling mortgage.

She had a town full of people who loved her. It would take time—lots of it—for him to be accepted by them.

She had an approved, well-established, classical product—truly exquisite French pastries that people had loved for centuries. He had a gimmicky product that might or might not take off in this more traditional area of the country.

But since she'd unwittingly given him an opening to the subject that was the cause of his dour mood, he wasn't about to let the chance slip away. "Yes, I've noticed that. In fact, I don't think your complaint about my taking business away from you has been at all substantiated by the people of this town," he returned.

Her eyes widened. In guilt? Or confusion? He wasn't sure.

When she remained quiet, he continued. "In fact, I'd say there's some sort of town-wide campaign to boycott my store." He clicked his tongue. "You wouldn't happen to know anything about that, would you?"

She met his gaze, met it honestly and openly, without flinching. When she spoke, her carefully enunciated words were soft, unemotional. "You moved in on *my* territory, Mr. Mitchell. I didn't move the Patisserie next door to your shop in LA. You moved your bakery next door to my seventy-year-old bakery in Stoneybridge."

He got her point and had to admit to himself that—even though America was a big land where people were free to move unhindered—there was some justification in it. But what he heard the loudest was that she made no attempt to deny that she was aware of the sanctions imposed on his shop.

Jumpin' Jehoshephat! His father's expression, when he was amazed by something, ran through his mind: A woman who came in such an attractive package, who could bake like he supposed angels might if they did such a thing and who didn't lie. No wonder he liked her in spite of her volatile reactions to his store.

She wiped her fingers across her brow as if, he felt, she was wiping him away. Then, turning her slender back to him, she started toward the service door. "Excuse me, but I've got some very important *macarons* waiting for me," she tossed over her right shoulder.

"Aimee, I'm sorry," he said again. He felt he owed it to her, even though he was beginning to think that all he ever did was apologize to her.

She paused, but kept her back to him.

"Most of all, I'm sorry I've upset you so much by moving here." He specified what he was apologizing for, although he knew she understood what he meant.

When she whispered, "Thank you," he was glad he'd said it. "I appreciate that."

Her words gave him hope. Moving as quickly as he used to on the football field, he stepped past her and said, "Aimee, please have a look at this." From the way her shoulders sagged, he could tell she didn't want to look, that all she wanted was to get back to her precious *macarons*. But he had to prove to her that she didn't need to think of him as her enemy. When he pulled back the parchment paper that covered his work-in-progress, she turned her head at the crinkle and the ruffling sound it made. "Our products really are very different."

She walked over to the frame of the cake, right now just a combination of wood and molding chocolate. Pointing at it, she asked, "What is that?"

"A cake in the shape of a Harley Davidson motorbike!" He was very pleased with its preliminary stage. He could already see the finished product. It was one of the reasons he was so good at making such large cakes; in his mind he could see what it would become from the very first. "Hank, my master sculptor, and I are making this cake for the display window." He didn't mention that he was trying to entice college men into his store.

"Did you say 'cake'?" she challenged and her lips twitched as she touched the wooden parts. "It doesn't look anything like a cake." *She couldn't see how it would be when it was completed?* That seemed unbelievable to him. "Tell me," she continued and he could tell that, although incredulous, she was also amused. "How many flavors does wood—" she flicked a fingernail against the frame "—come in?"

He ignored her sarcasm. "I'm trying to prove to you that we're not in competition. My focus is—"

"Big, brash and crass?"

Not exactly how he'd put it. "Sculpting large with cake."

She bent down to inspect it and asked, "Where's the cake?"

"When it's completed, there'll be enough cake on this project to serve seventy people."

"But will it be edible?"

He wouldn't dignify that with an answer. His cakes had won tasting competitions throughout the State of California, a hard market in which to sell sugary goods. "My point is we aren't competitors," he repeated. "We don't have to be."

She swiveled her gaze back to meet his. The light of having caught him in a lie flashed in her eyes. "Oh, really? And tell me, Mr. Motorbike Man, how many people in their big SUVs came from other towns to visit *my* store over the weekend?"

He couldn't believe it! She'd noticed that? Would it be worth it to explain that they'd been mostly his sister's friends and people he knew from when he'd lived in Nazareth or people he'd connected with in LA? So far, just a few people from neighboring towns had responded to the ads he'd put in their newspapers. No, looking at the self-righteous anger she now wore, he knew there wouldn't be any point in trying to explain. She'd already made up her mind. He remained quiet.

"Exactly. You keep your SUV patrons and let me keep my Stoneybridge clients, and we'll get along just fine." With that, she turned and walked out the back door.

Gerry glanced over at Doug.

The older man shrugged his shoulders. "She'll come around."

Gerry wasn't so sure.

Even though he'd tried numerous times, she'd made it clear that she wasn't interested in any sort of cooperation with him.

The gauntlet had been thrown, a formal challenge issued.

If they couldn't join forces and somehow make their products complement one another, at least in the eyes of patrons, then he'd have to work, if not exactly against her—because he really didn't want to blast her business out of existence—but not in collaboration with her, either. In the mood he was in right now, what he wanted more than anything was to ruffle the feathers of the woman next door.

He just had to figure out the best way to do it…

A thought was forming in his mind...

"Doug, if I were to bring the lady—" he nodded in the direction Aimee had just gone "—ten dozen eggs to replace the nine the power outage caused her to lose, would that leave us with enough to do the baking we have scheduled for today?"

Doug removed his gloves and reached into his pocket. "If Joanne can rustle us up a few dozen, we'll be fine." He called his wife's number. When not in charge of the shipping and handling of Uncle Gerry's nationwide on-line orders in what used to be the previous owner's home upstairs, Joanne ran the small organic-egg farm the couple had bought in the hills above Stoneybridge. "And I'm sure she can," he said and winked.

"Perfect." Gerry went to the fridge and, carton by carton, pulled out ten dozen eggs and placed them on a tray.

Doug said, "Bye dear," to Joanne and with a circular motion of his finger toward the clock motioned to Gerry that the eggs would be brought when she came in later.

Picking up the precarious load of cartons filled with twenty-four eggs each, Gerry said, "Be back in a few minutes."

Doug laughed. "I'm telling you, the lady ain't gonna like it!"

Gerry raised his eyebrows. "I'm counting on that!"

***

Aimee was studying the pistachio meringue that Becky had finished piping onto the trays. Flat, even disks about an inch and a half in diameter with a very attractive pistachio green color—something that wasn't easy to get right—covered the five trays. "They're going to be perfect, Becky. You're so talented at this," Aimee said and set them aside for an hour to form a hard crust before baking them.

"Can't have Miss Maggie's Carole Lombard disappointed when she opens the box and partakes of the 'cloud cookies' she loves so much," Becky said as she removed her gloves. "So…how'd it go next door?" she asked as she tossed her apron into the bin. "Do I even want to know?"

Aimee shrugged. "Let's say Mr. Baker Man and I both know where we stand."

"That could mean many things."

Aimee grimaced. "I think the song you were humming as I left was apropos. I think we're at war."

"Aimee, no!"

"Well, he wants his *huge* cakes and he wants to eat them, too!"

"Not at all," Gerry's voice objected from behind them, causing Aimee and Becky to jump at the unexpected sound.

Both women turned to see his eyes peeking out from behind a skyscraper of egg cartons that he was carrying through the alley door. "But I do want to replace those eggs I've ruined."

"I didn't ask you to," Aimee immediately shot back. "What are you doing?" she questioned as he maneuvered the fragile tower onto the counter space that had recently been taken up with pistachio *macaron* wafers.

Becky laughed. "I'd say it's a good time for me to go serve Carole Lombard her Belgian Drinking Chocolate and blueberry *macaron*. See ya." She waved to Aimee and let it include Gerry.

"Carole Lombard?" Gerry asked Aimee as he stood back.

"Long story." She gave the tray holding the eggs a slight push toward him. "Please take them back."

"Does it have anything to do with that Rolls parked across the street right now?" He ignored her comment about the eggs and went back to Carole Lombard.

Aimee nodded. "Miss Maggie's most important customer."

"Got it."

"She loves *macarons*."

"The very important *macarons* you had to get back to," he murmured and held up his hands. "And…hands off…" he didn't add, "your customer."

Aimee only nodded. She was glad she didn't have to spell it out. But she couldn't help keeping her gaze on his hands. Very attractive, strong hands, with minor calluses even. She supposed he got those calluses when he sculpted his so-called cakes. "Please take these eggs back."

"You said I ruined nine dozen. Here are ten," he replied lazily. Then in a butter-could-melt-in-his-mouth kind of voice and with eyes as deep and dusky as a fall day at twilight, he said, "With my apology."

Why did it sound like he was flirting with her? And why did her stomach flip-flop in response? "Are you going to make me carry all these eggs back to your kitchen?" Her voice was gruffer than she intended. But that was his fault for looking so good.

"I ruined yours. It's only fair."

"What's fair is you leaving *my* Main Street."

"That again." He reached around her and she couldn't believe it when he lightly tugged her ponytail. *Tugged it!*

"Hey!" she exclaimed and leaned away. No one had tugged her ponytail since Billy Boyd in the sixth grade. He'd done it to bug her when she ran faster than all the boys during a cross country race. She'd clobbered Billy—and thought about doing the same thing to Gerry now.

"The way I see it, Aimee, all that *our* section of Main Street needs now is a candy store. Then this stretch could be labeled the 'sugar district of Stoneybridge.'"

She examined his face carefully, looking for clues as to what was behind his coming over with the eggs. He was trying to give nothing away, but she saw the glint of amusement that shone out of his eyes and decided there wasn't much difference between him and Billy Boyd. "Did you come over here to give me eggs, or were they just an excuse to annoy me?"

A laugh grated in his throat.

She had her answer.

He'd mostly wanted to bug her.

That was it for her. She wasn't in the sixth grade anymore so she couldn't clobber him. She did the next best thing. She picked up one of his eggs and tossed it in the sink. The satisfaction of seeing shock register on his face made wasting that egg—something she really hated doing—worth it. "Take the eggs back or I'll do that to all hundred and twenty of them."

His eyes were hard now, probably as hard as hers. But only for a split second. Then an expression somewhere between amusement and revelation jumped into them, and she knew she'd regret turning down those beautiful eggs, which had been offered to the world by happy, free-range Connecticut hens. "If you don't want them I *will* take them back. And thanks. I just figured out what I'll do with them."

Oh, no! Something else to trouble her peace of mind, for sure. She watched him pick up the fragile tower and maneuver it back out the alley door. After he left, but not without sending a great big maddening smile over his shoulder—as if he had a secret he couldn't wait for her to discover—she walked over to the door and pushed it all the way closed. Hard. Then, she did something she'd never done during the day. She locked it. Two turns of the key.

Maybe that would keep him out of her life. But she already knew that a closed door would never be enough to do that. Because deep down—not even very deep—she wondered if she really *wanted* him out of it.

She stomped over to her worktable and got back to baking. It always calmed her down.

***

"Time for you to enjoy the great outdoors, little friend," Aimee said to Louis the next morning at nine when she came to collect him for his time in the treehouse. With his tail held high, he sauntered through the front door and started down the stairs leading to Main Street. "Wait for me," Aimee called.

"Meow," Louis replied, meaning "of course," and stopped on the fourth step down—always the same one—and waited for her to catch up. Aimee smiled down at him as they walked together in perfect synchrony. They stepped onto the brick-paved sidewalk of Main Street at exactly the same moment.

As Louis went over to greet Valery's mother at the florist shop next door, and her *nepeta cataria*—catnip plant—that Mrs.

Campbell put out each day just for his sniffing pleasure, Aimee looked around.

"Another glorious fall day, isn't it?" Mrs. Campbell said and took a deep breath of fresh New England air.

"That it is, Mrs. Campbell," Aimee agreed and let her gaze take in the October glory of red maple trees and Kousa dogwoods exchanging their shiny dark-green leaves of spring and summer for their autumn coats of gleaming crimson.

Noticing, Mrs. Campbell nodded toward the tree-lined street and said, "They're still in their early days of change but their orange-red coats are starting to come through."

"Granny!" Tommy Floyd ran up to Mrs. Campbell. Pink frosting was smeared all over his face.

"Tommy!" Mrs. Campbell leaned down to her grandson and pulling an ever-ready tissue from her pocket, began wiping his face. "Whatever do you have here?"

Tommy held up a half-eaten red velvet cupcake. "It's free!" he shouted with the glee all children feel on being offered something for nothing. "Uncle Gerry gave it to me!"

Aimee's blood pressure dropped. The sweet feeling of the day evaporated. Even though the sun was still shining brightly, as she took another step onto Main Street and looked at the shop on the other side of the Patisserie, she felt as if clouds had descended. There was Gerry standing behind a table—that he'd obviously just set up in front of his shop because it hadn't been there five minutes earlier—smiling broadly and offering free cupcakes, coffee and milk to everyone who passed by. *So that's how he used the eggs!*

Valery ran up to her son, a yellow frosted cupcake in one hand and a cup of milk in the other. She sent Aimee an apologetic grimace. "I'm sorry, Aimee. We were coming for

Tommy's morning *palmier* and cup of milk at the Patisserie when Gerry came out and offered us—"

"Free cupcakes!" Tommy shouted again and took a giant bite out of his, getting a new batch of rich, creamy frosting on his face.

Aimee knelt down to Tommy's level. Even though she now knew what was behind that teasing glint in Gerry's eyes yesterday concerning the eggs, she wasn't going to take it out on her neighbors. Taking the cup of milk from Valery, she said to Tommy, "But I'm sure he told you that you have to drink your milk with the cupcake, didn't he?" She glanced at Valery, who smiled her thanks.

Tommy wasn't so thrilled with being reminded. "Yeah," he admitted and pushed at the crack between the bricks with the toe of his tennis shoe.

"I've got an idea," Aimee said and directed him over to the bottom step. "Sit here, and for every bite of cupcake, you have one swallow of milk."

Tommy still wasn't too pleased that she'd reminded him about the milk part of the deal. "Can Louis stay and keep me company?"

Aimee nodded. "As long as you make sure your mommy puts him up in his treehouse afterward." She glanced over at Valery again, who nodded that she would.

Tommy liked that. More than anything in the world, he wanted a cat. "Okay!"

"All your milk. Got it?"

"Yeah…got it," he mumbled, a child who knew he'd been expertly outwitted.

As Valery's mother sat next to Tommy and started patting a very happy-with-the-attention Louis, Valery spoke to Aimee. "I'm so sorry—"

Aimee stopped her. Valery had too many big issues to deal with in her life. She didn't need to worry about Aimee's cupcake problem. "Please, don't give it another thought." She shrugged and smiled at her friend. "How could anyone refuse a free cupcake?"

Turning she walked toward the Patisserie. Using all the willpower she possessed—and then some—she kept herself from looking in the direction of the table. From the corner of her eye, she could see most of her morning-time clients hanging around it drinking coffee, eating cupcakes and talking animatedly. They acted as if they were at a fair. She swung open the Patisserie's door.

When she heard Cynthia whimper behind her—Aimee always greeted Cynthia at this time of day—she paused. The dog was understandably feeling slighted at being forgotten.

But Aimee couldn't say "Hi" to her right now. She just couldn't. Squaring her shoulders, Aimee entered the Patisserie. But the dog's continued whimpers cut her deeply. It wasn't Cynthia's fault she had such a shameless owner. Aimee promised herself she'd go out later—once Gerry had moved his table and free cupcakes away—and give Cynthia not one, but two doggie treats.

7—Neighbor Lady

"What are you going to do about that atrocity?" Mrs. Fonteyn sang out the second Aimee stepped into the café. She flung her ample right arm in the direction of the townspeople milling around Gerry's table.

Aimee regarded the four friends who sat with their cups of hot chocolate and escargots looking up at her.

"The ladies have been very upset by this development," Lucy stated from behind the counter. The frown that cut across Lucy's normally smooth brow said she was, too.

The cold shock of Gerry's betrayal evaporated as Aimee looked at these dear, sweet ladies who supported her even when she knew they wanted to be out there trying some of that red velvet cake being offered for free. *After all, who wouldn't?* She felt a smile pull at her face. "Thank you so much for being here. All of you." Her look included Lucy and Bob—who was hiding behind his newspaper but Aimee knew he was listening. "It means a lot to me."

"You want me to arrest him for theft? Stealing your customers?" Bob asked, proving that he was indeed listening. Putting the newspaper aside, he stood. There was a twinkle in his eyes that said he'd do anything for his almost-sister.

"Now there's a thought," Penny answered him and her smile widened as Bob nodded at her in agreement. Aimee noticed the flush that touched Penny's fair cheeks whenever Bob looked her way or spoke to her. How come Bob never seemed to notice it?

"Thanks," Aimee said and lightly touched Bob's arm as he passed her as he went out. "But I'll come up with something a little less…illegal."

"What would make Gerry do such a thing?" Mrs. Fonteyn asked after Bob left. "He seemed like such a nice young man the other day."

"He's just trying to introduce his product to the people of Stoneybridge. I guess I can't really fault him for that," Aimee said.

"Of course you can!" Miss Maggie insisted.

"Well, I think you should go out there and give him a piece of your mind," said Ruth Lovejoy. "His shop isn't even a café. He doesn't normally sell coffee and tea. It makes me so angry."

Aimee smiled over at Lucy, whose quick wink told Aimee she knew what she was about to say, then back at the ladies. "Actually, in a moment, I'm going to go do some baking. I've always found it to be my best therapy, the best way to stay calm."

As she tied her apron around her waist, she didn't want to tell any of them how, more than anger, sadness had gripped her. That emotion took her by surprise. She almost didn't want to analyze why it would be there. She decided it was her Uncle Cain's "business is business" attitude, regardless of the consequences to others. She hated that Gerry seemed to subscribe to the same philosophy.

But she wasn't sure.

For one person to make another sad, there normally had to be some sort of personal attachment, such as she had with her uncle. Uncle Cain, being her mother's younger brother, had been part of Aimee's life…forever. She hardly knew Gerry

Mitchell. Why should sadness be her main emotion right now? Shouldn't it be anger, as Ruth Lovejoy had said?

"Okay, Aimee." Ruth spoke bringing Aimee back to the moment. "But I still don't think you should let him get away with stealing all your morning customers," she admonished.

"They'll be back here tomorrow," Aimee said and smiled at Ruth. She wasn't really certain, though. When she'd knelt down close to Tommy, she'd gotten a whiff of that red velvet cake. It had smelled heavenly. But as she left the front of the store and walked into her therapy room—her kitchen—she had to believe she was right.

***

When, three hours later, Gerry was still outside giving away free cupcakes and coffee—how many cupcakes could ten dozen eggs make?—all thoughts of a peaceful neighborly existence, of trying to get along with her new Main Street neighbor, were obliterated as he bombed her store, figuratively speaking, with his red velvet confections. The door of the Patisserie seemed to have been sealed shut; it didn't open even once. Aimee was seething.

Mark was, too. He'd been standing by the window, blatantly staring out at Gerry for the last hour. If he'd had laser vision, Gerry would've been zapped out of existence by now. "He's going inside to replenish his supplies," Mark shouted as he ran back into the kitchen.

That was Aimee's cue, what she'd been waiting for. She wouldn't have a showdown with Gerry on Main Street for the whole town to see and talk about. No way would she bring their pastry war to the general population of Stoneybridge.

Gerry might be hoping she would—why else would he do something so deliberately public if not to entice her to battle it out with him on the Main Street stage?—but she wouldn't. Unlike Mrs. Fonteyn, Miss Maggie and Dr. Lovejoy who had no qualms about putting people in their place in front of an audience, Aimee didn't do public displays. She'd used up her allotted amount that day at church, when Professor Timothy Bainbridge had left her a bride without a groom in front of the whole town.

But Aimee had no problem with meeting Gerry Mitchell in his kitchen.

Taking a deep breath, she removed her gloves and her apron and tossed them into the bin. Fixing her ponytail, she walked into the front of her store. Mark trailed behind her. "I'll be back in a bit," she said to Lucy and Mark.

"Go get 'em, boss," Mark said while Lucy sent Aimee a thumbs-up.

She straightened her shoulders and marched out of her shop. After a few steps, she walked into Gerry's. With a nod in the direction of Doug and Hank, she headed directly for the kitchen.

"What are you *doing*?" she asked Gerry as she pushed through the doors, catching him in the act of decorating yet another batch of red velvet cupcakes.

"Thank God," he exhaled and tossed the spatula ten feet into the sink as if he'd just finished a competition. "I'm about to run out of eggs!"

Aimee wagged her head from side to side. Did he expect her to lend him some eggs? "What?"

"Why did it take you so long to come over?" he shot out, as if she were somehow responsible for—*what*?

She stepped back and blinked. "If you think I have any idea what you're talking about, I don't."

"I thought you'd come over when you brought Louis down for his mid-morning stay in the treehouse." *Gerry noticed she did that every morning?* "But you weren't even the one to put him in his treehouse today, which would've given me time to say hello. You didn't so much as glance in my direction when you marched into the Patisserie like some stoic soldier! Worst of all, you didn't say "Hi" to Cynthia! Poor dog. She couldn't understand that at all."

Aimee shook her head again. She felt bad about Cynthia; she hated ignoring her sweet whimpers and was only glad the dog had been sleeping when she dashed from her shop to his just now. But what else was he talking about?

"Look, it's true I wanted to find a way to get the townsfolk interested in my products," he continued. "But I only thought of giving away cupcakes when you gave me back all those eggs yesterday. I was only planning to offer them for free until you came over and tried one yourself."

"What?" Aimee whispered. With his words, the oppressive sadness that had been hanging over her all morning evaporated like mist from the meadow near the Old Stone Bridge in the mid-morning sun. *He hadn't been offering free cupcakes just because it was "business"!* He'd wanted to get her to come over and be neighborly. As she thought about it, she knew that acting neighborly, in spite of his opening a bakery next door to hers, was something Grand-mère would have done. The very first day. "Let me get this straight." She paused and licked her lips, "If I'd come over—"

"And been neighborly," he inserted.

Neighborly. Yes! She got that now. "You would've stopped offering cupcakes then?"

He nodded. "Or shortly afterward. I'd originally planned to give away three dozen." He motioned down at the latest batch. "I'm on my twentieth now! And I'm beat! And probably broke, too!"

Laughter bubbled up inside her. She felt carefree and giddy. "Why didn't you—"

"What? Call out to you when you might as well have had a 'keep away from me' sign on your back?" He chuckled. "Come on, neighbor lady, give a guy a break for having some self-esteem."

Neighbor lady? Was that how he saw her? The way he said it made her feel special. She liked it. "Why didn't you," she repeated, "*stop* giving away cupcakes after the three dozen were finished?" she asked. She knew she'd lost the battle to avoid smiling when she sensed both dimples dancing on her face. Grand-mère said her dimples always did that when she was happy. And she *was* happy right now.

"Because." He shrugged his shoulders. She could see his eyes looking between her right dimple and her left. "I don't know. I've always been a very determined kind of guy."

"Stupid, you mean?"

"Hey!" His gaze settled on hers. "Now you sound like my sister!"

"Believe me, Gerry. I don't *feel* like your sister." She knew what it was to feel like a sister. She felt like a sister to Bob. Not to Gerry. Not from the first moment she'd met him. But it was only as his eyes flashed in male recognition of what she'd just said and he came purposefully around the worktable and walked slowly toward her, that she realized what she'd admitted.

"I'm glad, neighbor lady." He spoke softly. "Because I don't feel toward you like I feel about my sister, either."

She took a step back. What was happening here? When had he gone from being Enemy-Pastry-Chef-Number-One to being…what? That wonderful Monday Gerry again?

"Aimee." His voice was smooth, as smooth as the red velvet cakes he'd been giving away all morning. "I really think we can–"

"Cynthia!" she shouted and took another step back.

He stopped moving toward her. Just as Cynthia might, he tilted his head in question. "What?"

"I promised myself that I'd give her two doggie treats—" she held up two fingers "—once we got this situation settled." She waved her hand between them.

He chuckled. "And do we have this 'situation' settled?" he asked. She knew he was talking on two levels. The Monday Gerry was asking about the feelings they had for each other and the Thursday Gerry was asking about their businesses.

Adrenaline coursed through her, invigorating her, making her feel alive and womanly and very optimistic. She could feel another smile forming at the corners of her mouth. Before turning away, just as the smile exploded from her, she decided to let her words be as honest as that smile. "Not by a long shot, Gerry Mitchell!"

The sound of his laughter followed her out the door. She had to shake the impulse to giggle.

***

That impulse to giggle hadn't left her by Friday morning when the clock tower chimed the hour of four, letting her know it was time to get up and start a new day full of possibilities.

Aimee had her preliminary meeting with the supermarket executive at ten o'clock. She was all set to go. She had to bake the raspberry *macarons,* chocolate éclairs and *St. Honoré* cakes now so they'd be fresh. But just to be on the safe side—in case of power outage, aliens landing on Main Street or, worst of all, an unscheduled visit from Uncle Cain—she'd already baked and packed away a successful batch of each yesterday. If she didn't do a thing other than dress the part of the Main Street entrepreneur Northeast Supermarket Chain needed, she was ready to go.

But that wasn't what had her senses soaring like freshly laundered sheets fluttering in a summertime breeze. It was Gerry.

Since their encounter in his kitchen, she'd only seen him at their six o'clock tryst yesterday morning. Due to a downpour of rain and equally strong gusts of wind, their pleasant exchange—over their identical brooms—had been cut short. Too short. But all day yesterday she'd been aware of him working on the other side of their mutual kitchen wall.

He'd called her "neighbor lady."

She was totally overwhelmed by how much she liked that, by how much she wanted to be a good neighbor to him, by how okay she was with it. She didn't think there was any real chance of becoming fodder for the town's gossip mill if people saw them as good next-door neighbors—and nothing more.

She worked hard to convince herself that the moment they'd shared in his kitchen had just been amiable bantering and not a step or two away from flirting. They'd both said they didn't feel like siblings to each other. Was that really so remarkable? After all, there were only two people who felt like siblings to her—Becky and Bob. And to her knowledge, Gerry had only one sister.

What that "moment" had been was actually a raising of the white flags, a truce, an understanding that they were neighbors and maybe on the way to being friends, just as she'd been with Mr. Wong. She would stop fighting the fact that Uncle Gerry's Cakerie was located on her Main Street and he would stop…what?

Kneeling on her bed she pulled back the lace curtains, said a cheerful, "Good morning," to the colorful array of pansies in the flowerbox—that seemed extra happy that a gorgeous day was dawning—and then made herself think about what Gerry had done to her other than not telling her who he was at their first meeting.

Annoyed her? Well, yeah. But that was *after* she'd treated him in such an unneighborly fashion.

No. His biggest crime had been setting up a bakery next door to hers. That was it. Nothing more. But it was a free country. Ten bakeries could come onto Main Street if they wanted to. She chuckled. As he'd said, if a candy store moved in, they could be called the "sugar district of Stonebridge." Was that really so bad? It worked for the many salt-water taffy stores along the Atlantic City boardwalk in New Jersey and for the fudge shops on Mackinac Island in Michigan.

As she reached over and cuddled Louis before getting up and starting her day, she pushed to the back of her mind that his biggest so-called crime hadn't been against her business at all. Surprisingly, what bothered her most was that he'd toppled her "stay away from men" rule. Her resolve against getting involved with men—until she was at least fifty—was being tested.

That disturbing thought tried to wriggle its way to the forefront of her mind where she'd mull it over again and again and consequently get more and more bothered by it. But instead of letting it have a place in her brain and agitate her soul, she said a quick prayer and released it.

She was in a good frame of mind now, thinking she could be Gerry's neighbor lady. She wanted to leave it at that and not tamper with that valuable state.

She could handle being his neighbor lady, she thought as she jumped off her bed and hurried to get dress. All she had to do was make sure she won that supermarket contract!

***

Aimee was on cloud nine! The supermarket presentation that morning couldn't have gone better and Lizzy Edwards, her contact at Northeast Supermarket Chain, said she was definitely one of the front runners. Aimee knew that didn't mean she had the contract. But the fact that she'd been allotted a final presentation date—November fifteenth—was encouraging. She had to believe that the contract would be hers. Especially since she needed it so badly…

To celebrate this successful round, she decided to treat herself to a new magazine. She'd just left the Book Nook with her shopping bag and its treasure—a travel magazine with an article on the churches of Paris—and was heading back to her apartment when she spied Lottie Fitzgerald tapping quickly along in her Manolo Blahnik heels, going in the same direction but on the other side of the street.

"Lottie!" Aimee called to her and waved just as the clock in the tower started chiming the hour of three.

Lottie didn't seem to hear her or see her. But then, Aimee realized, not only was the clock ringing but Lottie was attaching a surgical mask over her nose and mouth and was preoccupied with doing that. Since the outbreak of the world-wide pandemic, even with the Coronavirus mostly under control, these masks were often seen on Main Street. When people thought they might have a cold or illness of some sort, but still needed to leave their houses, they'd wear a mask out of respect for their neighbors. Aimee considered it a kind and caring practice. She did it, too. More than that, in the case illness, she stayed home and had made it the policy of the Patisserie that all her employees remained at home, if they thought they were sick or coming down with something.

The clock stopped chiming and Lottie seemed to have the mask in place. "Lottie," Aimee tried again. It was the perfect opportunity to remind her that they needed to finalize the theme for the triplets' fifth birthday party coming up soon. It occurred to Aimee that this might be the reason Lottie was out today and maybe she was heading toward the Patisserie. Aimee had baked the triplets' cakes every year since they were born. Elegant bespoke cakes decorated with piped icing was one of the things Aimee especially liked doing. She also happened to have a real talent for it. In the case of the triplets, she got to make three different cakes joined by a common theme.

Checking both ways for traffic, and seeing the street was clear, she crossed over.

"Lottie!" She tried one last time and was rewarded when Lottie stopped and turned to face her. *Did she see a glimmer of guilt in her eyes?*

"Oh, Aimee! Hi! How are you?"

"Great!" After her successful morning she really was. "And you?"

Lottie pointed at her mask. "I picked up a little cold from the triplets, but nothing serious. I don't have a fever and I'm almost over it now."

"That's good to hear." Aimee felt a little awkward asking, but since it was so important to the financial welfare of the Patisserie, she did anyway. "I was wondering... Have the triplets decided on their theme for this year's birthday party? I'd like to start brainstorming cake ideas."

Lottie laughed, a too-merry sound that sent warning bells pealing in Aimee's head even before Lottie answered. It was one of those nervous sounds people have when they know that something they say isn't going to please the listener. "Oh, Aimee..." From behind her mask came a twittering sound, "I'm afraid we've made other arrangements for the party." *Laugh. Laugh. Twitter. Twitter.* "The triplets requested a giant zoo cake this year."

Aimee felt as if she were sinking. *A giant zoo cake...*

Lottie went on. "It's going to be four feet by two feet and have six-inch edible sugar animals in cages. The triplets are so excited." She paused, then, "I'm sorry, Aimee, but my children are getting older and they want fun and whimsy now. Not pretty and elegant. They want an Uncle Gerry's Cake," Lottie said, confirming Aimee's fear, and waving bye, she turned and as carefree and nonchalant as characters in a nightmare, she continued tapping down the road.

Gone was the light-heartedness of before. In swooped all those feelings Thursday Gerry had brought her—that Uncle Gerry's Cakerie was going to steal all her business. It was happening already!

***

"No, Aimee," Becky said a few minutes later when Aimee heatedly recounted her sidewalk meeting with Lottie. "I disagree with you. It's not Gerry's fault. Lottie Fitzgerald was going to go to another bakery this year for the triplets' party anyway. People in her circle usually start investing in these over-the-top cakes for their kids by the time they're five."

Aimee stopped pacing back and forth. "You can't be sure she would've gone somewhere else."

"Yeah, I can. The triplets' birthday is on the second of November. Lottie always comes in by the twentieth of October to meet with you about possible cake ideas." She pointed to the calendar. "That was almost a week ago. She'd probably planned to go to another bakery long before Uncle Gerry's came in. The fact that he opened up a shop here just made it easier for her. And…" Becky paused and Aimee could tell she was wondering if she should say the following words. "Truth to tell, oh, friend of mine, having Uncle Gerry's Cakerie here is good for Stoneybridge. Good for our Main Street."

"*What*?" Aimee couldn't believe Becky had said that. Had she gone over to the enemy camp? "Why are you defending him?" It perturbed Aimee that Becky was sticking up for Gerry's shop.

"Look, Aimee. If Stoneybridge's Main Street is going to survive, it *needs* stores like Uncle Gerry's Cakerie to bring in people from the surrounding areas and also to entice Stoneybridge residents themselves to come downtown, wander around and shop here. Otherwise, our Main Street is going to end up deserted, full of empty storefronts like so many across America. Main Streets can't compete with mega stores, malls, pandemics and internet buying unless they have specialty stores." She paused. "Such as Uncle Gerry's Cakerie. Your store and his along with a few others make coming to Main Street an American *experience* rather than just a purchase."

"You mean," Aimee muttered, "we've turned into Disneyland?"

Becky chuckled. "Not a bad thing. Walt Disney was a man of vision. Knowing how important Main Streets were to America, he made "Main Street USA" the start and finish of his first theme parks. Good ol' Walt probably single-handedly saved Main Streets all across America back in the 1950s and '60s when people became more mobile and started driving everywhere, and developers responded to that trend with strip malls. Walt Disney reminded people how important and special our Main Streets are to our society, how they're a major part of a healthy community environment, where people know one another and care about each other. It wouldn't be far wrong to say that the loss of our Main Streets across America is one of the reasons so many kids get into trouble today."

Aimee couldn't disagree with that.

"And it's specialty stores like Uncle Gerry's Cakerie, the Treasure Trove, PJ Kabos Olive Oil shop and yours that draw people to our very own Main Street and keep Sam's Green Grocer's, Hale's Hardware and—" she motioned toward Valery's mother's store "—Mrs. Campbell's Flower Shop in business. Not to mention the totally regular places like the pharmacy and small grocery store."

Aimee smiled wryly. Her friend had made valid arguments. "When did you turn into such a good businesswoman?" In truth, Aimee knew that Becky was a natural at business.

Becky waved the compliment away. "Lottie will definitely still come to you for other cakes and pastries."

"True." Aimee conceded the point. Lottie could always be counted on to buy several pounds of *macarons* every month. "But it still hurts to lose this important contract," she couldn't help saying.

"Talk to Gerry about it," Becky suggested.

"Are you crazy?"

Becky's eyes danced with a secret knowledge. "Tomorrow morning. At your six o'clock greet over your identical 'autumn joy' orange brooms."

The same way a balloon at the bottom of a swimming pool shoots to the surface, that old fear of being the talk of town shot to the top of Aimee's mind. It was never too far away. "You know about that?" Aimee wasn't sure she liked it, even though Becky would never spread rumors.

"My new apartment mate and her 'Soothing Waves Crashing' YouTube channel does anything but help me sleep. I'm often up at six, looking out the window at the sun rising, the leaves turning crimson and orange and…maybe my best friend changing her negative attitude toward men?" She paused. "At least, maybe toward one particular man?"

"Becky! No!" Aimee shook her head in denial. "I don't want that sort of complication in my life. I just want to learn to be a good *neighbor* to the problematic Gerry Mitchell. That's all."

"Whatever you say," Becky said, and went back to piping rich Belgian chocolate cream onto the chocolate *macarons*.

8—Anything is Possible

His phone alarm went off. Gerry glanced at the clock. Saturday, October 26, 5:55 a.m..

He checked the timer for the cakes that were in the oven baking, grabbed his broom from the utility closet, his keys and Stetson from the hook by his office door. With the heavenly aroma of vanilla and blueberry following him, he ran from the kitchen, then rushed through the empty storefront to the Main Street door.

It was a crisp and chilly fall morning, but one that was sure to warm up nicely with the rising of the sun. As on most mornings, he'd brought Cynthia with him. She was happy to be tied to her very own dog house now. Gerry had moved her house, the same one that had stood under the palm tree outside his California store, to the dogwood tree in front of his shop here. Before swinging open the door, he watched her and smiled as she sat sniffing the fresh air. He knew she was waiting eagerly for the excitement of Saturday morning on Main Street to start. Such simple joy. Gerry understood; he liked it too, much more than he'd ever imagined he would.

Walking out, he greeted Cynthia, then looked up and down Main Street. Even compared with yesterday, the trees along the road had deepened in color, and autumn charm permeated the air. It was a glorious morning, made all the more wonderful because he was one step closer to getting that all-important supermarket contract. He was riding high this morning.

His meeting with the supermarket executives yesterday afternoon couldn't have gone better. His contact, James Monroe, had told him there was only one other serious contender, but that he felt Gerry's product had a much stronger appeal for their clientele. If James had anything to say about it—and he did—Uncle Gerry's Cakerie would soon be their new in-store bakery up and down the Northeast. To Gerry that meant becoming part of an established market, having a greatly increased internet sales presence and immense regional publicity. But it also would mean he'd be able to cut back on his over-the-counter goods in the Stoneybridge store. This would keep him from biting into Aimee's market—something that was becoming increasingly important to him the better he got to know his next-door pastry chef.

With his store part of the mega-supermarket chain, potential customers would visit Stoneybridge's Main Street, and the ripple effect would mean an increase in business for the Patisserie and for all the other shops in town.

He glanced at the Patisserie's pink-and-white awning. There was no doubt that it was a fixture in the tri-state area—New York, Connecticut and New Jersey—and he had no desire to usurp that. He still felt bad that Aimee was so threatened by Uncle Gerry's.

Aimee…

The thing that gave him pause this morning was realizing he wasn't alone in feeling there *might* be more of a future for them than just being neighbors. She'd given that away three days ago when she'd admitted she didn't have sisterly feelings toward him.

"Learning that was worth the work I put into baking and handing out all those free cupcakes," he sighed to Cynthia. She tilted her head, apparently listening intently, so he was quick to qualify. "Not that I came back East looking for a relationship. A romantic relationship with neighbor lady? No. No way. That's the last thing I want." Pulling his hat lower on his brow, he squinted towards the train station and added, "Or is it?"

Before Scarlett had dramatically decided against setting a date for their wedding the previous year, Gerry had wanted nothing more than to start a family of his own.

Scarlett.

The gorgeous Californian blonde who'd smashed his heart when she refused to set a date—she didn't want to be "tied down" and how dare he change their relationship by pressing her to "decide on a date." As if he'd committed a major faux pas in assuming that "engagement" led to marriage.

"I should've seen it coming," Gerry murmured to Cynthia. "In the end, there was too much of a difference between our personalities. I was too calm and traditional for her daredevil, live-for-the-moment ways. But worst of all," he said, kneeling down and rubbing Cynthia's chest vigorously, "how could she not love you, great dog that you are?"

The clock in the tower began to strike at the exact moment the key turned in the Patisserie's door. Cynthia jumped up, nearly flooring Gerry.

Aimee walked out and directly over to Cynthia. As she bent down to give the dog her favorite, cheesy treat, Gerry noticed again how lovely she was with her ponytail swinging and the blue silk scarf, which she'd tied just above her bangs, flowing softly around her shoulders.

Gerry stood and reached for his broom. "Good morning."

"Good morning," she returned, sending a tight little smile his way that made him wonder if something was wrong.

"How are you this fine morning?" he persisted.

She went back to her area of the sidewalk. "To be honest, Gerry, I'm a little perturbed."

"Not again." *Did he actually say that out loud?* Yep. One look at Aimee's face and he knew he had. "Sorry. What about?" Maybe she wasn't upset with something *he'd* done. He hoped not. He was getting tired of being the object of her anger. It reminded him too much of Scarlett.

She shook her head and, picking up her broom, started to sweep. "Oh, never mind. It's nothing."

That certainly wasn't a character trait of Scarlett's. Scarlett never let a subject go. He had to remember not to let thoughts of Scarlett upset his fragile relationship with his lovely neighbor. He walked over and stopped the energetic movement of her broom. "Aimee? What is it?"

She turned to him. He could see doubt and confusion in her frown. But he was relieved to see there was no anger. "Lottie Fitzgerald."

One name. That was all it took. He got it. Letting out a deep breath, he said, "She normally comes to you for the triplets' birthday cake," he stated. Didn't ask. He knew the answer even before she nodded.

"Always."

He could say he was sorry. But his memories of Scarlett reminded him that constantly apologizing was a bad idea. A habit he'd acquired with his former fiancée. He wasn't going to continue it with Aimee, unless he had a genuine reason to apologize. It didn't make for a healthy relationship, even if only a neighborly one.

Watching the play of emotions on Aimee's face, emotions that begged him not to lie or be flippant as she waited patiently for his response, he thought that someday, in the future, he might want more with her than just being neighborly. Not now, but maybe tomorrow, or next week, or next month, or in ten years, or even twenty.

Maybe.

What maybe? Definitely!

So he answered her with honesty and respect. "If it helps, when Lottie came to the Cakerie, she told me she had an appointment with a famous cake shop in New Jersey to meet with them about constructing a gigantic zoo cake for the triplets. But when she saw that Uncle Gerry's, which she'd heard about from friends in LA, had opened right here in Stoneybridge, she was happy to give her business to a shop on our Main Street. In our town."

Aimee's dark brown eyes searched his. After a moment, she did the unexpected. She sent him a smile, a true smile this time and murmured, "Our town." He heard no resentment in her tone, only acknowledgment that it was his town now, too. A feeling of victory coursed through him. "Becky, my best friend, thought it was something like that," she added.

An image, a very appealing one, formed in his mind of Aimee and her tall, very good-looking friend—a woman he'd seen around town several times since the day she'd come with Aimee to spy on his shop—talking about him. In his vision, there was flour in their dark hair, chocolate frosting on their noses. Whether the image was true or not, he was glad that Aimee's best friend showed herself to be fair and to have an ability to dissect business situations without letting emotion rule. It was good to know that she was a real help to Aimee. Only true friends did that for each other. "Sounds like Becky's a smart lady."

"The smartest person I know." Aimee gave him another honest smile and with genuine feeling, nothing flippant in her tone, said, "Present company excluded, of course."

He wasn't sure where that compliment had come from, or what had prompted her to offer it, but it was the first she'd given him. He liked the way it made him feel. He accepted it in the manner he'd seen his successful CEO father accept compliments all his life—simply, with a nod and a murmur of acknowledgement. "Thank you."

She went back to sweeping, and he was further surprised when she explained herself. "Before you moved here, I read about Uncle Gerry's Cakerie in a magazine and then checked out your website. I'm impressed that you sell online. Becky wants me to do that." A sudden breeze from the direction of Long Island Sound, some miles to the south, ruffled the curls that had escaped her silk scarf. The wisps were feminine and soft. And pretty. Very pretty. "You have quite a remarkable head for business. If you succeed in doing here what you did in California, you'll definitely become an asset to Main Street."

"Even if what I make is 'big, brash and crass,'" he bantered, using her own words.

As she continued sweeping, she nodded. "Even then. Besides, if you hadn't moved in, it was inevitable that someone else with your—" she paused and seemed to search for the right word.

"— talent," he supplied.

"Okay," she conceded with a skeptical twitch that made the dimple to the left of her mouth flicker. "*Talent* at making big cakes would move either here or to a town close by. With their growing popularity, it was inevitable, I guess." *Swish, swish,* went the broom.

A combination of that dimple and her concession made him want to whoop like a teenager at a football game. *Touchdown!* Instead, he started slinging his broom back and forth. He doubted that what he was doing could be considered sweeping, but it was a movement in conjunction with Aimee's steady strokes. And that he liked. "Well, I hope we'll be able to come to a real cooperation and make sure our businesses complement each other."

Without saying anything, she stopped sweeping, and walked to the recessed area leading to her door. Before passing through the three-foot entryway, which showcased the display windows on both sides, she stood for a moment and looked up and down the street. He could tell that the love she felt for this town ran as true and deep as the ancient river on which Stoneybridge was first settled by Mohegan one mile to the north. He was absolutely certain that Aimee would do anything to see the modern-day town, built around the colonial road that was now their Main Street, survive. And actually conceding that Uncle Gerry's Cakerie might be good for it was an "anything".

"On a day like this, Gerry Mitchell—" she paused, took a deep breath and slowly let it out "—I feel like anything is possible." She sent him a megawatt smile that made the elusive dimple to the *right* of her mouth show itself, then pulled open the glass door and walked through it.

"Anything at all," Gerry agreed as the door shut behind her and his on-top-of-the-world feeling was even greater now than when he'd awakened that morning.

A train whistle blew out a cheerful note somewhere off in the distant Connecticut hills.

It echoed how Gerry was feeling.

The Main Street Supermarket contract was almost his and maybe, just maybe, neighbor lady and he were finally on the same track, figuratively speaking of course.

***

As Aimee walked into the Patisserie and looked around the cozy, inviting space, she knew that the way she felt on the inside at this moment matched the comfortable, heartwarming decor in her shop. She lightly ran her fingertips over the embossed pink-velvet wallpaper and the worn, but still lovely, ornate oak counter. As on the previous morning, she unexpectedly found herself in a relaxed easygoing mood.

And it was hers to enjoy for a full two minutes.

Then thoughts swooped in like the Flying Fortress her grandfather had flown during the Second World War, bombarding her brain and demanding what in the world was she doing? She didn't want to get this close to Gerry. Not to any man and particularly not Mr. Next-Door-Baker-Man.

What had made her act so sickly sweet and forgiving? He'd taken a major cake contract away from her. Blast that nasty reflex again that had her not only smiling at him every morning but saying things she shouldn't.

The heat of embarrassment and disgust flooded her. Did she actually tell him "on a day like this anything was possible"? She peeled off her sweater, but still feeling her body temperature rise, she pulled off her long-sleeved T-shirt, too, until she was wearing only her tank top. How she wished she could redo their conversation. A second time around, she wouldn't be so understanding of his taking business away from her.

She fanned her hands back and forth in front of her face.

"It's simply a physical reaction," she tried to convince her reflection in the gilded mirror behind the counter. She'd forgotten how it felt to be so wonderfully aware of a man. She'd buried that sensitivity after Professor Timothy Bainbridge had performed his runaway-groom number. But when Monday Gerry had walked into her life two weeks ago, it had definitely been resurrected.

"Less than two weeks!" she groaned at her reflection. How could that be? How superficial did that make her? Was Becky's carefree attitude to dating finally wearing off on her? Gerry had definitely ignited feelings in her that she'd thought were long dead.

"What feelings?" she asked her reflection.

"Of caring for a man. A lot," she answered the too-pink woman in the mirror staring back at her. "More and more he's Monday Gerry, that wonderful first-meeting Gerry…when I thought he was just passing through. And that Gerry is very hard to resist." There. She'd said it out loud.

"Okay. Then what I'm feeling for Gerry is *more* than attraction," she stated, feeling very brave as she did.

But her courage only lasted a moment. Shaking her head and stamping her foot, she shouted, "No!" and grabbing her sweater and T-shirt from where she'd tossed them, she marched into the kitchen.

She had work to do.

She had to keep Gerry Mitchell, as anything other than a Main Street neighbor, out of her mind. Thank God he didn't *live* next door to her, too!

She couldn't let herself think of him as that perfect Monday Gerry again.

But how?

"Well, for starters, by avoiding him every morning at six. That's how!" she answered herself. "No more early greets over our identical brooms. Period." Besides, Becky knew about those meetings, so how long would it be until Miss Maggie did, too, and Mrs. Fonteyn, and all the other well-meaning but talkative ladies and gentlemen on Main Street?

She'd ask Lucy to start sweeping out front when she came in at eight. Yes, Aimee thought with renewed determination as she removed the first batch of croissants from the oven and continued her Saturday morning preparations. That was what she'd do from now on.

And she did.

But her conniving only worked the following day.

Because on Sunday night, as if by some preordained plan to thwart her scheming ways, when she went to close up at nine o'clock, she heard Gerry doing exactly the same thing. There was no escape. She didn't even have the excuse that she had work to do this late.

She *knew* she should've have taken a dozen more croissants to church that morning when she went to Sunday service. Was God making fun of her plans? Had she forgotten Proverbs 16:9 that the pastor had preached about that morning? "A man's heart plans his way, But the Lord directs his steps."

She must have, because she had a feeling that her plans and her steps were about to collide.

9—Frisbees, Dogs and Romans

As soon as she stepped onto the brick sidewalk of Main Street, Gerry called out, "Aimee!"

"Hi," she returned but forced herself *not* to smile. *Don't smile. Don't!* she commanded her lips over and over again. But they didn't pay any attention. She felt them turning up at the corners. *Nasty reflex!*

He walked over to her.

She was trapped.

He had a great big smile on his face.

She felt her own lips widen even more in response.

She was a sucker for men who weren't afraid to smile, whose eyes had even more of a smile in them than their mouths, whose entire bodies radiated an "it's so good to see you" look. She would take a warm and truthful greeting over a "dark assessing gaze" or "a sardonic twist of the lips" any day of the week.

And Gerry was walking toward her with just that kind of all-encompassing expression. In the mellow and soft glow of the streetlamps, she wondered if she'd ever seen a better smile. Despite deciding that she wouldn't encourage him, even in friendship—all she wanted was a nice, neighborly working relationship—his delight in seeing her warmed her heart. It made her believe things she didn't think were possible, made her feel like a woman again. A woman who just might be blessed in love this time…

Stop! Where had that thought come from? Had it caught a ride on Cupid's arrow? She didn't believe in Cupid! Go away! Go away!

Gerry held out a Cakerie box. "I didn't get these leftovers sent to the homeless shelter in time this evening. So I was going to take one box over to the police station for those fine men and women to enjoy as they keep our town safe tonight, and the other to the emergency room at the county hospital. Unless you'd like one of these? They freeze well."

He gave his daily leftovers to the homeless shelter! Aimee did, too, but she never had as much as two big boxes full. She suspected he didn't, either. He probably made fresh ones specifically to give and bring joy to people.

"They're peanut butter cupcakes with chocolate fudge frosting," he said enticingly.

Aimee loved peanut butter *anything*. Add chocolate, and she was ready to swoon. There was a reason she was a pastry chef. But she waved his offer aside, especially since he'd given her an opportunity to get away from him. *Was she crazy? Why did she want to get away from him?* that voice inside her demanded. She ignored it. "That's very kind of you, but I don't want to keep you from getting them to those deserving people. See you tomorrow," she said and turned away.

There. She'd done it. She was glad she'd taken Louis back up to the apartment at sunset, when the autumn temperatures dropped below an indoor cat's liking. This allowed her to walk quickly toward her stairs, away from Gerry, without pausing.

For the first time ever, as she listened to him unhook Cynthia from her dog house, she wished the Patisserie had interior stairs to her apartment, too. But the store and the apartment were totally independent spaces, and the outdoor stairs ensured that. She thought maybe Gerry had deciphered the message that she was trying not to cultivate any sort of relationship with him, other than that of neighbors. After all, she'd never sat and talked to Mr. Wong after they locked their doors at night. Or Mrs. Campbell.

When she heard Cynthia's *tap, tap, tap* as her claws hit the sidewalk behind her—and not going in the opposite direction toward the police station and the hospital—she knew she hadn't gotten the just-being-neighborly message across.

He was obviously stuck on the message she'd left him with the previous Wednesday, when she'd told him she didn't have sisterly feelings for him. And the one she'd given him Saturday morning, when she'd stupidly told him that anything was possible in their relationship.

She felt embarrassment heat her face. She was sure it was the color of the walls in the Patisserie again.

How could she blame the guy for being persistent in forming a friendship? If she were a traffic cop giving such mixed signals, cars would be running into one another all over Main Street.

Man and dog were close on her heels. To make matters worse, Aimee could hear the expectant joy in each prancing step of Cynthia's as the dog waited for her to turn around and do the polite thing—the thing Cynthia, with her great big doggie heart would do—and greet her.

Aimee groaned.

Animals were such pure creatures.

Many, if not most, so much kinder than humans.

She couldn't ignore Cynthia. She *wouldn't* ignore her. But she had to be careful of what she said to Cynthia's owner. *Careful, careful, careful!*

Aimee stopped walking.

Cynthia did, too.

But not Gerry.

Unlike Cynthia, he hadn't expected her to do the polite thing.

He plowed right into her.

"Whoa!" he shouted. The force of the collision twisted her around to face him. The look of horror on Gerry's face as his six-feet-something nearly mowed over her five-feet-five was worth the jolt it gave her.

"Aimee!" Gerry cried as his arms circled her waist and somehow kept both of them—and the two big cake boxes he held—from crashing to the ground. "Are you okay?"

Aimee nose was plastered against Gerry's neck. The scent of him! *Heavenly!* Like the Stoneybridge woods after a rainstorm, mixed with a day spent in the company of vanilla and butter. Her olfactory sense reeled. It was a heady combination for a girl who loved both the Connecticut woodlands and the scent of vanilla.

She tried to step back. But if Gerry hadn't still had his arms around her, she would've fallen. She looked down. Cynthia's lead was tangled around them. Their legs were tied together. *When had that happened?* She couldn't avoid a slight laugh. "Uh… I think we have a situation here."

Gerry chuckled. "Hang on." And to Cynthia. "Come here, girl. Let me undo your lead." He bent sideways, and at the click of the lead being released, the cord immediately loosened. Holding Gerry's shoulders, Aimee stepped over it.

She shivered. She suddenly felt cold.

Aimee watched as he untangled himself and reattached the lead to Cynthia's collar. "I'm really sorry about that." In the glow from the ornamental, early twentieth-century replica streetlamps that graced the now-deserted sidewalk, his eyes twinkled. *They really did!* "I wasn't expecting you to stop walking. I thought Cynthia and I were going to have to chase you all the way up your stairs."

Aimee knelt down and finally did what she should've done in the beginning. She greeted the lovely dog. "Not Cynthia," she said and rubbed her nose in Cynthia's fur. As always, its scent reminded Aimee of cherry *macarons*. She gave Gerry an exaggerated frown. "You? Maybe."

His lips parted in a carefree grin. "Do you like tossing a Frisbee?"

Where had that come from? She stood. "Frisbee?"

"Yeah. You know." He simulated throwing a disc and Cynthia jumped to attention. "Not now. Sit, girl," he instructed his dog. Cynthia sat.

"You mean the toy that was popular like…a million years ago?"

"No. I mean the toy that's still popular today."

"Seriously?"

"I have a special Frisbee for Cynthia. She's amazing at toss and fetch."

"There's a Frisbee just for dogs?"

"Well, actually, if the brand isn't Wham-O, it shouldn't be called a Frisbee. If it's another brand, it should just be called a flying disc."

Aimee shook her head and continued walking. She couldn't understand why he was being so talkative. And about Frisbees of all things.

Gerry and Cynthia fell in step beside her.

"But we," Gerry continued and smiled down at his dog when Aimee remained unresponsive, "play with a real Frisbee.

Don't we, girl?" he asked Cynthia, and Aimee saw he was rewarded with a doggie grin. "I mean, after all, that name comes from a bakery." He nodded back over his shoulder. "One that's located up the road in Bridgeport."

Aimee stopped. If that was meant to get her attention, it did. "Wait." She held up her hand. She'd just seen that name when she was looking for the old whisk during the power outage. "My grand-mère has a few old pie tins stashed away. I saw them the other day." For some reason she wouldn't even begin to contemplate, she didn't want to ruin the nice moment by telling him *why* she'd come across them. "They have 'Frisbie's Pie' engraved on them." She frowned. "Any connection?"

"Totally. The Frisbee toy got its name from those exact-same pie pans."

Despite her resolve to discourage him from an early-morning and now an after-hours neighborly friendship and not to continually send him confusing or contradictory messages, she couldn't help asking, "What do you mean?" She was intrigued.

"What happened was that kids in Bridgeport were using their moms' Frisbie pie tins as flying discs. Instead of shouting 'FORE,' like golfers do to warn people that a ball's in the air heading their way, they shouted, 'FRISBIE' to warn them about a flying Frisbie pie pan."

"I had no idea." Aimee loved learning tidbits about baking and bakeries. Add the fact that it was about a bakery in her home state…and she was thrilled. She decided then and there to hang those old pie pans up in the Patisserie. "So those kids invented the Frisbee from the Frisbie pie pan?"

"Nope. They were just kids making a toy out of a pie tin."

"So, who invented it, then?"

"A man in California named Fred Morrison. He and his future wife were on a beach one day in the late '30s, tossing a pie pan back and forth—"

"Grown-up kids," Aimee said and Gerry smiled.

"The best kind of grown-up in my opinion."

Yeah, you would think that. Gerry was definitely one. "Go on," she encouraged. She really wanted to know how a pie company, located a few miles north of them, gave its name to the world-famous toy.

"Someone offered them twenty-five cents for the five-cent pan, and Fred thought there might be a way to make some money out of it."

"Always about money," Aimee moaned. She hated big business.

"Well, in this case he was a deserving man. He served in World War Two as a pilot until he became a prisoner of war. When he was eventually released, he designed a more aerodynamic disc that he called the Whirlo-Way. Plastics were on the rise. In 1948, he and a business partner made the first plastic disc. He sold the rights to his latest design, the Pluto Platter, which is what all modern flying discs resemble, to the Wham-O Toy Company in 1950."

"But…how did it go from the name 'Pluto Platter,' to being called after a pie company in Bridgeport?"

He gave her a quick grin. "That's easy. Northeastern college students—like the ones we have here in Stoneybridge—heard kids shouting 'Frisbie' to warn others of a flying pie pan in the air. So they did the same thing. When the people at Wham-O heard about that, they decided to stimulate sales by giving their flying disc the additional name of Frisbee. People were already familiar with the name in conjunction with flying discs." He shrugged. "Just marketing."

Aimee nodded. "So that's why it's spelled differently. *Frisbee* with two "E"s for the toy and *Frisbie* with "IE" for the pie pan," she murmured.

"Yep. Trademark rights or some such."

"The Frisbie Pie Company... Wow…" The fact that it was a Connecticut bakery that had lent its name to the famous toy fascinated her. "How do you know so much about this?"

"My niece did a report on it last year and sent me a copy. So," he continued without pause, "do you like tossing a Frisbee?" He repeated his original question.

"Can't say I ever have." She laughed softly. "But now that I know its history, I think, as a baker, I'd be remiss not to try it."

"It's one of Cynthia's favorite activities. Maybe we can teach you some time."

"I'd like that." *No! Did she just say that?* What happened to her resolve? Gone like a puff of flour in a breeze!

"Our favorite place in Stoneybridge to toss one is out by the Old Stone Bridge."

"My favorite place in the world! Grand-mère and I used to go there for picnics all the time." *There! She'd done it again!* She was giving away too much information and the wrong signal, too. She continued walking toward her stairs. He continued next to her. *Why shouldn't he? Had she done anything to discourage him?*

"Do you believe the Stoneybridge legend? That the bridge was built by early Romans who might have lost their way across the Great Sea?" He motioned in the general direction of the Atlantic Ocean.

"Well, since it's not registered with the National Registry of Historic Places, I guess the experts don't think it is," she hedged. She, however, was a bit of a fanatic in believing it *was* a Roman bridge built by third century A.D. Romans who had crossed the Atlantic either by accident or on purpose.

"I didn't ask that. I asked what *you* thought about it. Since you've lived here and heard stories about what's left of the bridge all your life, I think *you're* the expert."

She looked at him. She couldn't tell whether he considered the Roman bridge theory a ridiculous one or not. But she decided to be honest. "I do. I believe it's the real deal," she declared. "Why not? Just because history books don't have anything about early shipwrecked Romans doesn't mean it didn't happen. Legend is based on oral tradition. In many cases that's as valuable as written tradition. Besides, as far as I know, the stones are placed in exactly the same way as they are in so many early Roman bridges—ones that are still in existence in Italy and France and Spain—and that speaks volumes."

"Yeah. That's what I think too."

"You do?" Timothy had thought it was ridiculous.

"Yep. As for history books, there probably was something written about it. But like so many other books throughout the centuries, it was lost or destroyed. But the bridge is still here. And stones are sometimes the greatest witnesses to history. Look at the Mayan temples or Stonehenge which, like the Old Stone Bridge, don't have early writings to back them up, either. None that I'm aware of, anyhow."

If she were a mother and he had just complimented her child, she couldn't have been more pleased. "My thoughts exactly." *He believed the same thing she did!* Inside she was like yeast expanding with happiness. *Get a grip, girl! Gerry's the enemy baker.* He was the nemesis to her peace of mind, the number one foe to her keep-away-from-men resolve.

Oh, forget it!

Trying to keep track of her resolutions was just too hard. And it didn't do any good anyway. As she discovered every year a week or two after New Year's Day…

She reached into her purse for her keys. What she *could* do right now was escape to her apartment. "'Night," she said. As her fingers continued to search for her keys, she started up the stairs.

"Wait," he called.

She turned back to him. "Your box of cupcakes." He held the box out to her. It was easier to take it than not. It had "Emergency Room" written across the top; tomorrow, she'd deliver the goodies there herself. She nodded and continued up the stairs.

"Are you going to be baking Halloween cookies?" he called after her.

She was placing her left foot on the fifth step when he asked. She paused. *Where did that question come from?* Stepping up, she twisted around. She was at least two feet taller than him now. She liked the advantage. "Of course. Why?"

He shrugged. "I sometimes do. But I don't want to take your business away from you."

"You *can't* take my business away from me," she retorted a bit more loudly than she'd intended. *No mixed signals in that though, right? Wrong,* she answered herself. She knew she'd superimposed Uncle Cain on the conversation. Since her uncle's visit, the refrain that he and his nasty wife were going to take her business away from her had resonated over and over in her mind. Gerry's choice of words brought that very real battle to the forefront.

But Gerry had no idea about Uncle Cain, and when a lazy gleam came into his eyes she was glad he hadn't caught the desperation in her voice. "Like I said yesterday morning, neighbor lady," he responded calmly, "there's no need for us to be direct competition. We can cooperate and let our businesses complement each other. That way, both of them will benefit."

That wasn't something she was ready to hear, either. "Why do you keep coming back to that C & C idea—Cooperation and Complement?" she asked. "Is it because of the Patisserie's age? Are you scared that maybe it'll cause your *new* store problems?"

Aimee watched as the lazy gleam turned into a humorous one. "Aimee Hart, there are very few things I'm scared of in this world." He walked three steps up. They were even in height now. "How about you? What are you afraid of?"

You! she wanted to shout. *For making my knees go weak and for smelling as good as a vanilla macaron! Go back to California and leave me and my Patisserie alone.* But she didn't say that. Instead she issued a challenge. "How about a friendly cookie competition?"

He took another step up. "A cookie competition?" It sounded as if he'd never heard of such a thing.

"That's right. The bakery that sells the most Halloween sugar cookies next Thursday—on Halloween—wins."

Gerry's expression morphed into the kind of look a man gives a woman when he sees her as a woman, not as a pastry chef and not as a competitor. Her heart started beating faster. "That depends." His words were low, intense, spoken mere inches from her face. "What does the winner get?"

"Pride," she shot out. Turning, she ran up the remaining stairs. She managed to pull her keys from her purse, but dropped them a couple of times as she tried to get the correct one into the lock. She could feel Gerry watching her.

She willed herself not to look back. "Haste makes waste." She whispered another of her grand-mère's often-voiced sayings, used whenever someone tried to do something too quickly and continually botched it. She slowed down and unlocked her door. In she went. She closed it behind her, then leaned against it, breathing heavily as if she'd just run five miles.

"Stupid, stupid girl," she chastised herself.

"Meoooow." Louis, with his tail held high, his usual evening greeting, ran over to her.

Picking him up, she cuddled him close. "Why do I allow Gerry Mitchell to make me feel like this?" she asked her cat. *"Mixed signals. Mixed signals,"* she wailed. "And even worse, I challenged him to a 'friendly' contest. Am I crazy?"

Louis strained his body in the direction of the box she'd dropped on the entrance table.

"Meow," Louis replied as he got a whiff of the cupcakes. He sniffed in their direction and then started purring. Cake always made him purr.

"Traitor," Aimee said as putting him down, she carried the Uncle Gerry confections into the kitchen and placed the box in the cupboard, away from Louis' reach. But not before she got a whiff of the peanut butter goodness within.

She was ready to purr then, too.

***

Gerry watched her go.

He smiled, but it was one tempered with a question. There was some sort of barrier between them, and Gerry was unsure how to proceed with the lovely Aimee. He didn't understand it and didn't know whether he was up to even trying. Scarlett's hot-tempered ways were still too fresh in his mind.

One moment he felt he and Aimee could be good friends—perhaps more than friends—and the next he felt she almost hated him. When he'd asked what the winner of a cookie competition would get, she'd reacted in a way he hadn't expected. He hated having to watch his words. He *wouldn't* watch his words with a woman again, not even a woman he liked. Liked a lot.

They'd had a true connection before she learned he was the proprietor of the new store. But since then, it had been an emotional ride filled with ups and downs. He looked at her front door and the autumn wreath that graced it, with its warm and inviting colors. The entwined brown branches were wrapped with a russet-gold velvet ribbon and decorated with evergreen boughs, tiny pinecones, acorns and sprigs of berries. Scarlett would never have put such a heartwarming wreath on her minimalist, white on white, glass and chrome house with its view of LA. People came to Scarlett's house to be impressed, not welcomed.

He sighed. He knew Aimee wasn't Scarlett. He didn't want to confuse them or let what happened with Scarlett keep him from being friends with Aimee.

He needed friends in town.

The chance to be part of a close-knit community, where your neighbors watched your back, was one of the reasons he'd returned to small-town life. Friendships like that were worth fighting for and overcoming whatever problems might have to be worked out. And if there *was* a chance of sharing more with Aimee—God knew the attraction was there—wasn't it worth at least trying?

The Cape Cod cottage he'd rented on a parallel road to Main Street had a white-picket fence, a huge oak tree in the front yard and a sandbox, swing set and bird bath in the back. He had to admit that despite his arguments and insistence to the contrary, someday he hoped a family would complete the picture. If a cute orange-and-white cat came with the deal, so much the better.

He looked down at his dog and as he so often did, mulled over his frustration with her. "There has to be something more bothering Aimee than just my owning the store next door."

"There is," Miss Maggie said from behind him. Startled, Cynthia rounded on her, all four legs planted wide apart. Although she was a standard poodle, a dog not normally associated with being a guard, she was one hundred percent Gerry's protector. She didn't like it when people snuck up on them. It rarely happened. Gerry was shocked that a lady of Miss Maggie's rather large size who favored long, flowing muumuus had come up behind them so quietly.

"Sit, girl," Gerry commanded Cynthia, and then said to Miss Maggie, "I beg your pardon?"

"There *is* something more bothering Aimee." The older woman paused thoughtfully. "And I think you should be aware of it, since it's common knowledge around town."

Gerry didn't want to hear gossip. He held up his hand. "Thanks, Miss Maggie, but I prefer Aimee to tell me whatever she wants me to know of her own free will."

"She won't. I love her and—" She paused and ran the tip of her tongue across her bottom lip, obviously wanting to take care in how she proceeded. "Although I haven't known you long, you seem like a fine young man." She waved a bejeweled hand in the direction of his store and then her own. "You opened the Cakerie across the street from my shop." She smiled, an older woman who was wise in the ways of the world. "I know where to find you if you do anything to hurt our Aimee." There was a friendly warning in her words. Gerry knew he wouldn't want to be on the receiving end of Miss Maggie's wrath; she'd make a formidable adversary.

Since she was offering him the information he needed and her friendship, he decided to accept it as the gift it was. He returned her smile and sighed out his frustration. "You're too late, Miss Maggie. I think I already hurt her when I opened my Cakerie next door to her Patisserie. There's a part of her that hates me for it."

"Don't be silly," she admonished and Gerry's brows rose. He hadn't been called *silly* since his nanny days. "Truthfully, about your bakery opening next door to hers and why it bothers her so much…" She tapped the toe of her ballet-style shoe and seeing it, Gerry understood why she'd been able to sneak up on Cynthia undetected. "I think there might be something going on there that not even *I* know about."

From the quizzical look on her face, Gerry could tell that very thought seemed beyond the scope of Miss Maggie understands. It amused him but he didn't let it show. He waited patiently for her to continue.

"Our Aimee is exceedingly close-mouthed about her personal business. She wasn't always like this. It was only after this…event, which I wish to tell you about, that she became this way. So, what the entire town knows, you should know, too, since you're part of Main Street now. It'll help you better understand Aimee and why she might be acting toward you in a contradictory way at times."

He ran his hand through his hair.

If Miss Maggie could shed some understanding on the subject, shouldn't he accept her offer? Decision made he said, "Tell me."

Without embellishment she quickly did so. "You've heard of a runaway bride?"

Gerry nodded.

"Well, in Aimee's case, the bride showed up."

"You mean—"

"Yes. It was a few months after Aimee's grand-mère died. All her friends—and that includes almost all the people who have shops on Main Street—were gathered at the church. The only one missing was the groom."

Anger, deep and swift, for the man who had committed one of the worst sins against a woman—and a woman he supposedly loved—rose in Gerry. He could understand calling off a wedding. That could be forgiven. But to ditch a woman, and a woman of Aimee's quality, at the church in front of all her friends and neighbors, and even worse shortly after her beloved grandmother had died... Well, that smacked of treason against all women.

"Sheriff Bob, who was to give her away, drove her around town three times hoping the groom was just late in getting to the church. Finally, as they started the fourth turn, his cell phone rang. Professor Timothy Bainbridge couldn't go through with it. No reason was given that I know of."

"I would have punched him," Gerry ground out and Miss Maggie chuckled.

"I had the sharp end of my umbrella ready for him." She paused. "He never showed his face on Main Street again."

"Coward." There were a few other choice words Gerry had in mind, but he pushed them away.

"Exactly." She paused. "Now do you understand why—"

Gerry reached out and took her hand. "Thank you, Miss Maggie. I'm glad you told me. Like you said, I needed to know. It explains a lot."

He could see relief that she'd done the right thing manifest itself in her relaxed and easy breaths. "One other word of advice. When you ask Aimee out on a date…" Her brows rose knowingly and he nodded back, not bothering to hide that it was something he wanted to do. "Don't expect her to accept the first or second time. It'll take at least three invitations before she does. But if you persist she'll eventually go out with you. So make it a good date!"

"You're a romantic at heart, Miss Maggie." Gerry wondered what her story was. She was a beautiful woman, ageless, graceful, charming. Had she ever been in love?

"Of course I'm a romantic!" she said, and checking in both directions, she gave him another wave and crossed soundlessly back to her side of Main Street.

Gerry smiled at Cynthia. "I think I've just made a friend." He looked up at Aimee's door. "And an ally."

As he started walking, taking his remaining box of cupcakes to the police station, he almost felt like singing. He'd made a decision this evening; Miss Maggie had helped him. Aimee had not only been hurt in love, but *mortified*. It was worse than the way Scarlett had treated him. Scarlett had removed his store from her electronic Rolodex and had instructed her thousands of connections to do so, too. Aimee had been humiliated in front of her friends and neighbors. Real time. Real space. Real wedding.

He would ask Aimee out. Definitely. Once, twice and maybe, just maybe, by the third time, she'd accept.

10—Halloween Bake-Off

Four days later Stoneybridge was all decked out for Halloween—*All Hallows' Eve* or *All Saints' Evening,* which was the evening before *All Hallows' Day*—as Pastor Samson had explained last Sunday during his sermon on the beautiful, if mostly forgotten, origin of the popular celebration.

Clusters of bright orange pumpkins held the place of honor in front of every store and within windows up and down Main Street.

Beautiful and colorful Halloween costumes fluttered in the fall breeze outside Jumbo Toy Store, inviting all to come in and enjoy their annual "Halloween Day, half-price sale." Stores in the malls put their costumes on sale the day *after* Halloween. Not Jumbo Toy Store in Stoneybridge. Mr. and Mrs. Georgian were the owners, and they wanted to make sure that any child who didn't have a costume yet—for trick or treat that night—would.

Halloween books and games filled the Book Nook's large windows for anyone who might not be able to make it out for trick or treat, while Otis's Organic Produce had small pumpkins for the taking stacked in little pyramids all around the shop. Otis had so many that even if every person who visited town that day took one—and many left the interstate and traveled the few miles up just to visit the historic center of Stoneybridge today—he wouldn't run out.

Miss Maggie's Treasure Trove had entire costumes arranged on the mannequins in her display window, mainly for "kids" over the age of fifty.

Best of all, the sky was as blue as everyone imagines fall days in New England to be. The maple and dogwood trees lining Main Street cooperated in decorating Stoneybridge for the popular holiday. Their leaves had faded to a shade lighter than that of pumpkin but they were, except for the occasional softly fluttering leaf, still clinging to the trees and today, that was what mattered.

Gerry had gone all out and created an elaborate window display showcasing his cookie creations. Kids of all ages oohed and aahed over the huge flying bats, brooms and sneaky-looking pumpkin cookies the size of Frisbees. His sophisticated decorating techniques made each cookie appear to be in 3-D.

The "wow" factor in his window display drew crowds into his store from early morning on.

Next door, Aimee's bite-size smiling jack-o'-lanterns, black cats with green eyes and friendly-ghost cookies looked so delicious that people were continually coming into her shop, too, and leaving with full boxes. Lucy and three others, who worked part-time on high-profile days, were kept busy in the café filling order after order, while Aimee, Becky, Tom, and Mark plus two other part-timers, an older man and woman who could always be relied on to provide tremendous help in the kitchen when Aimee needed it, worked Grand-mère's old ovens. They'd been at it from three that morning, baking, decorating and keeping the display cases filled with oven-fresh cookies.

Aimee was certain the Patisserie's cookie sales would beat Uncle Gerry's. Many of her buyers were repeat customers—

people who came from the tri-state area every year on Halloween just to get her cookies and experience Stoneybridge all decorated for the fun day.

Today, with its fine weather drawing in many first-time interstate customers, too, was a boon for her. It was encouraging to see the cookies flying into Patisserie boxes and out the door on their way to the homes of people from near and far.

Aimee took a midmorning break to check on Louis and see if he'd had enough of the commotion and activity along Main Street. Although sunny and bright, it was cool and she didn't want him catching a chill. If he preferred to go back to their warm apartment, she would take him.

"How you doin', fella?" Aimee asked and standing on the brick, reached up to rub Louis's nose. He bumped her hand with the top of his head and gave a mighty, back-arching stretch before he went around in a circle and settled down on his mat to watch everything from eight feet up. His soft purr told her he was happy right where he was.

"Louis is just like the cat in the window, Ms. Hart," Aimee heard Tommy Floyd say from beside her.

She nodded, thinking he was referring to Louis's reflection in her display window. "Hi, Tommy," she said and stepping down from her brick regarded the little boy. "Oh my, you're a very handsome cat today, too!" Tommy was dressed in a classic Sylvester the Cat outfit. Aimee glanced over at Valery and asked, "Didn't you wear this same outfit a couple of Halloweens when we were girls?"

Valery smiled. "Mom sewed it for me like…a thousand years ago."

"Ms. Hart! Look!" Tommy insisted, tugging on her arm. "It's just like Louis!" he repeated and ran over to Uncle Gerry's window display to point out the cat cake that had captured his attention.

Aimee's mouth dropped open. On the left side of the window of Uncle Gerry's Cakerie, Gerry and Doug had just placed a huge cake that was the image of Louis. In fact, the cat cake was identical from his orange and white fur to his green eyes and little white paws. Even Louis's typical wide-eyed expression that seemed to say, "What's going on, guys?" was perfectly depicted. Aimee walked toward the display. She was touched, astounded, flabbergasted. *Gerry had taken the time on their cookie bake-off day to create a cake sculpture of Louis?* "It's a masterpiece," she whispered. "Not at all crass." She was dumbfounded.

"That man is some kind of wizard with cakes," Valery agreed. "It's like a photo of Louis, and it really shows his personality."

"It's amazing," Aimee whispered as her eyes took in every little piped-on frosted star that had been used to "draw" Louis on the cake. She looked through the window at Gerry and smiled. He winked back, but when he put up his hand and motioned that he was coming out, she groaned.

Valery heard her. "Yeah, Aimee, it's *so* tough having a man like that interested in you."

"He's not!"

Valery shook her head and gave her a poignant smile. "Wake up, Aimee," she said as she herded Tommy in the direction of Hale's Hardware. "Or you might miss Prince Charming's kiss. And believe me, time's too short to miss even one."

Aimee knew she was talking from experience. Her words weren't frivolous or shallow but backed up by the great love and devotion she had shared with her husband for five years until death had prematurely parted them.

Aimee appreciated Valery's opinion, so, as she waited for Gerry, she tried to figure out if that was what she was doing. *Was she letting her mistake in having kissed a toad named Timothy Bainbridge cause her to lose out on a man who might just turn out to be her Prince Charming?*

Gerry was Becky's "hot guy" and he was Valery's "Prince Charming."

What was he to her? Enemy-pastry-chef number one? Or the impressive man who owned the store next door?

Yes, he was both of those.

But what else?

The man who made her feel like a woman again?

Yes, that too.

But what did *she* want him to be? That was something she needed to sort out.

She studied the cake. And what did this splendid likeness of Louis say about how Gerry felt for her?

She shook her head.

No! She clenched her fingers into tight fists.

She didn't want to sort anything out right now. She didn't want a man to complicate her life. Particularly not Mr. Next-Door-Baker Man.

Before Gerry came out, she had to remember why.

First—she poked one finger from her right fist as it hung by her side—romantic entanglements, and the trust they required of a woman, only resulted in making that woman weak, foolish and hurt when she finally learned that she couldn't and shouldn't trust her own heart. *Then whose heart should a woman trust?* a little voice inside her asked. Aimee quickly shooed it away and went on with her list.

Two—she poked out a second finger—a woman could lose her own confidence and even her self-respect for a very long time if she committed her heart to a man and then that man disappointed her. She waited to hear her inner voice disagree, but…it didn't.

Three—she extended a third finger. Added to reasons one and two was the fear of becoming fodder for town gossip again if things didn't work out. And what were the chances it would? Nil. Next to nil anyway. Number three should be reason enough to be a neighbor and nothing else to the enigmatic Gerry Mitchell.

There! Aimee squared her shoulders. She remembered. She felt triumphant.

She had to stick to her resolve that he was going to be no more than her Main Street neighbor and casual acquaintance. Nothing more.

She *had* to remember that.

Especially with repayment of the loan coming due in twenty-seven days. All her energy had to go into wowing the supermarket chain so they'd sign her for their Main Street Bakery contract. That was all she should think about now. That… She smiled, a smile not unlike the cat smile Louis wore on his cake. And winning the bake-off today.

She stretched her vertebra and stood even taller.

Her resolve was back in place.

Gerry walked out.

One look at him…and her determination melted away like sugar mixed with boiling water.

He nodded toward the cake. "You like it?"

"Yes. It's beautiful." Aimee motioned to Louis, who was staring down at it. "I think he knows he was the inspiration."

Gerry reached up and rubbed Louis's ears. As always, she was surprised her cat allowed that. "We're buddies, aren't we?" he said to Louis. Then to Aimee, "Here." He gave her a box she'd just noticed he was carrying. "I thought you might enjoy a jack-o'-lantern cookie the size of a Frisbee."

She took the box and held up her other hand. "Wait here." She skipped toward her door. "It's only fair for me to give you a box, too." As she went into the Patisserie, she tried not to think about how good he made her feel. She placed his cookie box on a table, and grabbing a box of oven-fresh, pumpkin cookies from the counter, she took it out to him.

"Thank you," he said and utterly shocked her when he immediately cut the ribbon with his pocket knife, flipped open the lid and plopped an entire pumpkin cookie in his mouth. His eyes closed as he chewed, and the sounds he made might have been considered rude if it wasn't obvious that he was testing a cookie. "You have added real pumpkin to the batter," he marveled.

She was pleased that he realized it.

"Yum, yum." He licked his lips, and she found herself smiling over the "yum, yum." She felt sure it was a sound he must have made as a little boy when he was delighted by a particular taste. "It's exquisite. Somehow you've managed to add a French twist to such an American classic. It's a sugar cookie through and through, but at the same time you keep guilt from being part of the culinary experience. You've combined the perfect amount of sweetness with the real taste of pumpkin. I don't believe I've ever had a better sugar cookie. It's sweet, but not so sugary that I feel the need to brush my teeth immediately after eating it."

Aimee stared at him. Was he really this nice? A crowd had gathered around him. Did crowds *always* gather around him? He seemed to attract people like a magnet does metal.

"Goin' to get me some of those!" A man with a Southern accent exclaimed from behind her.

"My mother would love them," said a young woman who sounded as if she came from Upper East Side Manhattan.

"I want some, too!" Another agreed.

Aimee looked at Gerry. "Did you do that on purpose?"

"Do what?"

"Get people to come into my store?"

"Why would I do that? Aren't we having a competition today?" he asked, and with a wink ambled back into his own store.

Aimee shrugged and walking back into her own store, she went directly to the kitchen. She had to think. Just when she thought she had her feelings for her neighbor figured out, he did something to confuse her. She was beginning to believe he baked such big cakes and cookies because it was a measure of his heart. But then, what did that say about *her* heart? Little cookies equaled teeny tiny heart? No, that was silly.

"This is delish!" Becky sang out. She'd broken off the upper right corner of Gerry's Frisbee-size jack-o'-lantern and put it in her mouth.

"I had no doubt it would be."

"Have you tried any of his baking yet?" Becky asked. When Aimee shook her head, Becky was incredulous. "Aren't you at all curious?"

Aimee was, but she wasn't going to admit it. "Uncle Gerry's Cakerie won all sorts of awards out in California. Culinary experts say he makes a high-quality product. That's good enough for me."

Becky opened her mouth as if to say something, then closed it again. With a smile, she turned back to the green eyes she was painting on the black cats.

***

"Those huge jack-o'-lantern cookies are leavin' the store faster than a hot knife through butter," Patrick, an eighteen-year-old scholarship student from down south, who studied all night and worked all day and didn't look any the worse for wear, shouted into the Cakerie kitchen. "We're gonna be a-needin' another batch in half an hour." His Southern accent and expressions had taken the Northerners a bit of time to work out, but after three days of working together, they all understood one another perfectly.

"Thanks," Gerry said to Patrick, then, with a satisfied grin on his face, took off his chef's coat. "That's it for cookies today, boys," he said to his team. Tossing his coat into the bin, he walked toward his office instructing, "We'll finish up with this batch, then get back to baking Halloween cakes."

The men looked at one another. Doug followed him into his office and asked the question they all wanted to ask. "You're not baking any more cookies?"

"Not today."

Doug tipped his head to one side. "But they're selling like hot cakes." He grinned. "Bad pun, I know."

Gerry grinned in response. "Isn't that great?"

Doug closed the door behind him. They'd known each other long enough for Doug to ask, "Just what game are you playing at?"

Gerry was honest. He nodded toward the wall he shared with the Patisserie. "Chief Chef, I want neighbor lady to win the competition so she can keep her baking pride intact."

"I don't think she'll like winning by default."

Gerry shrugged. "We're a Cakerie. We have to get back to making cakes."

"And she makes French pastries."

"Not today. She told me she always bakes cookies on Halloween. We didn't set a start and finish time to our friendly competition. Besides, the Halloween cakes are selling well, too. And that's what we need to push."

"Okay," Doug said. "But I don't think the lady's gonna like it," he repeated.

***

Aimee heard the clock tower strike two just as Lucy ran into the kitchen. "I don't know what happened, but business has picked up astronomically. We're almost out of pumpkin and friendly-ghost cookies!"

"Yes!" Aimee shouted while piping smiling faces on her seventieth batch of pumpkin cookies. "These are almost ready to go." She was not only making a lot of money today—much more than on previous Halloweens—but she was convinced she was beating Gerry at their competition.

"The ghosts will be ready in five minutes," Becky told her.

Mark opened the oven door, filling the room with more of the heavenly scent of baking cookies. "And ten more cookie sheets of all three are coming out now

"And ten more ready to go in," said Tom, one of the part-time college helpers.

Aimee glanced over at the cookies coming out of the oven. "Put them in the blast freezer, Mark." Then to Lucy, "They'll be decorated and ready in thirty minutes," she assured her. "But these pumpkins are ready now—" she finished piping the last smile "—and we'll bring the ghosts out in five minutes."

"Perfect," Lucy said, and taking a tray of the pumpkin cookies, she headed to the front.

Aimee loved the thrill of baking as a team. She didn't have a lot of employees but those she had were the best. They'd spent the last couple of days making the cookie dough and forming the cookies, then freezing them. Consequently, they had a large quantity that only needed to be baked and decorated. "Well done, guys! Doing a great job!"

Thirty minutes later, just as Lucy and Tom carried out the newly decorated pumpkins, ghosts and cats, Miss Maggie ran into the kitchen.

"If you need Becky now, Miss Maggie, I think we can manage," Aimee said sending a smile in her direction. Even though Becky should've been at her shop this morning—also a busy time for the Treasure Trove—Miss Maggie had lent her to Aimee. It was well-known that no one was faster and better at decorating cookies than Becky.

"No, dear. That's not it at all. You need to come and see something."

Aimee regarded the half-decorated pumpkin cookies, but she knew Miss Maggie wouldn't ask her to leave unless it was important.

She followed her through the café, which was filled with people waiting to order boxes of Halloween treats, and out the front door.

Miss Maggie nodded at the sign that had been placed on the window display next door that now contained *only* Halloween cakes. "No More Cookies. Visit the Patisserie—THE STORE NEXT DOOR—to satisfy your Halloween cookie cravings!"

Aimee suddenly felt as deflated as a balloon that had lost all its air. "What?" She frowned at Miss Maggie in confusion.

"I don't have the feeling that he's a baker who runs out of ingredients to make sugar cookies," Miss Maggie commented. But Aimee noticed an almost amused twinkle in her eyes, as if she was pleased by this turn of events—a sentiment she tried to hide by pointing over to where Gerry was putting a "sold" sign on the gigantic cake of Louis. A woman was looking over his right shoulder, obviously pleased to have found the cake and purchased it.

Aimee felt a passing sorrow that the cake had sold. When Gerry disappeared back into the shop, she whipped out her phone from her apron pocket and quickly took a photo of it.

Aimee knew she didn't have any right to feel sad about the cake, but what she did need to do was get to the bottom of this "No more cookies" sign. Waving bye to Miss Maggie, she opened the Cakerie's door and went in.

"Hey, Aimee." Gerry nodded in her direction. "I was just going to call you. Do you mind my selling the Louis cake? I made it for you, but this lady—" he smiled at the woman waiting beside him "—needs it for her party tonight. I promise to make another one for you."

So it had been meant for her? In spite of herself, it made her feel good. "No problem," she said to the customer and was rewarded with a relieved smile.

Aimee smiled back, then glanced around. Even though the Cakerie didn't have a single cookie—if those giant, plate-size things *could* be called cookies—left in the store, it was still crowded with out-of-towners buying Halloween cakes and cupcakes, all in sizes large, larger and jumbo. Aimee hated to admit it, but she knew that hardly any of the interstate people would be in her shop today if it wasn't for her Halloween cookies. She'd get a few who might want to try a pumpkin-flavored *macaron,* but those were the ones who were sitting in the café. She wouldn't have that long line of transient customers if it wasn't for the all-American sugar cookies. Grand-mère knew that. It was why they always took a step away from their normal French pastries and sold American cookies on Halloween, too.

But as she regarded the people in the store, it struck her that Uncle Gerry's Cakerie had people coming in *without* the cookie enticement.

When he'd finished getting all the pertinent information for the Louis cake's delivery, Gerry turned to her. "What can I do for you, Aimee?"

As if he didn't know! But she was proud of herself. She kept her cool. "May I speak with you?" She glanced around the shop. There were still several customers waiting to be served. But she saw that the man named Doug, who had helped with the electricity problem last week, plus a middle-aged woman as well as a college girl, were working in perfect rhythm and obviously had the store under control. "Privately."

"Sure." He waved her in the direction of the kitchen and his well-appointed office. It was neat and orderly, like the store. A place for everything, and everything in its place, even on this busy day. Nothing less than she'd expected.

When he closed the door behind them, and the noise from the kitchen receded, she whirled to face him. "What do you think you're doing?"

"What do you mean?" He acted as innocent as a two-year-old caught with his hand in the cookie jar. Even in her anger, she realized how apt that cliché was and almost had to grin. Almost.

"Come on, Gerry!" She slung her arm in the direction of the front and the sign on the window. "'No more cookies. Visit the Patisserie—THE STORE NEXT DOOR—to satisfy your Halloween cookie cravings!'" she recited.

He shrugged. "I ran out."

"And I was born yesterday."

"You were?" His grinned at her playfully. "You certainly seem like a grown-up to me."

She resisted the urge to act like a toddler and stomp her foot. "Please check your computer and tell me when you sold your last cookie. Our competition is valid only until then."

"Aimee, we never said what time the competition would end. What's the big deal anyway?"

"Do you think I'm a charity case?" *Well, she might be if she didn't land the supermarket contract.* But that had nothing to do with this bake-off. "I will not have you treating me in such a condescending and unbusinesslike manner." Did she actually use that dreaded term—*businesslike?* "Please check your computer now and tell me when you sold your last Halloween cookie. I'll run it against my records. Whoever made the most money until that time will be the winner."

He hesitated a moment. The gaze he ran over her was assessing. She sensed that he wanted to say something. Had he noticed how unaffected his store was by the lack of cookies in stock? And how desperately in need of them the Patisserie was to keep up her sales today? If he did, she was glad he didn't say anything, glad when he turned to his computer and started tapping on his keyboard to bring up the information. "I sold my last cookie at exactly…13:48."

"And the tally?"

When he told her the amount, she did some quick figuring in her head. "It's going to be close."

"Okay."

She half-turned from him but stopped, and glancing back, asked, "Why did you do it? Why did you stop making cookies and put up that sign?"

A lazy smile formed on his lips. "I was done baking all the cookies we'd prepared in advance and stocked in the freezer. I needed to get my staff back to baking and decorating cakes." He shrugged again. "Is it so bad to recommend that people go to a neighboring shop?"

"But we had a competition going on!"

"Cooperation also starts with a C, Aimee. You know, as in getting along with each other for the common good of our Main Street stores. To be nice and neighborly." He paused. "Besides, we didn't say for how long," he repeated.

"I assumed it was for the entire day."

"Don't assume things, neighbor lady. It always leads to problems and misunderstandings."

He seemed to be speaking from experience rather than mouthing a phrase. And she had to admit he was right. She'd shot out the bake-off idea the other night without suggesting any boundaries. She'd *assumed* it was for the entire day. But how could he have his people baking and decorating cookies when he needed to keep his cakes in front of his customers, especially on such a high-profile day?

She nodded. "I'll remember that."

"Remember this, too." His eyes softened. "It's not bad to do something nice for one's neighbor. It is not charity. It's being friendly." He laughed. "And more often than not, as Pastor Samson pointed out last Sunday, whatever you do to be good to another person comes back to repay you a hundredfold." A twinkle settled in his dark eyes. "So, actually, what might seem to be for another's benefit is, in the long run, equally for one's own."

She slowly nodded. He couldn't know it, but he'd just expressed her grandmother's philosophy of life. When had she forgotten to practice it, she wondered? Somewhere along the way of being a bride without a groom, of losing out on buying this property and Uncle Cain's declaration of a takeover, she supposed.

But as she turned and walked out of his office and through his kitchen toward the back door, sensing she'd been busted made her skin grow hot. She knew it hadn't been Gerry's intention to make her feel guilty, and yet she did. What had she done to help him, a new business in town? Absolutely nothing. Just the opposite. She'd accused him of things at every turn.

Grand-mère would not have been happy about that.

As Aimee slipped in her key and unlocked the back door of the Patisserie and walked into her own kitchen, she knew she wasn't happy about it, either.

11—La Vie en Rose

"He beat me by twenty dollars," Aimee told Becky fifteen minutes later when she left her office. "I sent him a text telling him." Aimee was actually happy about it. He and his generous attitude deserved to win. Besides, sugar cookies weren't his product any more than they were hers. While they'd helped her today, she now suspected they'd probably hindered Gerry's business.

"He likes you," was Becky's only response.

"He likes everybody," Aimee stated, and as she did, she realized it was true. Gerry really did seem to like everybody. One thing for sure, she hadn't met a single person who didn't like him.

"He likes you differently. As a woman," Becky persisted.

"Don't go there," Aimee said. She needed to fill a special order of two hundred orange pumpkin cookies and was placing them in a huge box—the Patisserie's largest.

Becky pointed at Aimee's box, which she was actually filling with *black cat* cookies. "You expecting those cats to turn into pumpkins?" Becky asked her with a knowing grin.

Aimee looked at the box. Twenty pairs of green cat eyes stared back at her, mocking her attempts to ignore the truth of Becky's words. Aimee knew that Gerry liked her. What surprised her was that she was finally listening to her own heart, which was screaming that she liked him too.

Later that evening when the kids started coming around the shop for trick or treat dressed in their various outfits, it was a lot to think about. Especially with hearing Gerry next door kidding around and having fun with every child who came to his Cakerie asking for a treat. Treats he gave, with the biggest being his personality and his ability to turn every moment into an extra good one.

Yes, she had a lot to consider, she thought as the beautiful sound of children giggling and tittering in pure delight over something Gerry said or did wafted over to her. Liking Gerry was a complication she might not be able to push aside.

***

Aimee woke up at three o'clock Saturday morning, an hour earlier than usual. She glanced out the window. The moon and the stars were hidden behind fog and gray mist, but the color of the softly rustling leaves in the light from the stoic streetlamps touched Main Street with good old Connecticut magic. She felt the window pane; it was much cooler than yesterday. Winter wasn't far off.

"This is perfect weather for an early-November Saturday morning," she said to Louis who answered by opening one eye, then nestling farther into his quilt. "Don't worry. I won't get you until it warms up later this morning."

Aimee was glad that it wasn't sunny and bright. When Saturday mornings in fall and winter were dressed up in weather like this, most of her regular customers wanted to do exactly the same thing as Louis—come to the Patisserie later.

Getting up and going down to her kitchen now would afford Aimee time to experiment with a couple of the recipes she'd found late last night in Grand-mère's handwritten cookbooks. The final supermarket presentation was less than two weeks away, and Aimee wanted to make sure she went through all her grandmother's recipes to select just the right ones to present. Her only concern about her menu was that it leaned more toward French tastes than American, not a surprise since it was a *French* Patisserie. The people who came to her shop liked that, but she wasn't sure how it would translate to a supermarket environment. The cookie sales on Halloween had brought that point home to her.

She remembered Grand-mère making a certain *tarte aux pommes*—apple tart—that she thought would be good to include with a variety of *macarons,* croissants and her grand-mère's famous caramel cream *mille-feuille.* She hopped off her bed and hurried to get ready. She didn't want to miss even a minute of this cozy predawn time in her kitchen.

Fifteen minutes later, sitting in her office with Grand-mère's recipes before her, Aimee felt her resolve strengthen. She was going to win that contract and save the Patisserie! With care, she ran her fingertips over the handwritten words her grand-mère had left behind. It was a connection with the dear sweet lady, something that somehow transcended the veil between heaven and earth.

Flour, butter, baking powder, cream, etc might be the ingredients used, but it was a lifetime of Grand-mère's personal dedication to quality and care that made the recipes special. And that was what Aimee had inherited from her and what she recreated every day in the Patisserie. It was what had made the Patisserie successful enough to support Grand-mère's family for all those many years, and it would win Aimee the supermarket contract now, so she could continue sharing her grandmother's legacy with the people of Stoneybridge and beyond. *She had to.*

Aimee couldn't let the Patisserie die. She just couldn't. It would be like losing Grand-mère all over again.

Nearly three hours later, the Patisserie was filled with the heady aroma of *tarte aux pomme*—which Aimee decided would definitely be part of her presentation menu—croissants, and blueberry *macarons*. She pulled on her bulky sweater, grabbed her orange broom and headed to the front of the store.

She had a 6:00 a.m. date with Gerry to keep.

Gerry was already outside sweeping.

"Good morning," she called. Her glance touched on his square jaw and the ready smile that softened it. Gerry could be described as exuding virility—Becky's initial description of "hot guy" was right—but it was toned down by a personality that didn't take his classic appearance seriously. Even as an old man, bent with age and faded by years, Gerry would epitomize the masculine man. Masculinity wasn't about appearance as much as personality and outlook. When Gerry was around, it was as if the sun was always shining. Few men understood that was how most women wanted them to be. Bright, cheerful, optimistic men made for strong, secure, confident ones—fabulous lifetime companions.

Before walking over to Cynthia to offer her a treat, Aimee quickly scanned the sky beyond Gerry's left shoulder. Although the sun would soon rise above the eastern horizon, thick low-lying clouds kept it as dark as midnight.

"Good morning," he returned and gave a slight shiver. "Chilly today."

"Too cold for you?" she countered but unlike that first morning they'd met outside, there was a friendly challenge in her voice.

"Bring it on," he replied, a hint of amusement in his voice.

Their eyes held for a moment, silent, yet silence was the perfect setting for the awareness that crackled around them. Cynthia started jumping, changing the charged air back to its normal six o'clock one. He nodded toward his dog and chuckled. "She's been waiting for you."

How about you? It was on the tip of her tongue to ask, but she didn't have to. She knew he had been.

She looked at the sidewalk. Even though the wind had been blowing and there should've been at least half a container of fallen leaves to sweep on her thirty-two-foot wide storefront, there weren't any. There weren't any leaves on Gerry's sidewalk, either. Her glance landed on the container by the curb. It was nearly overflowing ready for the daily curbside compost truck to come by and collect. Conscious of his searching gaze, she asked, "Did you sweep my sidewalk, too?"

He shrugged.

She was touched. Very. "Thank you." It was a heady sensation not fighting her growing feelings for him. She motioned toward the Patisserie. "Would you care to come in for a croissant or two and a cup of hot chocolate?" Croissants had been Monday Gerry's breakfast.

His grin told her he was remembering, too. "Are they fresh?"

"What do *you* think?" She opened the door and the yeasty aroma that rushed out with the store's interior heat answered for her.

He breathed in deeply, set his broom against the tree, and followed her inside, holding her unused broom.

***

While Aimee prepared their tray, she watched Gerry set a fire in the old stone fireplace. "For someone who's spent the last several years in Southern California, you sure know how to do that well."

"It's not something one ever forgets. I'm a born-and-bred Connecticuter, don't forget."

"Which town are you from?"

Standing, he motioned over his shoulder in the direction of New York City. "Nazareth."

"So close," she murmured. Relatively speaking, they'd grown up just a few miles apart. It seemed strange that they'd never met before.

"My high school still plays Stoneybridge East High each season."

"Were you a football player?"

He held out his hands and motioned to his size. "Do you think the coaches would let a kid who was this size by the age of sixteen *not* play?"

"I went to all the home football games from when I was in the fifth grade. How old are you?"

"Thirty-six."

"I'm four years younger. So that means I probably saw you. Which position did you play?"

"Quarterback."

"Quarterback! Then I definitely saw you!"

"Small world, isn't it?" he said and sank down on the *fauteuil* next to the fireplace. Just as he had that first Monday when he'd sat in the matching chair by the window, he stretched out his long legs. "Ah…the most comfortable chair in town. I feel like I'm in Paris whenever I come here."

"I take that as a compliment," she said as she placed his croissants and hot chocolate in front of him.

"Meant to be. I guess you've spent many a summer holiday in France."

She sat across the small table from him and shook her head. "No. Never been."

"I don't believe it." He gestured around the café. "The ambience is just too perfect for you not to have been inspired by a familiarity with the place."

She looked around, seeing it through his eyes—the light-pink tinge to the embossed antique wallpaper and how well the wrought-iron chairs and tables blended with the old oak counter, gilded mirror and faded carpet. "That's all Grand-mère's doing. She was French. She grew up in France and lived there until after World War Two, when she moved to the US with her first husband, my grandfather, who was an American serviceman. She met Fredrick when she was sixteen and married him at seventeen."

"What a fascinating history."

Aimee continued to look around. "I haven't changed the café since she died." She hadn't. Even after making the repairs last year, she'd put everything back as it was before.

He nodded toward "Miss Maggie's table" and said, "Miss Maggie mentioned that it was your dream to live in Paris."

He remembered that? "I have lots of dreams."

"It's good to have dreams."

She shook her head. "Not if they never come to pass. Then they can be a bit of a downer." The sudden force of his gaze told her that wasn't a philosophy he subscribed to. She didn't want to hear it, though. Not with *his* store, the property she'd wanted to own, occupying one of her dreams. She was trying to get beyond that. No. She *was* beyond that. She quickly changed the subject. "Did you go to Paris to learn French?"

He laughed. "Far from it. I actually went to study at Le Cordon Bleu. Cuisine and Patisserie baking."

Aimee couldn't stop her jaw from dropping. She reached for her hot chocolate and took a sip. It nearly scalded the roof of her mouth.

"Whoa, there," he admonished and helped her set the cup down. "It's hot."

She hardly felt it. Here she'd been ranting at him about his "big, brash and crass" cakes and he was the one who had the best qualifications to own and operate a *real* patisserie. Other than sitting at Grand-mère's feet and learning everything she'd had to teach her and attending a local culinary school, she had no such grand qualifications. "Studying at Le Cordon Bleu has always been my dream." *Did she really use that word again? Dream?* Yep, at the amused look in his eyes she knew she had. "I mean," she quickly went on, "I'd feel honored to study there someday." Still not quite right. She tried again, and in the tone her mother, who'd been an officer in the military might have used with someone under her authority, she all but commanded, "Tell me about it."

Eating his croissants, he did.

"It sounds ideal," she said as he finished. "Paris is truly the culinary capital of the world." She couldn't help the sigh that came out with the last word.

He sat back and said the unexpected. "Well, one of them anyway."

"How can you say that? Paris is *it*!"

"Every area of the world has its own special cuisine, Aimee. To say that Paris with its open-air markets, bistros and *boulangeries* is *one* of the culinary capitals of the world would be more accurate." He motioned down at the fresh Connecticut blueberry jam and the local honey on the jam tray. "If we take what Connecticut has to offer, we can—along with what the five-star B&B down the street and Joe's Diner are both already doing—contribute toward making Stoneybridge one of the culinary 'capitals' of the world."

She flashed him a dubious half-smile. "I love Stoneybridge, Gerry. But it's so not Paris."

"No, it's not. It's something better. It's home."

She closed her mouth on her words. She couldn't argue with that. "You're glad to be living back in Connecticut?"

"Very."

"And your sister is still living in Nazareth?"

"Yes."

"Why didn't you move back there?"

"And save you the aggravation of having *moi*—me—as your neighbor?"

"Well, yes, of course. There is that," she returned with a smile, and his quick grin was full of wry amusement.

A log dropped in the fireplace, and Gerry got up to reposition it. "To answer your question, it was simply a case of finances," he answered after fixing the log and shutting the grate. "Being so much closer to New York City, Nazareth was just too expensive." Aimee knew there was no denying the truth of that, so she didn't say anything. "Now it's my turn to ask a question."

"Oh, no," Aimee groaned good-naturedly.

"Why a patisserie?"

Relief. That question was easily enough answered. "My grand-mère. Her mother was Parisian and had a little bakery in

Montmartre, so she grew up in the trade, just like I did. After my grandfather died—he and Grand-mère were living in Manhattan then—Grand-mère had to support her daughter, my mother. She claimed she had only one talent—French pastry-making. With no living relatives on either side of the Atlantic, the only thing she knew was that she had to find a good town where she could raise her daughter."

"A lady of spunk. But how did she settle on Stoneybridge?"

"One day she and my mother, who was just a little girl back then, boarded the train in Grand Central Station. They sat together, looking out the window. They checked every town the train went through to see if maybe it could become home. They both liked the look of Stoneybridge. They got off the train, saw this property—and the apartment upstairs—and bought it a week later, then set about opening the Patisserie." She pointed out the window. "Grand-mère always told me she and her little girl, my mother, opened it when the 'white leaves of the dogwood trees planted all along Main Street looked like a bride's wedding veil.'" Aimee waved a hand to indicate the café's counter. "My mother, her younger brother, and I all grew up here. It's where we ate our meals, where we did our homework, where I learned about running the Patisserie."

He whistled. "So for your mother to have a younger brother, your grandmother must have remarried."

She nodded. "A fine man from Stoneybridge. But he died when his son, my uncle, was just a teenager."

"So where's your uncle?"

She did *not* want to discuss Uncle Cain. "We're not close," she murmured. "Never have been."

"I feel sorry for him."

"Don't be." She cautioned. "My Uncle Cain would neither understand nor appreciate that."

"He's missing a lot. I doubt I could love kids of my own any more than I love my sister's kids."

Aimee gave her head a little shake. "Do you know how special that is? For you and your niece and nephew. I would love to have my uncle in my life." *Well, she did have him in her life.* "In a good way, I mean," she qualified.

When Gerry frowned again, Aimee was afraid she'd said too much. She didn't want to discuss her uncle, and she definitely didn't want to say anything about the loan. Trying to keep things light, she said, "You mentioned at your grand opening that your niece and nephew named your store."

"It started out being called 'Cakes Galore.'"

"*Ouch*! Seriously?"

He grimaced. "My sister said it sounded like 'gory.'"

"I agree with your sister!"

"The kids just called it 'Uncle Gerry's Cakerie.' I guess because it rhymes with bakery. I finally realized that's what it truly is—a bakery specializing in cakes—so I changed it. Business boomed after that."

"It's a good name." Aimee had liked it the first time she'd read about it. She remembered wishing she had an uncle who loved her so much that he'd name his business after their relationship. She also remembered her image of what Uncle Gerry looked like. She gave a little giggle. Gerry was the total opposite.

"Okay. What's amusing you?"

She licked her lips, "I remembered picturing 'Uncle Gerry' as an older, red-faced, pseudo-Santa type who wore a big white apron over a big belly. Definitely not—" *the cowboy-sleek man Uncle Gerry actually was* "—you!"

He chuckled. "Sorry to disappoint."

"Not a disappointment."

"That's good to hear."

She tried to think of some remark to break the spell that was wrapping itself around them like a down comforter on a snowy day. But her mind went blank.

"You don't have a clichéd pastry-chef appearance yourself," he commented after a moment and from the way his eyes narrowed, she knew he wanted to say something else, perhaps something more personal. She wouldn't have minded if he had. But how could he know she'd welcome that? She'd given him all the opposite signals ever since he'd moved in next door. Even so, she was a little disappointed when he changed the subject and asked, "Was your mother a pastry chef, too?"

The image of her mother attired magnificently in full-dress military uniform went through her mind. She had looked larger than life to the young girl Aimee had been. And beautiful. Very, very beautiful. "No, no. Far from it. Following in *her* father's footsteps, she was career military. That's where she and my dad met."

Gerry shook his head as if to clear it. "I didn't see that one coming."

"Believe me, I don't think my grandmother did, either. But perhaps she should have. Her first husband, my mother's father, had been a West Point graduate. Both *my* parents graduated from to the Coast Guard Academy in New London," she indicated the easterly direction of the famous Connecticut coastal town. "They had me when they were in their early forties. Unfortunately, they both died when I was very young."

"I'm sorry."

"Yeah, me too." She'd always missed not knowing them for more than a few early childhood years. "But at least they didn't leave Grand-mère or me alone. They left us the gift of each other."

"And…" He looked around the Patisserie. "You were like your grandmother and great-grandmother… A born-and-bred French pastry chef. That's not something that can be taught in any school, Aimee."

Grand-mère always said that. But Aimee had never believed her. Maybe not until this very moment. With Gerry speaking it. "For a graduate of Le Cordon Bleu to say that is very sweet."

Gerry groaned. "Oh, no! " He fell back as if he'd been shot. "I've just been called 'sweet'!"

Aimee laughed. "No! I mean what you *said* was sweet!" she qualified. "There's a difference." *Note to self: don't ever call Gerry sweet—even if it describes him perfectly!*

"Okay. I'll accept that." He flashed that wide and giving grin, then said, "So, it was natural for you to start working at the Patisserie."

"Well, I don't think I had much choice. After waking up one too many times to Édith Piaf singing *La Vie en Rose* on Grand-mère's old record player and helping Grand-mère pipe rose-flavored cream centers into pale pink *macarons,* the love was kind of transferred to me. By osmosis, you could say."

"La Vie en Rose," Gerry repeated. "Now there's a song I haven't thought about in a while." She heard a wistful quality in his voice and it seemed the most natural thing in the world when he sat back in his chair, gazed into the fireplace and in a

strikingly expressive baritone began singing the hauntingly beautiful tune.

His voice was that of a ballad singer, and it filled the Patisserie with the emotion people all over the world feel whenever they hear the song that's synonymous with Paris. Aimee was spellbound because Gerry wasn't just singing the song but *feeling* it, living it, with all its wistful notes suggestive of deeper truths about finding love and surviving hardships. For Grand-mère and Piaf herself, those hardships had been, among other things, losing the men they loved, and the extreme difficulty and deprivation of the war.

Aimee was captivated. She closed her eyes, and with the glow of the flames in the fireplace dancing on her eyelids, she listened, and let herself feel the extraordinary notes once again.

Something about the way Louiguy's music flowed always brought tears to her eyes. The words and the melody combined to make it an experience, a melancholy one to be sure, but one filled with hope too. After learning about the singer, Édith Piaf, who wrote the lyrics and whose throaty voice made it famous, Aimee knew that it was Piaf's very sad life that touched her soul. It was as if Édith Piaf was searching for love, searching for the perfect world.

Grand-mère always maintained that Édith was inspired by God to write those lyrics. *La Vie en Rose*—Life in Pink or Life in Rosy Hues—was a song that gave and gave to the world long after Édith went to be with the Lord. The last notes of Gerry's magnificent voice, which spoke the very title of the song, faded from the rosy walls of the Patisserie, leaving only the sound of the fire crackling softly before them and the breath of the wind blowing crimson leaves from the maple and dogwood trees onto the street below.

After a moment, Aimee opened her eyes and with her head against the back of the chair, turned slightly to look at Gerry.

His eyes were already resting on her. Their gazes held for an eloquent moment while he dragged in a deep breath, then let it out.

"That was beautiful," Aimee whispered.

"It's one of my favorite songs," he admitted. "A song of love, a song of hope, a song of life."

"That's why my grand-mère played it almost every morning before starting her day, why she liked it so much, too."

Gerry's hand reached out across the small table. He was asking for hers.

As if she'd done it a million times, Aimee placed her hand in his. It felt right, perfect, at home.

His lips curved into a smile. *Did he feel the same sense of coming home that she felt?* She was sure he did.

The moment was too special for words. It was as if their spirits and their souls had, through the emotional beauty of the song, finally found common ground. The width of the table separated them, but with each passing second, their newfound intimacy brought them closer and closer. The tug of his hand, the sound of—

Cynthia crying!

Reality struck.

Gerry jumped up.

Aimee did, too.

"I wonder what's wrong with her," he threw over his shoulder as he ran out the door, leaving Aimee momentarily stunned.

12—A Cosmic Event

Cynthia was fine—only waging war on her tangled hair. But as Gerry bent down and tried to work out the latest worrisome knot, he wondered about his jumbled emotions.

Aimee had been holding his hand, but it might as well have been his heart.

How could he have let that happen?

How could a woman he hadn't even known for three weeks affect him so deeply? What was it about Aimee that went beyond her appearance, her touch, the sound of her voice, to make him feel for her in a way he'd never felt before? Not even with Scarlett. Was it because of the vulnerability he sensed in her, or was it because of her strength? There was no doubt that she was a woman of ability and talent, a woman who stood up for herself and shouldered responsibility in spite of the tough breaks she'd been dealt.

Or was it because of something as simple as their shared passion for baking, for creating confections that brought smiles to the lips and sparkles to the eyes of both young and old? She liked small and delicate; he liked big and bold. From the first, he'd seen how that difference could actually become an advantage. And not just in a business sense…

But were these reasons to have fallen in love with her? To believe that, together, they might find "life in rosy hues?"

Was this what the proverbial "love at first sight" was all about—that age-old combustion between a man and a woman that went beyond rational explanation? Was that why the historic and Biblical Jacob had worked a total of fourteen years for Rachel, the love of his life? Was this what his own parents had felt when they'd married only four months after meeting, and was it what had kept them best friends and companions all these years? Even with his parents as role models, he'd never believed in love at first sight. He certainly hadn't experienced it before.

He thought about his sister. Sabrina had told him that she and Logan had fallen in love at first sight—but what good had it done them? After eleven years of marriage and two children, they were now estranged.

Gerry shook his head. It was confounding. He and Aimee had no history. But then, maybe that was what love really meant—making a history together. Loving another person was something that probably took a lifetime to do correctly. To make a long-lasting, beautiful love—the greatest emotion in the world—had to be a combination of words, actions and those quiet, companionable moments exactly like the ones he and Aimee had just shared.

After all, wasn't that a version of what he did when he made cakes? he thought, easily seeing the comparison. As long as he had the right ingredients, enough patience, the correct blending speed and the accurate amount of heat at different times in the baking process, he could make the tastiest, prettiest and most astounding confections in the world.

Could the passion he felt for Aimee, an attraction he'd sensed from the very first, continue, and then with the mellowing of time, turn into that comfortable, sustainable love that might well stretch out over the years, the decades, to equal a lifetime together? Was that what had made his parents' marriage so strong? His grandparents', too?

Cynthia gave a loud whimper and moved away from Gerry when he pulled too hard on a strand of her hair. "Sorry, girl." He rubbed the sore spot.

"Let me take her to be groomed," Aimee said from behind Gerry. He hadn't realized she'd followed him outside. "There's no way you're going to get all those knots out." She bent down. While cooing reassuringly to Cynthia, she ran her hands through the dog's matted hair. "She needs to be trimmed. Properly."

He stood, watching Aimee and Cynthia together.

Aimee's nose touching where he supposed Cynthia's red-brown bob nose was located under all her scraggly hair while Aimee's long and capable fingers dug through Cynthia's hair to gently rub her canine shoulder blades.

As Aimee continued to coo in soothing tones to his dog, his mind shouted at him,

This is the woman I love!

This is the woman I want to build a future with!

This is the woman I want to vow before God to love and honor for as long as we both shall live!

At that moment, Gerry was one hundred percent sure of it.

But he knew better than to scare Aimee by putting his thoughts into words.

He might know he loved her, but he had no illusions as to Aimee's feelings for him. She might be warming to him, but he'd too recently been only the enemy-pastry chef who'd moved into the store next door. He would follow Miss Maggie's advice and take care in how he proceeded with the lovely Aimee.

Aimee looked up at him, impatience in her eyes. "Gerry, I mean it. You have to let me."

What did she mean? Have to let her what? Oh, yes, the dog. "I've taken her to groomer after groomer." He felt he had to tell her how he really had made an effort to trim his dog's hair. "They've all tried, but they all claim they can't do it unless they tranquilize her."

"Tranquilize her!" She was obviously appalled.

"I've never let them," he was quick to assure her.

She patted Cynthia's head and talked softly into her ear. "I've got a friend, Cynthia, who's the best doggie hair-dresser in the world. You'll like him. Let's see if we can get Gerry to let me take you to visit him?" she said to Cynthia but looked up at Gerry. "Do you trust me?"

With my life, he wanted to say. "Of course."

She stood. "Okay. So, when you see that Cynthia's missing this evening, don't call out the National Guard."

He chuckled and patted Cynthia's head as she sidled back up to him. "Cynthia would call out the Guard if anyone other than someone she trusts tried to take her away from me."

"Does she trust me?"

"From the first day." Like him, Gerry thought, on that first wonderful Monday before life intruded on their romance. Because Gerry accepted now that what they'd shared that perfect Monday had been the beginning of a romance. But their working life had encroached on it. That was what often happened to couples; day-to-day life usually invaded—and sometimes altered—it. It hadn't been like that with his parents, though; they'd always been careful not to allow the cares and stresses of life or even two children who sometimes felt left out because their parents only had eyes for each other, diminish those loving feelings.

"Good. I'll phone Colin—" Stoneybridge's best dog groomer "—and take her later today. He works out of a van, but he often has it set up at the dog park."

"Thank you, Aimee." He really meant it. "If you can get her trimmed, that'll be a huge relief."

"Sometimes animals let other people do things for them that they won't allow their families to do." She shrugged her shoulders. "Besides, it's something I can help with, to be nice for a change."

Gerry reached out and tucked a strand of hair that had escaped her ponytail behind her ear, and as he did, he let his eyes make a feature-by-feature study of her face. He could see that she was extending an apology for her past accusations against him, and he forgot about every single one of them in the face of how much he cared for her. "You're always nice."

She guffawed. "No I'm not," she spoke louder than she intended. She lowered her voice. "But I hope that from now on I will be, Gerry," she said as Otis at the Organics Shop and Hale at the Hardware Store unlocked their front doors to start their working day on Main Street.

***

"Cynthia! You gorgeous girl, you!" Gerry exclaimed fourteen hours later as Aimee and Cynthia tapped up Main Street toward him. He was just locking his store for the night.

Aimee laughed as Cynthia jumped up and placed her front paws on his shoulders as if to say, "Do you like my haircut?"

"You gorgeous girl, you!" he repeated. "Wait until Benji and Pattie see you!"

A gust of wind blew down Main Street, and Cynthia gave a whimper. "I think she's cold."

"After losing ten pounds of hair, that's probably true. I should be getting her home and out of this chill."

Aimee nodded. "Good idea," she said.

But she made no move to head toward her stairs, which told Gerry more plainly than words that she didn't want the day to end, either. He considered Miss Maggie's advice and said, "I'm starving. Let me take Cynthia home, and then would you like to join me at Joe's Diner tonight?" He watched as her eyes widened. Pleasure jumped into them before another emotion, something related to fear, overpowered it. Her shoulders tensed, her chin lifted. "Thanks," she replied softly. "But I've been up since three this morning."

Gerry knew the real reason. Miss Maggie had said it would take at least three attempts before she agreed. "You must be beat."

She nodded and turned toward the stairs. "I am. But thanks, anyway."

"Maybe some other time," Gerry suggested.

"Yes," Aimee said and with a small poignant smile she turned and walked away.

"One down," Gerry said to Cynthia as he and his now perfectly groomed standard poodle walked along Main Street. "Two to go."

***

Gerry had just finished eating his favorite dinner—bacon and eggs with carrot cake for dessert—when the phone rang. Cynthia was happily snoozing on the hearth, absorbing the fire's warmth, as he watched a football game on TV. He lowered the volume before answering, first glancing at Caller ID. It was Sabrina. There was a smile in his voice as he greeted her.

"Hey, sis. What's up?"

"Just wondering how Benji's birthday cake is coming along?"

Benji's cake! Gerry hit his forehead with the palm of his hand. "Great!" he said and cringed as he thought about the six-foot, solar-system cake his nephew was expecting next Saturday for his eighth birthday party. Gerry had intended to work on it that morning after his 6:00 a.m. visit with Aimee. But he'd found that whenever he had a few extra minutes, instead of working on the cake he sat and thought about Aimee. Those strong feelings of wanting a family of his own—urgings he'd been suppressing for the last several months—had gleefully jumped to the forefront of his mind.

"Fib, fib, call the fib doctor!" Sabrina sang out the ditty they'd used to accuse each other when they were kids and knew a tall tale was in the making.

"It'll be ready by Saturday. I promise."

"You can bring *her* along, too," Sabrina said, and Gerry looked around as if Sabrina were sitting behind him. *How did she do that?* His sister always seemed to know when he was interested in someone. It was as if she had him wired…

"Bring who?"

Sabrina laughed. "The special lady in your life, of course. What's her name?"

"No idea what you're talking about."

"Fib, fib, call the fib doctor!" she sang out again.

"Sabrina! How old are you? Five?"

"Yeah, okay. Keep your secret for now, little brother." She laughed again, and Gerry wondered how she could be asking about *his* love life when her own was such a shambles. In spite of everything, did she still believe in the power of love, that it could overcome seemingly insurmountable obstacles? He hoped so.

He wanted to ask. But he said, "Is Logan going to fly home for the party?"

At the hurt pitch in Sabrina's voice when he mentioned her husband, he wished he hadn't said anything. "I don't know. Benji called him and practically begged his dad to leave his bicycle, get on a plane and come home for his birthday. But Logan said he couldn't. He told his nearly eight-year-old son," she spat out, "that he had to get across the Rocky Mountains before winter sets in. I mean, really? Can you believe that?"

Gerry frowned. As ready as he was for marriage, he knew that Logan hadn't been when he and his sister got married. Gerry was only glad Logan was on a bicycle trip across America rather than totally calling it quits on a life he hadn't wanted in the first place. Four years younger than Sabrina—even younger than Gerry—Logan had tried to tell her that he'd wanted adventure before settling down. But Sabrina hadn't wanted to wait. Well, Logan was getting his way now. "He just wasn't ready for marriage and kids, Sabrina. He'd wanted a life of freedom and exploration, of doing different things first."

"Eleven years too late for him to realize that!" she snapped.

"Sabrina. He knew it then," Gerry softly reminded her. "And he tried to tell you."

"I know," she whispered and Gerry could picture her. Regret always made her shoulders slump, her spine compress and her head hang, shrinking her normal five feet six by at least two inches. "I shouldn't have pushed him. It came back to bite me."

"Just be patient."

"I am. For myself. But I can't take him abandoning the kids!" she shot out. "That practically drives me crazy, Gerry."

Gerry was glad Logan had given the kids a cell phone number that he promised he'd answer…as long as they didn't call too often. "That's why I'm here." Along with the prospect of the potential contract with the supermarket chain and wanting to escape his ex-fiancée's mean ways, *this* was the reason that had tipped the balance in his relocation to Stoneybridge. He wanted the kids to know that their uncle wanted to live close to them, so he'd rearranged his life to do it.

"I know. And it's made a great, big, wonderful difference to them. They want to see you every day."

The guilt Gerry felt over not living in Nazareth and being within walking distance of his niece and nephew was intense. Even the forty-minute drive was almost too much with the store and its huge responsibilities at this crucial time.

"I'm sorry," Sabrina rushed to say. "I shouldn't have said that. You're not their father."

"No. But I *am* their uncle. It's a role I take seriously. And I promise, soon I'll come out at least twice a week and have dinner with you all."

"I've told them. They know you have to get the Cakerie running first." She gave her rich, deep, optimistic laugh. "They're more patient than their mom."

"When have you ever been patient?"

"That's my problem," she moaned. "Logan asked to wait for two years before getting married. I was impatient."

"Maybe it's not too late."

"Maybe." But more and more he could hear doubt in his usually positive sister's voice.

"Do you still love him?"

"I'll always love him," she replied quickly.

Too quickly?

"Oh, not in the same way," she went on to explain. "But in a better way. A more mature way," she qualified and this was something Gerry liked and appreciated in his sister. She was rational and always saw the big picture. "At least I hope so. One thing I've learned, Gerry, is that there are many different stages of love between a man and a woman. I just want the chance to move forward to the next one. Just like Mom and Dad always do so seamlessly."

"We think it's seamless. But is it really?"

"Good point." Her voice had its natural buoyancy again. "You know what? I think I'll ask them when they come to the party."

"So they're definitely coming?"

"Yes. Flying in from Mexico Saturday morning. Even bringing a piñata for Benji's party."

Gerry was glad. He'd been angry with them for not moving back from their Mexican hideaway to Nazareth when Sabrina's life fell apart. Family should stick together even if it was inconvenient. "It's time they shared their world with us in a bigger way. Especially since we're older than they were when they got married, and we need their help to sort out this marriage business!"

"So… What did you say her name was?"

"Good try, sis."

Sabrina laughed. "Have you figured out who'll help you transport the cake?" He had told her that Hank and Doug were already occupied with deliveries on Saturday, and his college students needed to run the store and decorate cakes. "Are you sure you don't want me to come and lend you a hand?"

"What are you? An octopus? You'll have your hands full enough that afternoon. Don't worry. I've got it covered." He really didn't, but he knew he would. Maybe hire someone to help. It was a last resort but he'd do it if he had to.

"Fib, fib—"

"Sabrina! Enough already!"

"See ya next Saturday, little brother! Love ya!"

"Love ya back!"

Gerry signed off and flopped across the sofa. He had a dilemma. Who could he ask to help him deliver the cake?

As Aimee's face flashed into his mind—for about the millionth time that day—he felt a grin, something like the Grinch's in the Dr. Seuss children's book—spread across his face. Aimee did say that morning that she wanted to be "nice" to him from now on. And if he asked in the right way, maybe it could count as Miss Maggie's second "date," without Aimee's even realizing it, getting them to that all-important third asking that much faster.

Gerry jumped up.

Cynthia did, too.

"Time to run," he said to his dog and put on his jogging shoes.

Despite looking the part of a very expensive dog now, Cynthia gave an excited bark, then ran for her lead, the same as always.

As Gerry attached it to her collar, grabbed his florescent jacket and fastened Cynthia's matching one around her, he said, "Life is good, Cynthia. Life is good!"

Ruff, ruff! she agreed and out the door they went. He didn't feel the near-freezing temperature, and he was sure, as Cynthia sped next to him, that she didn't, either.

***

Gerry didn't ask Aimee the next morning at six, or the following one. He waited for three days before broaching the subject while they chatted over their identical brooms. "I have a bit of a problem I'm hoping you can help me with."

"What is it?" Her eyes were bright, and he loved the friendship that had been shining out of them since they'd shared that very special breakfast the previous Saturday.

"My nephew's eighth birthday party is this coming Saturday afternoon. He's asked me to make a solar-system cake for him."

"Don't tell me you need my help to make it?"

"Ah, no," he deadpanned. "To deliver it."

"Why?"

"I'm in a bind. All my employees are going to be busy delivering cakes or making them or selling them. I need someone to ride in the back of the van to make sure Benji's cake doesn't fall over."

"Will it take long?"

He grimaced. "That's the thing. We'll have to stay for the party. That's why I didn't want to ask just anybody or hire someone."

"I see..."

And *he* could see that she was wondering if this was a date. "Please think of it as one pastry chef helping out another," he prompted.

She glanced over at the Patisserie. "Saturday afternoon is actually my slowest time…" she murmured.

He knew that. One of the reasons he didn't mind asking her. Could it have been providential that Benji chose Saturday afternoon to have his party? His birthday was actually on Sunday, a busy afternoon for their shops. "Benji would really appreciate it. He wants to be an astronaut when he grows up."

"An astronaut!"

"Or a cake-shop owner."

She smiled. "Just like his uncle."

"Yep."

"I love the close relationship you have with your niece and nephew."

He knew she did. He was counting on that, and right now, he didn't mind exploiting it. "So will you help me?"

A slow nod, then the words he was hoping for. "Sure. Count me in."

"Great! Thanks!" *Miss Maggie's date number two! Done!*

***

If anyone had told her two months earlier that she'd be sitting in the back of a van making sure a six-foot replica of the solar system—made out of sugar and flour and lots and lots of uncle love—wasn't dislodged from its pedestal and come crashing to the floor, Aimee would've said the idea was "out of this world."

But here she was with a model of the sun, the earth and the other planets bouncing around on wires like so many bobbing heads, driving over to Gerry's sister's home, for a birthday celebration. How was it that the owner of the store next door, who had been her nemesis for the first two and a half weeks of his time in Stoneybridge, was now so important to her?

Last Saturday night she'd been one simple word away from agreeing to go to the diner with him. She'd *wanted* to go. Dear Lord, how she'd wanted to. Instead, she'd climbed the steps to her apartment and spent the night with only her cat for company; a lovely cat but a cat none-the-less.

She and Gerry had started that special day together with the most intimate breakfast she'd ever shared with a man, and she would've liked so much to have the day end with another meal together.

If she'd said yes, it would have. But she hadn't.

Why?

Because of the loan repayment hanging over her head? Or because she feared making her life more complicated than it already was?

Maybe both.

But that was only part of it. More than anything, she felt that old dread of becoming the talk of the town again. If people saw her going out with Gerry, tongues would wag, and soon questions and innuendoes would fly up and down the street. Added to that was the terror of getting involved with her neighbor on Main Street and having the relationship turn sour. She couldn't go through that. Not again. At least Timothy had left town. Gerry wasn't going anywhere. He'd made that abundantly clear.

"And I'm glad he's not," she whispered to the replica of the solar system. "Agh," she moaned. "What's wrong with me?"

When she'd asked that of Becky the previous night, Becky had said, "Simple, boss. You want to have your cake and eat it, too!"

Well, she did! What pastry chef didn't? Her stomach growled. She examined the cake in front of her. It looked delicious, while the scent of the vanilla, chocolate and orange that filled the back of the van was an exquisite form of torture.

For the umpteenth time she studied the lower right corner of the cake. Wasn't there a bit of extra sheeting there? Could she nip a tiny morsel without the whole solar system collapsing? After weeks of not eating even one slice of Gerry's cakes, she was desperate to see how it tasted.

She reached out with tentative fingers to pull that little bite of cake away when the van came to a sudden and bone-jarring, screeching halt. Aimee grabbed hold of the baseboard the cake sat on. Using all her strength, she managed to keep the solar system from shooting, at the speed of light, off its pedestal to decorate the rear door of the van with red Mars, giant Jupiter, elegant Saturn and the rest. "Hey!" she shouted, after her nerves settled back in place.

Her phone rang. "You okay back there?" She could hear concern in Gerry's tone but also humor. "By any chance, are you now wearing the sun? Should I come back and rescue you from a cosmic event?"

"No. The solar system and I are still in orbit. Just." She checked the stand. It seemed secure. "What happened?"

"A dog darted out into the road. See why I needed you? If you hadn't been back there, the cake would've been a goner and Benji would've been sad."

She smiled. He didn't care about the cake—even a fabulous one that took him twenty-six hours to bake and create. When the life of an animal was at risk, even his nephew's special birthday request was expendable. One of the reasons she was coming to love this man.

Love? Whoa! She looked at the phone as if she'd caught something from it. Where had that come from? Cupid's nasty arrow again? But was it really so bad? Maybe it was made of sugar and it was an arrow that could sweeten her life. The scent of the mega cake must be intoxicating her.

"Let's do this," she somehow croaked out and switched off her phone. She cleared her throat over and over again. She had to sound completely normal before she met Gerry's sister. Sisters could see right through other women. Aimee wasn't sure *what* Sabrina would see when she met her.

13—First Kiss

Sabrina was the best. If Aimee could choose a sister, it would be Sabrina. She reminded Aimee of a dragonfly, always in hovering, darting motion. Aimee had always liked dragonflies. And the more Gerry's sister talked and moved—she was a hostess who exuded a boundless, joyful energy that encompassed all around her—the more Aimee liked her.

"Thanks for helping my brother bring the cake. So tell me, what can I do for you in return?" Sabrina asked and searched Aimee's eyes. She really meant it.

Show me how to love your brother. Aimee's wanted to say. She didn't, but that didn't stop Sabrina from seeing the question anyway. A sister's intuition?

Leaning closer, she whispered for Aimee's ears only, "Gerry is the real deal, Aimee. What you see is what you get." She waved her right arm toward him and said, "The nicest guy in the world."

"This is the most awesome cake ever!" Benji exclaimed when his eyes landed on the sweet replica of the solar system. He jumped on Gerry's back.

Gerry hitched his nephew up and with his Stetson firmly on his head, started "broncoing" around the yard like an unbroken horse at a rodeo, with Benji "yahooing" in delight. The twenty kids at the party, including Pattie, Benji's sister, started shouting and running around them. Sabrina nodded over at Aimee, as if it was the exclamation point to her comments about Gerry.

Aimee laughed. She couldn't remember the last time she'd had such fun. "I sure wish my uncle had been like that."

"Uncle?" Sabrina nodded toward the middle-aged, distinguished-looking and very attractive couple who sat to the side watching the proceedings. They were at the party physically but not mentally, not emotionally. "I wouldn't have minded if our parents had been more like that!"

"They seem nice."

"They *are* nice," Sabrina agreed. "And we love them dearly. But they've always only had eyes for each other."

"Sounds like a great love."

"It is." Sabrina sighed. "One of the greatest. But they never should've had kids. They didn't have room in their lives or their hearts, for children."

"Wait a minute. You're their *daughter*! Wouldn't their 'not having kids' have made life a bit, shall we say, unattainable for you?" She pointed to Gerry, who was in the middle of a moving, giggling crowd of seven and eight-year-olds. "And Gerry."

Sabrina sighed again. "There is that," she said. "And we have to be grateful that they did. Twice." She shuddered. "I'd hate to think of them stopping with me, leaving me an only child, without Gerry. Gerry and I have always been family to each other. Our parents are just people who visit every now and then, stay and talk pleasantries, then fly or sail or drive out of our lives. In fact, it was like that from the beginning. Don't get me wrong." Sabrina held up her hand. "We love them dearly," she repeated, "and we know, in their own way, they love us, too. But long ago, Gerry and I learned that there was only so much our parents could give us of themselves. They provided for us in grand fashion." She motioned to her neighborhood in

Nazareth, an exclusive one by almost all standards. "And we had a wonderful nanny." Now she glanced over at an elderly lady who'd been, as Aimee had learned during introductions, their beloved nanny from the time Gerry and Sabrina were quite young. Audrey now lived with Sabrina and helped with her kids. "Gerry and I learned when we were very little to accept the fact that our mother and father gave what they could of themselves, but we shouldn't expect anything more. When we finally got that, it...made everything less complicated."

"To accept them as they are," Aimee said, mulling over the words. "That's good. If more people could learn to do that, expectations that aren't met could be avoided. And lots of pain, too." She realized as she spoke that she had yet to do that with her uncle and aunt. It was about time she did. *Accept them for who they are and don't expect anything else from them.* She knew that, at this stage, only a miracle could change her uncle, anyway.

"That's the main reason Gerry moved back to Connecticut. To be with the kids and me after—" she swallowed and Aimee knew it pained her to say it "—my husband left us, and our world fell apart."

"I'm so sorry."

Sabrina shook her head and smiled bravely at Aimee before indicating her brother, positioned on all fours, his cowboy hat now safely tossed on a nearby table. The kids were all surging around him and three of them had clambered onto his back, shouting, *"Uncle Gerry Mountain, Uncle Gerry Mountain!"* while the others waited for their turn. Sabrina and Aimee laughed together, and after a moment of cheering the kids on in their bid to climb the "Uncle Gerry Mountain," Sabrina continued. "How many brothers would upend their whole professional life for their sister, niece and nephew? Even though there were a couple of other good motivations for him to move back home, nothing short of family need would have made him close up his business in LA and start all over in Stoneybridge. Some people called it business suicide. If it hadn't been for his online presence, I don't think he would've made it this far."

"Online sales... Of course," Aimee said, remembering again how Becky had been trying to get her to branch into online sales for the last two years.

Sabrina nodded. "It's kept him afloat."

And Aimee had been so mean to him! So self-absorbed. If she'd been asked, even a week and a half ago, she would've said he'd come on a personal mission to destroy her business. She had a lot of "being nice" to do.

Gerry chose that moment to rumble and shake. The whole yard seemed to tremble, too.

"Volcano!" the kids started shouting and dancing all around.

"Volcano!"

"Volcano!"

"Argh! Uncle Gerry Mountain is about to blow!" Gerry roared.

"Yippee!" The kids lying across the Uncle Gerry Mountain squealed even more gleefully as Gerry's preliminary tremor turned into a giant one. He straightened to his knees, and then slowly, so none of the kids fell off too hard, he stood. He caught Benji, who clung to his neck, and held him up in the air before lowering him to the grass and tickling him. All the kids cheered.

"Hang on," Sabrina said to Aimee. "I think I should rescue Uncle Gerry Mountain before the kids start jumping all over him again." She started to go, then paused. "Oh, would you do me a favor?"

"Sure," Aimee said but fingers of fear that it might have something to do with Gerry—was Sabrina throwing them together in front of an audience?—curled around her spine.

"When it's time for the piñata—after I serve the cake—would you help blindfold the kids and be in charge of the game?"

Did Sabrina know that offering her that job made Aimee feel like she belonged? She was sure Sabrina did; she was as kind and caring as her brother. "I'd love to."

Sabrina turned to the happy children, put her fingers to her lips and blew out a super-charged whistle, the kind of sound a lumberjack might make. Certainly not something one would expect from a lovely Connecticut mom. Once she had their attention, she shouted in her best mom voice, "Who wants cake?!"

"Cake!" The happy kids totally forgot about Uncle Gerry Volcano. Jumping up and down and sounding more like a herd of buffalo than children, they clapped their hands and chanted over and over again, "Cake! Cake!"

Sabrina pointed to the playroom and said, "Everyone inside! Time to see if the solar system tastes as good as it looks!"

It did. Aimee found that out twenty minutes later with a large slice of Saturn in her hand. She closed her eyes and savored the rich vanilla and orange pound cake. It had a quality she couldn't quite identify. Buttermilk? No. It was something else. But what?

"Do you like it?" Aimee's eyes flew open. A very flushed Gerry was standing next to her.

"Gerry! I love it! But what's that taste—"

"Extra virgin olive oil. From PJ Kabos."

She took another forkful. Yep! That was it. Olive oil. "It's so tasty and moist."

"Something I learned on a trip to Greece. I couldn't believe it when I saw that the same brand I used to buy online was sold in Stoneybridge on our very own Main Street."

Our very own Main Street... Aimee savored how appealing that sounded to her now. Particularly the *our...*

"I use their olive oil in almost all my recipes now, rather than butter," he said.

"Shh." Aimee glanced over her shoulder as if someone were listening. "You shouldn't tell your baking secrets."

He shrugged. "Why not? I don't mind sharing my recipes. This journey called life is too short not to tell others about things learned."

She shook her head and smiled. "You really are a nice man."

His eyes darkened, and when he spoke, his voice was a little husky. "That's good to hear. Coming from you."

"I..." She paused. There was so much she wanted to say—how full her heart was, how much she loved his family, how much she was coming to love him. "Gerry, I—"

"Piñata! Piñata!" The kids started chanting, and Aimee looked over to where they were now congregated around the huge, colorful, exquisitely crafted paper mâché donkey. The excited children could hardly wait for the fun to begin.

"That's my department." Aimee gestured to the Piñata. "I...promised your sister...I'd be in charge of..." Her voice trailed off.

He nodded. But his eyes said, *I know what you were about to say and I feel it, too. Go. There'll be a time for us.*

As she walked away, she was beginning to think so, too.

***

Sabrina came up to Gerry and handed him a glass of homemade pink lemonade. His favorite drink and one she always had on hand for him. "I think you could use this, little brother."

"Thanks." He took a large swallow. "That's good," he said, looking over at Aimee as she kept the twenty blindfolded kids from pandemonium.

"She's fabulous," Sabrina said. "Definitely a keeper."

Gerry grinned and gave his sister a quick hug. "I'm working on it."

"I'm glad!" They laughed as Pattie swung the stick and almost hit the antique English lamp post instead. Aimee quickly turned her, avoiding a possible accident. "What about that other project?" Sabrina asked. "Have you heard anything from James Monroe about the supermarket contract?" When James had come into Gerry's Cakerie in California the previous year and encouraged him to relocate back to Connecticut and to try for the supermarket contract, they hadn't realized he was Sabrina's best friend's brother-in-law.

"I have a presentation on Friday afternoon. I hope to find out then." He slanted a glance at his sister. "Why? Do you know something?"

"Just that it's down to you and one other pastry chef. And you're the stronger contender. They were impressed with your gumption. Specifically, how you relocated back east in order to qualify for the contract—never mind your personal reasons, which are none of their business. That you went to all the trouble to move proved to them how badly you want it. To their fiscally-focused minds, it translates into your making a success of their new venture, the in-house "Main Street Bakery," and therefore increasing their revenues."

"Sounds hopeful."

"Sure does," Sabrina said. "And it would relieve me of the guilt I feel about the fact that you closed your business in California, too."

Gerry turned his eyes away from Aimee and the children and looked directly at Sabrina. "Don't ever feel that way, sis." He motioned toward Pattie and Benji. "It was stupid of me to be so far away. These two were going to be all grown up, and I wouldn't have seen them except on special occasions. Even if I don't get the contract, I'm glad I moved back home. I love my store in Stoneybridge." His gaze returned to Aimee. She was laughing and as much at ease with the kids here as she was with those who came into her café. "I love it," he replied firmly.

"Good," Sabrina said. "I love *her* too. I'd like to see you make a family of your own. With Logan's defection, our family needs another member."

Gerry and his sister smiled and nodded at each other before turning back to the party scene before them.

***

When the lights along Main Street had been lit for five hours, and all the stores, including their own, were closed for the night, Gerry and Aimee arrived back in Stoneybridge.

Remembering the events of the day, Gerry grinned. His eyes followed the gently swaying motion of Aimee's perky ponytail as she walked up the steps leading to her front door, which now boasted an inviting and cozy Thanksgiving wreath with a miniature Pilgrim couple.

Aimee stepped up onto the landing. Gerry did, too. She turned to him. The scent of vanilla wafted around her. He'd figured out that it was the scent of her body lotion. He loved it. Loved *her*.

With all his heart, he wanted to hold her in his arms…and kiss her. The day had been perfect. Benji's party perfect. Sabrina, perfect. Aimee, perfect.

He fought the urge to wrap his arms around her. Yes, everything about the day had been right, and he wanted it to stay that way. So he stood even straighter.

Suddenly, standing on her tiptoes, she rose several inches higher. In an instant, less than an instant, she was leaning against him, and then her lips were on his, warm and generous. She wasn't demanding a response, nor seeking one.

But he was glad to give it, anyway.

As if they'd kissed a hundred times—they had in his thoughts—his lips moved hungrily over hers, answering her questions, asking his own. "Aimee," he whispered and breathed in sharply as he kissed her eyelids, her cheeks. *Aimee, I love you,* his mind said over and over as his arms encircled her, and he pulled her closer as his lips found hers again.

Aimee gave and received, then gave some more…

He was shocked at the intensity of his feelings for her. He knew he loved her but this went beyond anything he'd ever felt for another woman, not even Scarlett. They were standing outside her door. He wished they were inside. But that wasn't a threshold he would cross. Not yet. Especially knowing how badly she'd been hurt two years earlier.

He dragged his lips away from hers, kissed her forehead, the top of her head. "What just happened?" he whispered into her hair.

"I don't know," she gave a small, teasing, confidential laugh. "My…my…knees went weak. I had to lean somewhere, didn't I, so I wouldn't fall over?"

"You can lean on me anytime you want," he said—and he meant it, in more ways than one.

"Blame it on your sister's punch." Aimee had had a small glass of the spiked wine punch after all the guests had left, and Benji and Pattie had gone to bed.

"Nah," he drawled as his eyes absorbed the happy light in hers, "Something this great doesn't need an excuse. Come here." His lips returned to hers, and this time he kissed her with all the longing he'd felt for the last few weeks. What weeks? All his life. This was the woman he'd been searching for his entire adult life. After a moment, he spoke into her right ear. "I'm so glad I finally found you."

She lifted her mouth to his right ear and, so softly he almost wasn't sure of her words, said, "And I'm so glad you weren't just passing through town, my wonderful Monday Gerry."

He wondered what she meant by "Monday" Gerry. But he didn't wonder enough to ask. "I'm staying put, Aimee. Staying put on our Main Street."

"I like the way that sounds," she said and kissed him again.

***

As the days passed, Aimee knew she should've been thinking only about her all-important presentation on Friday morning.

But even more than the presentation, which she was mostly prepared for, she was thinking about Gerry.

After he'd seen her to her door on Saturday night and they'd kissed, it became natural that they'd meet as they closed their shops each evening. Natural that he'd accompany her up the stairs to her apartment door, where—beneath the chaste eyes of the little pilgrims on the Thanksgiving wreath—they'd kiss good night. This happened on Sunday night, Monday night and Tuesday night, too.

As Aimee turned on her dishwasher Wednesday morning, she wished it could always be like this. Gerry's arms around her felt so good. Had she ever felt so cherished, special, safe? Gerry put no pressure on her for anything else—not even a proper date. He was taking things slow. *If falling in love within weeks could be considered slow!* She loved that about him, too. A lot of men pushed too fast and expected that one or two kisses should lead to an immediate physical relationship.

But not Gerry.

He cherished her in the old-fashioned way—as she did him—that really wasn't as old-fashioned as the media and TV shows and movies sometimes presented. But Aimee knew now that she was ready to take their burgeoning relationship a step farther. When Gerry asked her for a date—and she was certain he would soon—she'd accept. She *wanted* to go on a real date with him. The prospect lent an extra spring to her steps.

And…if their becoming a "couple" caused tongues along Main Street to wag, so be it. Gerry had proved he was worth letting her guard down, and trying for a "life in pink." The haunting tune, as he'd sung it that special Saturday morning, played over and over in her head, and she knew Grand-mère would have wanted her to try to find that rosy life. After all,

Grand-mère had found it. Twice. Even though she'd lost both men, she'd often told Aimee that she'd never regretted opening her heart and her life to them. The only thing she was sorry about was that she and her first husband, Aimee's grandfather, hadn't had the time to reach that stage of companionable love that was normally a result of years spent together. Death had taken him from her when they were still young, when their love had been based mainly on the physical passions of youth and not the more mature love that only the passing of years and its mellowing can bring.

Aimee was coming to realize that with Gerry, she was on the way to discovering a love that could go the distance, like the one Grand-mère had shared with Aimee's sweet step-grandpa, Harry, Uncle Cain's father.

Aimee had thought she'd found that love with Timothy. She now knew that what she and Timothy had shared was a pale reflection of the real thing. Coming to feel so quickly and deeply for Gerry, she finally accepted that Timothy had been right to cancel their wedding. If Timothy were to come to town today, she'd probably thank him for not going through with it—although certainly not for the manner in which he'd called it off.

Later in the afternoon, while Becky was filling *macarons* with blueberry filling and Aimee was whipping up a new batch of meringue for rose-flavored ones, Gerry sauntered through the back door. Aimee had started keeping it unlocked again in the hopes that he *would* use it.

"Hello, ladies!" he greeted them, and Aimee felt as if the sun had come out on this very wet, cold fall day.

He smiled over at Becky, then flashed Aimee a look that made her feel special all the way down to her toes. If she'd been a step or two closer, she would have kissed him. She didn't even mind that Becky was there.

With a chuckle in his tone, he held out a measuring cup. "Do you by any chance have a cup of honey I might borrow?"

Aimee grinned and laughed inwardly. "Don't tell me you ran out?"

"Nah. It's just an excuse to come over and ask if you'd like to go out with me tomorrow night. On a date?"

She didn't need to think about it. "Love to," she answered. "But I can't," she continued and his facial muscles instantly deflated. She'd be getting ready for her presentation all Thursday evening and into the night.

But didn't she have to eat? a little voice inside her asked.

"How about lunch?" she suggested, before she could question the wisdom of going on her first real date with Gerry the day before her crucial appointment. But she didn't want to turn him down. This was at least *as* important if not, in the scheme of things, *more* important than her meeting with the supermarket people. And she was prepared; she knew exactly what she was making to present to the board.

He seemed content with the alternative she offered. "Lunch it is. Noon okay?"

"Perfect."

"See you later." He winked. *At closing time.*

She nodded and smiled. *At closing time.*

Satisfied and fully at ease, he turned and walked out the door. She could hear him whistling, *La Vie en Rose.*

"Wow!" Becky said after he left.

Aimee gave a little giggle and did a mock show of swooning. "Double wow!"

"I'm happy for you, girl." Becky sidled up and lightly bumped her hip against Aimee's.

"Me, too," Aimee said and bumped Becky back.

14—Picnic by the Old Stone Bridge

For at least the tenth time, Aimee checked the early-American clock that ticked on the wall of her living room. It was now five minutes to noon on a day that was more like mid-September than mid-November.

She glanced out the window.

The clouds and rain of yesterday had blown away sometime during the night. They'd had a surprise in tow—a sunny, warm, pristine day. Grand-mère always said days like this were like a postcard sent straight to Connecticut from Florida. Seeing it was a "Postcard from Florida" day and knowing it might be the last before the cold Connecticut winter set in, Aimee had forsworn her normal attire and dressed in her favorite Diane Von Furstenberg wrap dress—from Miss Maggie's Treasure Trove—and suede Isabel Marant ankle booties.

Checking her reflection in the Chippendale mirror, she leaned this way and that to make sure her dress was wrapped properly around her legs, grabbed her grand-mère's sixty-year-old black Chanel bag from the table—it went perfectly with her vintage dress—and checked her ponytail one last time.

She was ready for Gerry to knock on her door.

Well, physically, at least.

Mentally, she knew the thirty-one-year-old woman staring back at her in the mirror was having second thoughts. She wanted to go out with Gerry—she really did—but now that the date was here, she'd started to worry again. As soon as her neighbors on Main Street saw them going to the historic, eighteenth-century Maple Tree B&B—she assumed that was where they'd go since it boasted a five-star, Colonial-themed restaurant that brought in people from near and far—she knew their relationship would be the talk of town. That was true for any couple who went there. It was the "serious couple" place in town.

She didn't mind so much, as long as everything went well for them. But what if things didn't work out? Could she stand having people look at her in that sympathetic way again? It had nearly driven her crazy after Timothy left her.

"But," she reminded her reflection, "with Gerry everything's different. What I feel for him is deeper and more mature than what I felt for Timothy. Timothy was there when Grand-mère died and when I was scared." She paused and glanced around the apartment that still had memories of Grand-mère all over it, "And I was very lonely." She looked back at her reflection and was finally honest about why she'd agreed to marry Timothy when she knew that neither of their hearts was really in it. "I thought that building a family with a man, any decent man—and Timothy was very decent until the end—would solve all my problems. Gerry is different. With Gerry—"

The doorbell chimed. Aimee stopped talking to her reflection and turned to the solid front door.

Gerry was standing on the other side of it. The man she loved. Somewhere between disliking him for moving his cake business next door to her pastry shop and admiring him, she'd fallen in love.

Love…

She took a deep breath. "This is it," she murmured nervously. "Once I open the door and walk hand-in-hand down

Main Street with Gerry, and go into the Maple Tree with him, everyone will know we're a couple." Her heart pounded and her ears registered the rushing of her blood.

She glanced over at Louis. Snoozing. No help there.

She had to move forward. She couldn't stay in this place of emotional anxiety any longer—one that was more about how other people would react to this relationship, not about her love for the man on the other side of the door. She had to trust him. She had to trust her own judgment.

Squaring her shoulders, she walked resolutely across the parquet floor and threw open the door.

"Wow!" Gerry said and the approval in his eyes at her spruced-up appearance shooed all of Aimee's fears away. He extended his arm.

Aimee glanced to the left of Gerry's shoulder and down the wooden stairs. When they kissed at night, no one had ever been around. But this was broad daylight. And there was Mrs. Campbell, standing in front of her store just as Hale came toward her carrying a new garden trowel. They both stopped. They looked up at her dressed in her "Sunday best" and at Gerry. He was still wearing jeans but not work jeans. Rather, jeans that probably cost more than a suit from Brooks Brothers. He had on a dark-blue Herringbone wool sport coat, dark-brown cowboy boots and the same Stetson he'd worn at his grand opening.

Taking a deep breath, she smiled at Gerry and, stepping forward, boldly wrapped her arm around the one he held out to her.

She didn't see Mrs. Campbell's reaction or Hale's because the feel of her arm snug within Gerry's was all that mattered. Just as when they'd held hands that wonderful Saturday morning, and when they kissed by her door at night, it felt perfect, like the smooth, flawless fitting of the last piece of a thousand-piece jigsaw puzzle.

They walked down the stairs, greeted Mrs. Campbell and Mr. Hale. Then Gerry did something she wasn't expecting. He led her to his truck.

Cynthia was in the back and greeted Aimee grandly.

"Hey, girl!" She gave Gerry a questioning look.

"I had reservations at the B&B. But when I saw on the weather report what a nice day it was going to be, I thought you might not want to be inside any more than I do. You once said how much you enjoy picnics." He motioned to the wicker picnic basket on the back seat of the truck. "So—"

"A picnic! Gerry, what a great idea!" She scratched Cynthia behind her ears. "And best of all, Cynthia can come with us." She liked that. Having Cynthia along would make everything easier, more natural.

He opened the door for her. She paused before climbing in and motioned to her dress. "Should I go change into jeans?"

"Please don't. You look lovely," he said and closed the door behind her. She was glad. She liked how the dress made her feel; she liked Gerry liking her in it.

***

After a few minutes, Gerry drove onto the road that led to the Old Stone Bridge. "You remembered!" Aimee said.

She turned to him, and when he saw the "I'm-important-enough-to-you-for-you-to-do-this-for-me" look shining in her eyes—awe, wonder and admiration at the fact that he hadn't forgotten that it was her favorite place—he knew he'd made a good choice in packing a picnic lunch rather than going to the Maple Tree B&B. "Of course."

"There's nowhere in the world I'd rather be, Gerry, than right here with you—" she motioned to the back of the truck "—and Cynthia, going to the Old Stone Bridge."

"I feel the same, Aimee." Miss Maggie had said to make the initial date a good one so Aimee would agree to a second and a third. But Gerry hoped for so much more. He wanted to be on the road, not just to the Old Stone Bridge and their first date, but to a lifetime together. He wanted to make this such a memorable *rendezvous,* as Aimee's grand-mère might have said, so that in retrospect—sixty-some years from now—they'd be able to look back on it and proudly recount this magical day to their kids and grandkids.

"The trees are dressed as if they're attending an autumn ball," she commented, as she watched the land pass by them out the open side window.

Gerry nodded and breathed in their rich scent. "It's like a warm burst of color before the white and the quiet of the frost and snow set in, which are as much a part of this land as your autumn ball is today."

"So you really don't mind that winter's coming?"

"I love Connecticut, Aimee. It's home."

Cynthia started barking, quick, excited sounds that made them both glance back at her and chuckle. "She's letting us know we're almost there."

"I hope you remembered to bring her Frisbee!"

Gerry reached under the seat and pulled out the blue disk that had Cynthia's teeth marks all over it. "Sheriff Jones could've brought me in on a 'cruelty to animals charge' if I hadn't."

They turned a bend in the road. "There it is!" Aimee shouted, sounding like an excited ten-year-old. Gerry loved her exuberance.

He stopped the truck, and for a poignant moment, the three just sat and stared at what was left of the Old Stone Bridge. Rising from granite boulders that were scattered around like stepping stones for giants, was one perfectly arched segment of a bridge, which at one time had had at least two other arches, on either side of the remaining one. Roman concrete could be seen under the dressed ashlar stones that had fallen from its façade. Tall weeds were growing from between the stones on its surface. The structure was situated in the middle of the now-shallow river, so it didn't connect the two banks, but it did speak of the passage of time, and of an epoch that recorded history either didn't know or recognize.

"I really do understand why you hold fast to the belief that it was built by shipwrecked Romans. It's exactly like some Roman arched bridges in Europe that I've seen," Gerry said.

"The thing that keeps experts from accepting it, however, is that there are no Roman roadways visible on either side of the river."

Gerry shook his head. "But why would there be? Just because a bridge was built in the Roman way doesn't mean they had to build roads, too. Maybe those stranded Romans used it as a defense, as a safe place to live where they could build their shops and homes. Or else to have something from home to make them *feel* at home. A bridge to connect the two banks of the river was practical and beautiful and secure. They were very much builders, after all."

"Exactly."

"I guess we'll never know."

"All *I* know is that it's here for us to dream and wonder about, to stretch our imaginations. That's enough for me."

"Me, too." He removed his jacket and took the Frisbee off the seat. "And the green pasture over there—" he nodded in the direction of the grassy meadow that was about the size of a football field, "—is the best place in town to play Frisbee with Cynthia." He was careful to keep the Frisbee out of the dog's sight as he came around the front of the truck and opened Aimee's door. He helped her out, and then together they went to the back of the truck. "Cynthia." He opened the tailgate and motioned for her to jump down.

Bringing the Frisbee out of hiding and holding it high in the air, he said, "Who wants to play?" Cynthia went wild with excitement and darted off in the direction of the meadow. Gerry took Aimee's hand in his own, and together they walked along the modern-day stone path toward the waiting dog.

***

After about fifteen minutes of fun and hilarity, Gerry told Cynthia to go to the river and lap up a drink while he, after guzzling down a whole Thermos of cold water, turned his attention to setting up their picnic.

The only thing he allowed Aimee to do was select the table—and Cynthia promptly parked herself underneath.

She'd chosen one in the shade of five golden-leafed, white-barked birch trees with her favorite view of the bridge; it was also far away from the other picnic tables, two of which had other couples enjoying the "postcard from Florida," day. While she sat on the cushion Gerry produced for her, he set out an exquisite lunch, complete with an Irish linen tablecloth and matching napkins, crystal wine glasses and sterling silverware. The centerpiece was the biggest surprise of all. On a silver-and-crystal dish, he placed a stunning miniature cake, one he'd made to the exacting specifications of classic French baking. Just as the bridge was a testimony of third-century Romans having lived in this land, the cake proved that Gerry was an outstanding graduate of Le Cordon Bleu.

"It's *beautiful,*" she whispered and had to clear her throat. She couldn't believe he'd gone to so much trouble for her. She knew that this sort of cake took a great deal of time and effort to create. She reached out to touch the miniature pink roses and their green leaves. But when he jokingly slapped her hand away, she couldn't help her too-loud, self-conscious giggle.

"Shall we eat?" he asked as he took the lids off the tin boxes to reveal chicken kebabs, buttermilk biscuits, an authentic Greek village salad with a small bottle of PJ Kabos extra virgin olive oil to complement it, plus grilled veggies and fresh baguettes.

Eat they did to the melody of the ancient river, the sound of cardinals singing in the trees, red squirrels scurrying around as they gathered nuts, the light breeze swaying the golden leaves around them and Cynthia's steady, contented breathing as she lay under the table. When it came time to slice the cake, Gerry picked up his cushion, came around the table, placing it on the bench next to hers, and sat close beside her. She watched as he put a slice on her dessert plate, another on his own.

He turned to her, and when he looked at her the way a woman hopes a man will, at least once in her lifetime, the cake was forgotten. His eyes crinkled at the corners as his fingertips ran along the sides of her mouth. "Have I told you how much I love your dimples?"

She shook her head. *Have I told you how much I love you?* she wanted to ask. But instead, she challenged, "How much?"

With a moan, she felt the warm touch of his lips, and he whispered, "Let me show you."

That was it for Aimee. During the next minute or was it ten?—Aimee couldn't tell—he did show her. She could have gone on kissing him for a hundred hours if he hadn't slowly pulled back.

But not completely. With his forehead resting against hers, she felt his chest rumble as he chuckled softly. "I'm so glad I persisted with you, neighbor lady."

She cringed. "Was I really that difficult?" She knew she was, but she hoped that by now he didn't remember.

"Totally disagreeable," he groaned. "A logical man would've run in the opposite direction. But owning the store beside yours, I had nowhere to go."

She lowered her head in remorse over how she'd treated him during those first days. "Grand-mère used to say that my temper sometimes rises higher than the temperature of melted caramel."

"Good image!" He grinned. "I think your grand-mère was probably right," he added.

"I'm so sorry, Gerry. She would've been very disappointed in me for not welcoming you."

"No. It was wrong of me not to tell you the first time we met that I was opening a cake shop next door to your patisserie. You had reason to be wary of me."

Aimee knew then that if she wanted a future with him—and she'd known for the last few magical days that she did—she had to be honest about the other reason she'd been so careful not to give in to her attraction to him. "Gerry." She sat back, putting a few more inches between them. "It wasn't just about our shops," she began.

Running her tongue lightly across her lips, she paused.

It was much harder to tell him about Timothy than she'd expected. She didn't want Timothy's betrayal to sound like a pathetic sob story, even though it was. Except for Becky, she'd never told anyone how mortified Timothy's leaving her at the altar had really made her feel. She'd downplayed it to everyone. Although she accepted now that he'd done the right thing, it still didn't diminish the terrible embarrassment she'd carried around with her for the last two years.

"Aimee?" Kindness could have taken a walk on his tone. "Are you going to tell me about the whole runaway-groom thing?"

She blinked. "You know?" Her instinct was to feel upset that her privacy had been breached. But as she looked into his eyes and read only gratitude that she wanted to tell him, all she could feel was relief that he already knew.

He nodded. "Miss Maggie told me. She thought I should know why you were sending me mixed signals."

"Mixed signals..." Aimee blew out a long sigh. "That's putting it mildly." His eyes widened. The surprise in them that she'd admitted it made her laugh. "Well, it is!"

"It's not that." He shook his head. "I just appreciate the fact that you acknowledge it."

She shook her head, confused.

He grimaced. "Let's just say it's a pleasant change," he qualified. Then, as if he'd come to a decision, he said, "My ex didn't see things quite that way."

So there was an ex, was all Aimee could think. Had he been married before? Aimee suddenly realized she didn't even know. "Ex—?" she asked.

"—Fiancée," he supplied, and Aimee was relieved. Somehow, it put them on the same level when it came to failed relationships. Having things go bad when you were engaged was hard enough, but she couldn't even begin to think how difficult it would be if marriage had been involved. For either of them. "A fiancée who was offended that I actually wanted to set a date for our wedding."

"Seriously?" Aimee couldn't imagine putting off being married to a man like Gerry and planning a life with him… It seemed like the most wonderful of dreams to her. For the first time in two years, she was allowing herself to have such pink-tinged thoughts again.

"Oh, there's more," he said and grimaced, bringing her back to the moment. "When Scarlett called off the wedding—because after two years together she didn't want to be 'pressured' into setting a date—she told me she was going to keep the ring as a parting gift."

As he continued to tell her about his ups and downs with Scarlett, he made it sound more like a comedy show he'd watched than a real-live event he'd lived through. "You actually seem more amused by it than upset," she said when he finished.

He breathed out deeply. "I *was* upset in the beginning," he told her. "But more with myself for thinking that a woman travelling in the LA fast lane would want to settle down and have a family. She wanted the fun of being engaged, the security, always having a guy at her beck and call. Never the actual marriage with all the changes she felt it would bring to her very full and active life. I really wasn't too bothered when I figured that out. What got me the most was how she called off everything—because I asked her to set a date—then used her extensive PR skills to make me the fall guy and did her best to ruin my business."

Ruin his business? "What do you mean?"

"Let's just say if I hadn't had a healthy online sales presence, Uncle Gerry's Cakerie would have closed down," he said confirming what his sister told her at Benji's party. "Scarlett took me off her electronic Rolodex and all her social media accounts and instructed all her 'friends' to do the same."

"So she was a woman with clout?"

"Vice-President of one of the top PR agencies in LA."

"That's a pretty big deal."

"I'm the first to admit that it certainly helped Uncle Gerry's Cakerie in the beginning." It didn't surprise Aimee that he'd own up to such a thing.

"Makes my own sob story sound lame," she commented. "At least my business wasn't involved. If anything, more people came to the Patisserie afterward to support me."

"No. Not lame. Just different," he said. "Scarlett's retaliatory actions went after my business. Your fiancé left you in the lurch…" He paused and using a much lighter tone, continued, "or rather, left you in—"

"*—the church!*" they said together and both started laughing.

"Electronic Rolodex?" Aimee said between laughter.

"Runaway groom?" he returned in the same manner.

After a moment, they stopped laughing and looked deeply at each other, understanding in hindsight, and with this new and wonderful love wrapping itself around them, how unimportant to their future together their past romances were. In many ways, they were humorous even.

"Dear Lord, but it felt good to laugh," Aimee said. "And about this," she added. "It's like I'm finally free."

"That makes me very happy, Aimee. It's an important step. I've been free, as you say, from Scarlett for quite some time."

Aimee placed her hand on his cheek and rubbed her fingers down the pleasant roughness of his skin. "Well, I'm glad Miss Maggie told you about Timothy's runaway-groom gig."

"Something I hate the man for doing to you," he said.

She took his hands in her own. She liked the way his fingers automatically wrapped around hers. "May I tell you something I haven't told anyone else?"

"I'd like that."

"It's…it's something I've only come to understand during the last few days."

He gave her hand a squeeze and prompted, "Tell me."

She spoke slowly. "For the first time since my almost-wedding, I understand that Timothy didn't so much desert *me* as he did a marriage he realized didn't have the correct elements to make it the one we both needed. A forever marriage. He was right to call it off." She frowned. "Wrong in how he went about it," she was quick to insert. She still didn't forgive Timothy for that. "But right to do so. We didn't love each other the way a couple about to be married should."

"How did you come to understand all this now? Nearly two years later?"

Here it was! The do-or-don't moment. As she sat just a breath away from the man she knew she loved, was she going to be brave and tell him the truth? Or was she going to hedge?

"From being with you, Gerry." Courage won.

When his arms wrapped around her, she was thankful it had. With the crimson and gold leaves fluttering to the ground, the birds chirping in the trees above, and a now wide-awake Cynthia elegantly standing guard over them, Aimee knew there was a reason candor was so highly lauded. If the sound of Gerry's heart beating beneath her ear was anything to go by, this was the correct course to follow. As naturally as the river that flowed below the Old Stone Bridge, he kissed her and she kissed him back. Over and over again.

15—Cloud Nine

Friday morning was as beautiful as the previous day had been. Aimee gazed up at the fluffy white clouds poised, as if in a still life painting, over Stoneybridge. She pointed at a particularly splendid cloud formation that had sunrays radiating from around it, asking Becky, "Could that be Cloud Nine?" They'd just finished packing up the Patisserie's van with pastries. The presentation was in an hour and a half.

"Can't be," Becky said jokingly. "You're already riding Cloud Nine."

Aimee laughed. "I am! After yesterday with Gerry," she admitted, "I don't see how anything can go wrong."

"Did you tell Gerry about your meeting this morning?"

Aimee carefully shut the delivery van's back door on its precious cargo of *tarte aux pommes, mille-feuille, macarons* and the "butteriest" and "flakiest" croissants in all of Connecticut. She paused and looked at Becky. "Actually, I never even thought about it." She was a little shocked to realize that. "Not once." On a personal level, the importance of having Gerry in her life had supplanted even this all-important business meeting.

Becky laughed. "I'm happy you found each other, girl!"

"Yeah, me too."

"Your pastries are baked, crafted and safely tucked away in the van. Now it's time to get *you* all spruced up!"

They had just entered Aimee's apartment, and Becky was removing her makeup kit from her bag to give Aimee "the perfect business look" when Aimee's cell phone rang. She glanced at caller ID. "Uncle Cain," she groaned and left her phone sitting on the table. Nasty black flies seemed to bombard the walls of her stomach, making her feel sick.

"Don't answer it," Becky warned.

Talking to Uncle Cain was the last thing Aimee wanted to do. "Argh," she groaned as the phone continued to ring. She extended her hand to pick it up, but pulled back. She reached out a second time, but again pulled her hand back. Never had a ring sounded more offensive to her. "I'm afraid he'll come out to Stoneybridge if I don't."

"Good point." Becky grimaced. "Okay. Answer it. But hang on to your cloud-nine feeling."

"Yeah, right," Aimee said dubiously. Ignoring her queasy stomach, she picked up her phone, slid her finger across the screen to connect and said, "Hello, Uncle Cain."

"I know there are still two weeks, less two days, until the loan deadline." He spoke without so much as a hello. "But I hope you'll be available later today. I want to bring out an architect buddy of mine so he can get a jump start on the redesign of the Patisserie. We hope to have Stoneybridge's Play Ball Sports Bar up and running in time for the Superbowl—"

"—I don't *believe* this!" Aimee cut in.

The line went quiet, then, "My dear niece, you must face the inevitable." His voice was rife with condescension. "The clock is ticking. You don't have the money. The store space will be mine in less than two weeks."

"Why would you assume I won't have the funds to repay you?" she shot back. She was angry. How dared he destroy her cloud-nine feeling on this all-important day!

The sardonic sound of what he probably thought was laughter came through the phone. "Why do you think I lent you the money? I was, and still am, one-hundred-percent certain you *won't* be in a position to repay me. A win-win situation for a businessman, dear."

From downstairs, from the direction of Uncle Gerry's Cakerie, Aimee heard the sound of a small saw starting up. She knew that Gerry was making a wooden frame for one of his big, brash and crass cakes. She smiled. As much as she'd disliked those cakes before meeting Gerry, she could appreciate his craft now. In fact, she was even beginning to like them. Just knowing that Gerry was in her life and was, at this very moment, so close by, gave her the courage to do something she'd never done before. She stood-up to her uncle. "No, Uncle Cain. You may *not* bring your buddy out to the Patisserie."

In the stunned silence that followed, Aimee watched as a gleeful Becky pumped the air with her fist and mouthed, "Yessss!"

"Aimee." His voice was hard now. "I do not need your permission. We could just come."

"If you or anyone who seems to be looking at the Patisserie with an eye to redoing it comes in, I will consider it trespassing. I will call *my* buddy, the sheriff of Stoneybridge, and have you and *your* buddy thrown out."

"My mother should never have left the store to you," he whipped out, like a cobra striking. "You have no idea how to run a business."

"That's not true! What I don't have any idea about is how my only living relative can be so mean to me. Goodbye, *Uncle* Cain," she said and cut the connection before he could say one more venomous word.

Aimee turned to Becky. She dropped the phone on the sofa as if it still held the viper's voice. She thrust out her hands. They were shaking violently. Becky took them in hers. Aimee laughed. Then she giggled. "Becky! I stood up to him! For the first time ever! I didn't let him walk all over me!"

"I'm so proud of you, girl!"

Aimee looked over at the Chanel business suit—another vintage item that had come to her from Grand-mère—hanging on her bedroom door. She took a step toward it and ran her hand over the dark-gray boucle fabric. She remembered her grand-mère wearing this suit on special occasions and to church. Back when her five foot, two inch Grand-mère was taller than she was. She swiveled back to Becky. "Give me a hand with my makeup! I'm glad he called! It's only made my resolve to go out and win this contract greater!"

"That's the spirit! Ride Cloud Nine, Aimee, and don't step off it again!"

***

Four hours later Aimee ran into the Treasure Trove. A quick look around the shop, and she could see that Becky was alone, so she shouted, "Cloud Nine has risen to the stratosphere! The presentation went *great*!"

Squealing with delight, Becky ran out from behind the racks of Jimmy Choos and Louis Vuitton bags that she was careful to keep fresh and looking like new with a daily dusting. Holding the feather duster in the air like a flag, she wrapped Aimee in a big hug. "I'm so happy for you, girlfriend! Tell me! Tell me all," she said and, ditching the duster, she led Aimee to what Miss Maggie called the store's front parlor. Miss Maggie believed in making her patrons feel special when they came into her "home away from home." Besides, as she always told everyone, it had the best view on Main Street. The Patisserie with its pink-and-white striped awnings, flower boxes in the upper three windows and Mansard-style roof was directly across the street.

"Well," Aimee began. She was excited about recounting the meeting to Becky because Becky had been part of it all since the beginning. "There were two women—Lizzy Edwards, the lady I've been in contact with was one—and two men," she said. "Both women loved the concept. At first I wasn't sure about one of the men, their head chef, but by the end, after eating the coffee macaron, he definitely liked the products, too. The other man—James Monroe—had some questions about my ability to deliver the quantities they need," Aimee paused. She didn't want to tell business-minded Becky that he was the CEO of the company. She knew Becky would put too much weight on his having more of a say in who was awarded the contract whereas Aimee truly believed he'd take the advice of his marketing experts and head chef who liked her samples. So, excluding that detail, she went on. "But I gave them each a copy of my feasibility study, which shows that by cooking around the clock and turning the Patisserie's storage room into extra kitchen space I'd definitely be able to fill all the supermarket's orders. He pointed out that by giving up my large storage room, it would mean I'd have to depend on daily deliveries of supplies. Which could in turn cause problems in their picking up Patisserie orders for their supermarkets should there be a glitch in my receiving basic goods." She grimaced. "It would've been *ideal* to have had the store next door to expand into..."

"Yes." Becky playfully punched her arm. "But then you wouldn't have had Gerry to expand your life. Now you can *bake* your cakes and eat them—or at least Gerry's kisses—too!"

Aimee giggled. "So true!" she agreed, then shook her head and continued. "*Anyway,* Lizzy Edwards pointed out that I'd also have Northeast Supermarket's kitchen facilities at my disposal."

"Oh, good."

"And in fact, part of the contract would require me to train their chefs to bake Patisserie items in the supermarket's kitchen. So my facilities being small really wouldn't be an issue for long." She recalled the skeptical frown that had cut across James Monroe's craggy face. Aimee knew he hadn't been convinced, but she pushed the thought to the back of her mind.

"That's something that's bothered me," Becky admitted and Aimee had a moment of wondering what she meant. "Are you okay with sharing Grand-mère's recipes with others? Especially a *supermarket* franchise?"

That had been Aimee's concern for quite a while, too. Gerry's words to her at Benji's party, about how he shared what he'd learned with other people, and that included his professional recipes, had a great deal to do with her being okay with it now. "Becky, how often have you heard that things are lost to history?" She pointed in the direction of the town's landmark, the Old Stone Bridge. "If someone had written down the bridge's history, even chiseled the date it was built on one of the stones, we'd know it today. If I don't share Grand-mère's recipes with others, they'll be lost to later generations. There's just too much secrecy in the world today."

"Whoa." Becky laughed. "Look who's talking about secrecy. If you just *told* the townspeople what HurriCain's doing to you and what he's planning on doing to the Patisserie—I mean, turning it into a Play Ball Sports Bar—don't you think they'd come to your aid?"

"That's entirely different." Aimee really believed it was. Telling the townspeople would make her look pathetic, show that, unlike her grand-mère, she really didn't have what it took to run the Patisserie—thereby proving HurriCain's point.

"No. It's not. Secrecy is secrecy is secrecy. It's not a good thing," Becky insisted.

"Becky…the die is cast." Aimee could feel her cloud-nine sensation disappearing. She'd heard all this from Becky before and really didn't want to hear it on this day of all days. Even though she *said* she didn't mind giving Grand-mère's recipes away, it was still hard. She had to remind herself that it was the only way to save the Patisserie. She was sure Grand-mère would agree.

Becky held up her right hand. "I'm just saying. But I won't say any more," she rushed on and taking Aimee's hand, repeated, "I'm happy for you, Aimee. I think you might have saved the Patisserie today. When will you know?"

Aimee took a breath and let it out, glad to get back to the wonderful event of the day. "Lizzy Edwards said within the next couple of days. There's only one other contender. But she thinks the age of the Patisserie—and that many people in the tri-state area already know about it—will be the deciding factor."

"So she's hopeful."

"Very."

"What are you going to do now?"

"Pray," Aimee laughed. But she was serious. "And look forward to Sunday."

"Sunday?" Becky's nose scrunched up in a way that would look ridiculous on anybody else. "To go to church and pray harder?"

Aimee giggled. "No, silly." She giggled again but quickly put on a serious face. "I mean yes to going to church—you know how much I love Pastor Sansom's sermons and worshipping with a group of believers—but that's not why I'm looking forward to this particular Sunday. This Sunday, it's what's happening *after* church. Gerry and I are going to take his niece and nephew to the pumpkin farm."

The door chimes sounded. Aimee and Becky glanced at the lovely fifty-something woman who walked into the Treasure Trove. Neither recognized her. Most likely someone from a nearby town. They always bought something; it was time for Becky to get back to work. They both rose from the sofa.

"So glad for you," Becky repeated and lightly squeezed Aimee's shoulder before walking over to the stunning woman, who was almost as tall as Becky but twenty pounds heavier, which on such a tall figure still made her seem very slim. "May I help you?" Aimee heard Becky ask.

Sending the woman a friendly nod, Aimee walked out into the bright sunshine of the glorious November New England day. Looking both ways, she crossed over to her side of Main Street and climbed the stairs to her apartment. Right now, she needed to change out of Grand-mère's Sunday best, and get back to work just like Becky. She smiled as she swung open her door.

She couldn't wait for Sunday.

***

Even though a cold front was due to hit sometime later that afternoon, Sunday began relatively warm and bright; church service that morning was extra-special, and the afternoon was great fun for all four of them. Benji and Pattie enjoyed the hayride at the farm, ate too many funnel cakes and cuddled the baby animals at the pumpkin farm's petting zoo. Aimee and Gerry had a delightful time keeping up with the kids' nonstop movement. Finally, Benji and Pattie were happily playing in the Enchanted Forest, surrounded by giant pumpkins, apple trees and multidimensional haystacks, while Aimee and Gerry watched from the surrounding stone wall.

"Wow! Do they ever stop?"

Gerry took Aimee's right hand and squeezed it. They'd been careful not to be too demonstrative in front of the kids. "My sister calls them the 'kidnadors.' Exactly what a tornado would be if it was a kid. That's why she's treating herself to peace and quiet today. She's not doing a thing. Sitting and reading her Kindle or just lolling in bed. Whatever she feels like doing. She said she might even enjoy a movie with some adults in it." They glanced over at the kids and watched as they and a couple of other children started climbing to the top of the ten-foot-high haystack.

"Come here," Gerry said after a moment and pulled Aimee close. With Gerry's left arm around her shoulders, tucking her firmly against his side, Aimee reveled in the feeling of belonging, that feeling of coming home. He nodded toward the happily squealing kids and then focused his dark eyes on her again. "But I don't want to talk about the kids right now, or my sister."

"Oh." She tilted her head further back so she could look directly at him. "And what *do* you want to talk about?"

"This," he said and lowering his head, he kissed her. It was a kiss unlike the kiss they shared every night, and unlike the ones they'd shared at the Old Stone Bridge. She felt that immediately. This was a kiss that demanded the next level in their relationship, a kiss that was asking for a future together, a kiss whose main ingredient was love. With her entire being, she moved her lips in rhythm with his and kissed him back until, finally, he whispered, "I love you."

The words surged in her head and in her heart, making her feel dizzy and faint. Could he really love her? Did he really say the words she'd given up hope of ever hearing again? Words she'd resisted even wanting to hear again?

"I love you," he murmured again just when she thought she'd dreamed them. "Aimee," He held his forehead against hers. "You know that, don't you?"

Tears flowed from her eyes. Happy tears, healing tears, thankful tears. "I know."

"I'm not asking you to say it back. I can wait. After all, we're neighbors." She heard a low sound coming from his chest, something resembling a chuckle. "I'm not going anywhere," he whispered hoarsely and smiled at her. "But when you do say it, *if* you do, you'll make me the happiest man—" he paused and grinned mischievously "—in the solar system."

She blinked back her tears. "Solar system? *Only* the solar system?" She knew what he was doing—lightening the situation. She loved him all the more for it. *Loved him!* There it was again, the thought, the feeling, the impulse, the words. She *did* love Gerry!

He shrugged. Even with desire coloring his voice and its tone, she could hear laughter. "It's a pretty big place—as Benji's cake proved."

"And my telling you 'I love you,' would make you the happiest man in it?" she quipped.

His eyes darkened; there was no humor in them now. Only want and need, need for the life they both dreamed of. "Absolutely."

"Well, then..." Feeling the figurative walls she'd built within herself turn into something as ethereal and delicate as those made of sugar, she whispered, "Gerry Mitchell, I love you...with all my heart."

He groaned and gathered her close. They clung to each other, just as she knew they always would as they faced life together. She felt free, grateful, trusting, happy. She felt... She laughed softly, and Gerry moved back an inch and asked, "What?"

"It just occurred to me, my love," she said and ran her fingertips over the five o'clock roughness of his face, "that you are the man—" she let her fingers move to his lips "—I never knew I was waiting for."

His hands cupped her shoulders, and he drew her closer. "Aimee..." he breathed into her ear. "That is the nicest thing you could've said—"

"Uncle Gerry! Look at me!" At the sound of Benji calling out at the top of his voice, Gerry and Aimee exchanged a smile, and then looked toward the boy. Benji was standing on the highest part of the haystack waving his arms madly. "Watch me jump into the pile of leaves!"

"I've already done it," Pattie said, suddenly standing before them. She had leaves sticking out from her hair and the waistband of her yellow parka. "Hey, Aimee!" Pattie pointed and laughed. "You're face is all red."

Aimee covered her cheeks with both hands.

"What did you do to get so hot?" Pattie asked with a frown. "I think sitting up on that old stone wall would make you cold." She gave an exaggerated shiver. "It's getting colder."

"You're right," Gerry agreed, drawing his niece's attention away from Aimee's flushed face. "The cold front's moved in and the temperature's dropping." He nodded over to Benji to jump. The boy immediately leaped into the leaves, squealing in delight. Then to Pattie, "Now let's get you two 'kidnadors' home to your mom."

"Can I do it one more time?" Pattie asked, hopping up and down.

"Sure. But be quick," Gerry said.

"Me, too! Again!" Benji hollered from the bottom of the haystack.

"Okay. Go!" Gerry answered him and said quietly to Aimee, "Let's take these rascals back to their mom. Then how about coming over to my place for dinner? I'll make a Cordon Bleu special."

"You're on!" This was a day Aimee never wanted to end. She glanced up at the five o'clock sun. With its waxing, the sky was painted every imaginable shade of pink.

"Look, Gerry!" She motioned up.

His gaze followed where she pointed, and he nodded. "Life in pink… It's ours to accept, Aimee. Ours."

"Amen to that," she said and as she rested her head comfortably against his shoulder, they watched the ever-changing and lovely Connecticut sky together.

16—Love and Hate

By the time they arrived at Gerry's house, the temperature had dropped another twenty degrees. "This weather's perfect! It's like Connecticut's welcoming me home," he said, vigorously rubbing his hands to warm them enough to unlock the door. "This is how late fall is supposed to be. The way it was when I was growing up," he qualified as he grabbed two white birch logs from the stack beside the door and motioned for her to enter first.

Aimee looked around. His house was comfortable and cozy, decorated with early-American furniture that appeared to be newly bought reproductions. They fit perfectly into the small Cape Cod cottage.

"I sold my house in California furnished. When my parents moved to Mexico, they gave me a lot of their furniture. I kept it in a storage facility near Nazareth. Most of this comes from when I was a kid."

"I was just thinking how new it looked."

"Yeah. When we were growing up our house was more like a museum than a place for kids to play. The reason Sabrina's is not." He laughed. "It's neat and tidy, but definitely geared to kids." Aimee nodded as she remembered the large dollhouse and child-size table and chairs in Sabrina's otherwise exquisitely decorated living room.

The fire was now burning, and Cynthia was sleeping nearby, enjoying the sweet slumber of a dog who'd spent a whole day playing outside with two children and two doting adults. After making them each a cup of steaming hot chocolate, Gerry went to work in his small country-style kitchen. Aimee sat at the kitchen bar and watched. His movements were the exacting ones of a great chef. Not one step—neither one whisk of the sauce nor the crack of an egg—was wasted. Pots were soon bubbling on the stove, and a fresh pumpkin pie was in the oven. He knew his way around the kitchen like a ballet dancer did a stage. Aimee was watching a pro at work.

And when they sat at his small, but elegant cherrywood dining table and she tasted the *gougères* and *coq au vin* and *ratatouille,* she certainly wasn't disappointed. "If you ever want to open a Parisian restaurant here in Stoneybridge, I'm sure you'd have people coming from Manhattan just to dine there." She took the last bite of the creamy potatoes au gratin. "This alone is fabulous. It's rich and full-flavored without being too heavy."

"Truthfully, I had a hard time deciding between opening up the Cakerie with its over-the-top cakes—" he flashed a smile, and she sent him a self-conscious answering one "—or a Parisian-style restaurant."

"But the Cakerie won. Why?"

"Its lack of pretense," he replied without hesitation, and she knew it must have had something to do, in a negative sense, with his upbringing. She'd liked meeting his parents, but could see, even after spending just one afternoon in their company, that although polite, they weren't easy people to get close to. It wasn't that they were cold, exactly, more aloof. "The Cakerie is a place for all people, all ages, to come and have a good time. I want to encourage people to use their imaginations, to indulge in whimsy. And to give and share." He chuckled. "For instance, next Thursday I'm taking three dozen cupcakes to Pattie's class for their early Thanksgiving Day celebration. What's really special is that Pattie and her friends drew pictures of what they thought their Thanksgiving cupcakes should look like. I'm going to recreate what each child drew."

"That's a lot of work," she said, impressed by his generosity.

"But when you see the kids' faces light up at the tangible creation of what was only in their minds—well, that makes it worth every minute."

"Early Thanksgiving Day celebration?" She'd never heard of it being celebrated so far in advance. "When I was in school we used to celebrate on the Wednesday before Thanksgiving." Aimee's favorite day of the year. *Deadline day this year,* she reminded herself. But somehow, she knew it was going to be a good day. Just as it always was. She placed her napkin on the table.

"Yeah. Many teachers like celebrating Thanksgiving early now. Before the kids get tired of all the partying," he said and as they stood, she gave him a questioning look. "Hey! I'm just the baker," he answered with a who-am-I-to-judge shrug. "Besides, it's our job as adults to make kids feel special. The themed cupcakes will not only make Pattie feel good—because her uncle's offering them to her friends—but every one of her classmates, too."

Once again, Aimee was struck by his loyalty to his family. She placed her arms around his shoulders, whispering, "I sure wish *my* uncle had been more like you."

Gerry wrapped his arms around her waist. "Tell me about him."

Aimee shrugged. "Not much to tell." Even as she said it, she knew she was lying. There was so much to tell about Uncle

Cain, about how he was trying to take the Patisserie away from her, about how if she didn't win the contract with the supermarket chain he'd succeed in doing exactly that. And how she often felt her life would have been better without him.

Gerry's eyes narrowed. "For some reason, I don't think that's true."

She couldn't help sighing. "It's not."

"Tell me." It was a command, but one flavored with love. He was asking only because he wanted to know everything about her, including the negative things in her life. It made her feel special, important.

"Someday I will. But not tonight," and as if she'd done it a million times, she took his hand and gently led him to the sofa. "I really don't want Uncle Cain to intrude on this night—on this special day—when we both admitted—" She didn't dare say it, somehow afraid it would disappear like a puff of flour in the wind.

"Loving each other," he finished for her as they sat together.

"Yes. Loving each other," she repeated and as he put his arm around her shoulders and she leaned comfortably against him while the wood crackled in the fireplace, casting a cozy glow, she said, "I'll tell you all about Uncle Cain and his even worse wife," she promised. "Another time, though."

He rubbed her shoulder. "Okay. I won't push. But tell me one thing. Did he abuse you?" he asked softly. "Physically, I mean?"

"No, Gerry, no." She turned to face him. "I'm sorry if I gave you that impression. Nothing as serious as that. Never." It occurred to her then that she really didn't have as much to be angry with Uncle Cain about as she thought. She was even beginning to understand why Grand-mère seemed to set bounds on her anger toward her son. Yes, Uncle Cain was selfish, uncaring and ambitious at all costs. But he wasn't evil. "No. He's always been…" She paused and searched for the correct words. "Neglectful...aloof…selfish…mean-spirited. I guess that's the best way to describe him. He never seemed to have any family feeling toward Grand-mère or me. If anything, my biggest complaint is that he left us alone more than we wanted to be."

"Kind of like my parents?"

Slowly she nodded. "Yeah, kinda. Except your parents, in spite of the tunnel-vision love they share, are nice. Ignoring you and Sabrina wasn't something they did on purpose to be mean. That's just who they are. Uncle Cain, well, he *cultivated* being mean. He believed it made him tough. It might have been fine in the business world, but he shouldn't have let it carry into his personal life." She laughed. "Especially since Grand-mère and I were his only relatives."

He nodded. She could tell that her words had set his mind at ease. "Okay. More about your uncle another day. For now…" His arms closed around her and hers around him. The wind blustered and blew outside, the rain—or was it now sleet?—beat against the windows, the dog snored and the fire in its stone hearth sang its ancient song. As they held each other, all thoughts of Uncle Cain, the Cakerie, the Patisserie, the Old Stone Bridge, niece, nephew, sister, Main Street and the sun and stars were far from their minds.

Sometime later—Aimee couldn't have said how much later—the alien sound of a phone ringing punctured the cocoon that had become Gerry's house that stormy night. Reluctantly, Aimee lifted her head from his chest and listened.

Was it her phone? She was expecting to hear from Lizzy Edwards any time now. Wouldn't it be wonderful to be able to share the news with Gerry on this day of all days? But no, it wasn't her phone. It was Gerry's.

"You've got to answer that," she whispered.

"No, I don't."

She sat up. "Gerry. Check Caller ID at least. It might be Sabrina."

He took a deep breath. She knew that his loyalty to his sister would get through to him. She loved him all the more for it. But she also treasured how he took hold of her hand while reaching for his phone, as if he didn't want anything separating them from their special moments together. He picked it up and glanced at it.

"Whoa!" he said when he saw who was calling. "This could be good news!" he shared with her as he opened the connection. The hopeful expectancy on his face made the resemblance between him and his eight-year-old nephew stand out. She knew then what Gerry had looked like as a young boy. She smiled at the image. He really wasn't all that different today.

"James! What's the good word?" Aimee could feel, even before Gerry spoke again, that the word from "James" was indeed good. "That's terrific news! Thanks for calling." A pause. "Are you kidding? You could've called me at 3:00 a.m. with this news!" He gave Aimee a wink and an excited nod before answering James. "Believe me, it couldn't have come at a better time. I have just the person with me I want to celebrate with," He squeezed Aimee's hand, and she tilted her head in question. *What was going on?* Aimee couldn't wait to find out.

Gerry ended the call as the clock tower could be heard through the pounding of the rain, ringing out the hour of nine.

He picked her up from the sofa and spun her around the room. Cynthia leaped up and started barking in delight, while Aimee found herself squealing just as Pattie and Benji had earlier that day when they were jumping into the leaves. Aimee felt like a kid again and loved it. "Gerry! What is it?"

Putting her down and looking at her with what she knew was love, he said, "You are my lady full of blessings, that's what." As he rubbed his fingertips over her face, his eyes were bright with relief.

"I am?" *She'd never been called that before! She hoped he'd always feel that way about her.*

He held up the phone. "Other than wanting to be close to Sabrina and the kids after Logan, Sabrina's husband, left which was shortly after my ex's adverse actions toward my business in California, the main financial reason I felt I could make such a drastic move and transfer my Cakerie to Connecticut was that I'd been more or less assured of a contract with a major supermarket chain if I did." He gestured with his phone. "That was the CEO of the company."

Cold surged through Aimee's body. CEO? James? *James! James Monroe*?

She stood back from him. Did he mean *her* contract? *No! No! This couldn't be happening!* Gerry continued, too excited to notice her shock. "When James happened into my California store last year and found out I was originally from Connecticut, he suggested I try to secure a very lucrative contract with his company. When I later found out that Sabrina's best friend is James's sister-in-law, well, she put in a good word for me, and it might have been…the icing on the cake. So to speak…" he added with a grin. "That's the reason I had to open a shop on a Main Street in a New England state—it's called Main Street

Bakery and it's with—" He stopped speaking. His eyes narrowed in concern. "Aimee? What's wrong?"

Her phone rang. Holding her hand up, she stepped away from him and over to her purse. Gerry followed.

"Aimee?"

Her hands started shaking as she fished the phone out of her bag. She looked at the screen. It was Lizzy Edwards. She answered it. Somehow, she managed to speak. "Hi, Lizzy."

"Aimee," Lizzy said, and then began talking a mile a minute as if trying to get what she had to tell her out of the way. "I'm so sorry to have to inform you that Northeast Supermarket has decided to go with another bakery. I didn't expect it. I honestly thought you had the contract. It's no reflection on your product. The other bakery has a product that the members of the board believe will have a wider appeal to our customers. More…American. It has larger facilities, too, so they can supply our needs immediately. The owner also proved his desire for the contract to our CEO, James Monroe, by moving his business from California to Connecticut, his home state, to be eligible. Mr. Monroe liked that. A lot." She finally paused. But Aimee didn't say anything. Couldn't say anything. "I'm truly sorry, Aimee," Lizzy repeated. "But you know how it goes. It's just business."

There it was again! That terrible expression! "It's just business." Would it always haunt her? "Thank you, Lizzy." Aimee somehow managed to break through the paralysis that was threatening to overtake her and spoke politely. "I appreciate everything you've done."

Lizzy continued to speak, but Aimee didn't hear a word she said as her own mind screamed, *"No! It's happening again! And because of Gerry this time!"* Gerry, the man she loved with all her woman's heart. She had only herself to blame. She'd pushed aside rule number one—romantic entanglements and the trust they required only resulted in making a woman weak, foolish and hurt. She'd given her heart free rein, and here she was. Duped by a man again! But this was worse, a million times worse, than Timothy. This was Gerry. She loved Gerry in a way that didn't come close to the feelings she'd had for Timothy.

No, she didn't. Her heart instantly hardened. *She hated Gerry! Hated him!* Timothy had only humiliated her. Gerry's crimes were worse, much worse. He had stolen her heart *and* her grand-mère's seventy-year-old business. The day Gerry moved to *her* town, *her* Main Street, had meant the end of all her dreams, not the beginning as she'd talked herself into believing.

But Lizzy was continuing to speak, and Aimee forced herself to listen. "Let's get together for lunch sometime. And maybe in the future—" Lizzy let the insinuation that they might form a business relationship at some undefined distant time dangle. But as Aimee murmured a vague answer and somehow managed to say good-bye and end the connection, she knew that any moment past this one wasn't something she could think about.

There was no future. Not for the Patisserie. Not for Gerry and her.

Those dreams were dead. Dashed. Gone.

And the insidious thought formed in her mind… Through his personal and private connections with the CEO of Northeast Supermarket—the one he'd made with James Monroe last year and the one he had through his sister—had Gerry known all along that she was his competition for the contract? And if so, why hadn't he told her?

It did occur to her that she'd said nothing, either, but why would she? For one thing, she hadn't seen Gerry as a threat to the contract—he'd just moved to town. For another...she'd been thinking of other things when she was around Gerry—direct sells and most silly of all, her attraction to him—and...it just hadn't come up.

Although she hadn't gone out of her way to tell others about her bid for the supermarket contract—she had in fact downplayed her need for it—it wasn't top secret either, not like the financial mess the Patisserie was in. So if he hadn't heard from James Monroe that she was in the running for the contract, he'd surely found out through the town grapevine.

When the bell on the clock tower had tolled nine, and Gerry answered his phone, her whole world changed. She would never be able to hear the chime of the clock again without thinking about it. The Patisserie would soon become Stoneybridge's Play Ball Sports Bar and Gerry, the man she loved, had stolen not only her heart but her dream of being able to repay Uncle Cain and keep Grand-mère's Patisserie. Gerry had destroyed her on multiple levels.

And with that, the thought that it had been Gerry's mission all along worked its poison though her body. Gerry had kept his real reason for moving to *her* Main Street a secret. How he must have been laughing at her with his baking buddies. Here she'd been afraid he'd take away her direct business when all along, all along... *It was the contract with Northeast Supermarket Chain that he was after!*

She felt tears of rage rise within her...

Her contract!

Had all the words of love, of caring, just been a ploy to keep her distracted?

Definitely! Those poisonous thoughts answered her. *What else?* If she hadn't been distracted she would have done better. She would have given her menu a more American appeal. She would have—

"Aimee?" As if it came from a million miles away, she heard his voice. *The voice of a traitor, an imposter!* She would've preferred him to *be* a million miles away. In California, at least. She couldn't look at him.

All she could think was—

Bathroom!

She had to get to it. *Fast!* The supper Gerry had cooked for her wasn't going to digest.

Clutching her stomach, she doubled over and ran toward it. She slammed the door in his face, and just managed to lock it before turning and heaving up all the food—and all the lies Gerry had been telling her for the last several weeks. The lies of omission he'd woven around her heart that had made her lower her guard. Never mind that she hadn't told him about the sought-after contract. Again, why would she? She hadn't changed her entire life and moved across the country to go after it. No. That was what *he'd* done. He'd moved to *her* world, *her* Stoneybridge, *her* Main Street and he had destroyed her life.

Uncle Cain, Timothy, Gerry. There was no difference, none at all. She should have known better than to trust a man again.

17—Broken Hearts, Broken Dreams

"Aimee!" Gerry pounded on the door. "Are you all right? What's going on?" At first, as Gerry stood outside the bathroom door, totally shocked at the turn of events, and listened to Aimee moaning and gagging, he had no idea what had just happened.

But as he started to put together the various pieces of the last few minutes, the insidious thought formed in his mind. Had Aimee been going after the same Main Street contract? Had *she* been his major contender?

But she couldn't have been. She was all about small and elegant, dainty and quaint, with old family recipes that he seriously doubted she would want to share with the world.

The idea that she'd been in the running for the same contract was preposterous.

And yet…what other explanation could there be? He'd seen her Caller ID. He knew who Lizzy Edwards was. What else *could* it be? But no, the idea was absurd, he told himself again. The coincidence was just too great to be a real possibility. It had to be something else.

"Aimee, please…" He felt helpless. He wanted to knock the door down. He could easily do that. But he quickly crushed the caveman instinct and forced himself to stand back and wait. It was the hardest two minutes of his life.

When Cynthia sidled up to him whimpering, he knelt down. "I don't know exactly what's wrong, girl. But I'll fix it. I promise." He stood as he heard the *click* of the door being unlocked.

"You can't fix it," Aimee said as she opened the door. Her voice was soft but not her tone. The whites of her eyes were red and there wasn't even the hint of a sparkle in her brown irises. Her face was pale. But still, she wore dignity and pride, character traits he suspected she'd inherited from her remarkable parents and grandparents. Her heart seemed to be breaking, and yet, her grace remained. He admired her—loved her—for it. And also for the way she knelt down to reassure his dog.

"It's okay, girl. But I've got to go home now."

"Aimee, what exactly is wrong?" She was in agony, and he didn't know how to help, what to say.

She stood and looked at him. She might as well have reached out and slapped him. Hatred burned in her eyes, as did that intense pain he'd seen the first time she'd come to his shop. His heart felt as if it had dropped straight to his stomach. He wanted to take her in his arms, tell her that whatever it was, if it was indeed about the contract, they would work it out. He wanted to tell her to trust him, trust their love and give it a chance. But her words, her ridged posture, didn't allow that.

"As if you don't know," she ground out, and dismay touched by anger worked its way around his shoulders, around the muscles in his jaw.

He tilted his head upward. She didn't realize it, but she was echoing the very same words Scarlett had spoken to him when they'd broken up. Using every ounce of willpower he had, he only asked, "What do you mean?" He needed to find out precisely what he was dealing with.

"You were just told that you were awarded the Northeast Supermarket Chain's Main Street Bakery contract. Right?"

He nodded. Until a few minutes ago, he'd thought that was cause for celebration. With her.

"The future of the Patisserie depended on *my* winning that contract," she said and Gerry felt as if he'd just been clipped by a fast-moving Harley.

"I was under the impression that you owned the Patisserie outright. I thought your grand-mère passed the business on to you."

"She did." She wouldn't look at him. "But the storm last year, coupled with the worldwide lockdown—"

Storm damages on top of the lockdown. He got it. A double hit for a small business. "I didn't know."

"I took a loan from my Uncle Cain."

Uncle Cain! He'd figured there was a lot more to that story than she'd told him. He should've insisted on learning what it was. The man might not have physically abused her—and for that Gerry was grateful—but he'd gone after her business. Hadn't Scarlett done something similar to him?

"Due date is the day before Thanksgiving. If I don't pay him back every single cent by five, he'll take the Patisserie from me. He's going to—" she started hyperventilating, still looking anywhere but at him "—turn it into a Play Ball Sports Bar. I needed…the contract…with the supermarket—"

"—to repay him," Gerry finished. And he knew what he had to do. "Don't worry, Aimee. You'll get the contract." He walked back into the living room and reached for his phone. "I'll pull out." He loved her. There was no question of his taking the contract now. Online sales had improved. He would manage.

She ran up from behind him and with the skill of a linebacker blitzing a quarterback, she snatched the phone from his fingers. "Do you honestly…" She tried to take a deep breath, but only managed shallow ones. "Do you honestly," she repeated, "expect me…to believe…that you didn't know I was in the running for it?"

If she'd slapped him physically, it couldn't have stung more. "What exactly are you accusing me of?" He fought to keep his voice calm. But accusation had returned to her tone, her stance, and he no longer saw Aimee but Scarlett, accusing him of things that fit no logical pattern.

"You found out either from James Monroe or through talk around town that I was going after the contract. Then you orchestrated everything to persuade me to let my guard down, so I wouldn't get it."

He ignored the James Monroe and town grapevine comments—which he really didn't understand. He'd certainly never heard she'd applied for the contract from either source. Instead he went straight to the more important statement. "What do you mean by 'orchestrated'?" This was personal. This was between them. He was beginning to believe that it was a problem he might not be able to "fix" by refusing the contract. There was something much deeper going on here, something that had to be addressed if they were ever to have a future together. "Orchestrated what?" he repeated.

"Why did you ask me out on our first date the day before the presentation? I mean, any time within the last few weeks would have done. But no, the day *before* the presentation you took me out and—"

In that instant he saw what had happened. Because of one phone call and because of a situation that could have been logically explained, Aimee had defaulted to what she'd believed of him in the beginning. Back then, she'd thought he'd come to steal her business on Main Street. Now she was accusing him of—falsifying his love for her in order to win a contract? *A contract?* Seriously, what was wrong with women these days? Was business all they thought about? First Scarlett, now Aimee. He'd been so sure Aimee was different, that she hated the "It's just business" attitude as much as he did.

He'd had enough... Two women he'd expected to spend his life with... Two women who had disappointed him beyond measure.

No, that wasn't true. He'd known where he stood with Scarlett. Deep down, he knew—even then—that he'd been trying to turn her into something she didn't want to be. A wife with a doting husband, a mother, and a traditional family. He'd never had a problem with her need to work, to maintain a successful career, but he'd hoped marriage and family would be *at least* as important.

But Aimee was different. She wanted the same type of life he did—dogs, cats, a house with a white-picket fence, kids, and their shops on Main Street in a small town. *This* small town. She was the one reneging on their dreams, dreams that were still so new, so fragile, not much more than a wisp of mist. But that didn't matter. They were real, those dreams, and if she hadn't stopped trusting him, they would have grown, matured, become their intermingled lives. He took a deep breath. He had one card to play. He hoped it would work. He'd vowed never to beg, but Aimee and their love was worth it. "For us to be neighbors on Main Street, Aimee Hart, there has to be trust. Please." He repeated what she'd said to him that first week. "Trust me."

She blanched. If possible, even more color left her face as her eyes darted to meet his. "How dare you throw my words to you in my face? *You* are the one who broke *my* trust."

He looked deeply at her and shook his head. "I didn't." She might not believe him, but he had to defend himself from such a false accusation. "As God is my witness, I had no idea that the Patisserie was the company Uncle Gerry's Cakerie was in competition with to win the contract." There. He'd said it in plain English. "You never told me."

"You never told *me* that was the reason you moved here, either! That was a lie by omission. You led me to believe it was because of Sabrina, your niece and nephew and Scarlett's attack on your LA business. You *never* mentioned that another reason you moved back to Connecticut was because the CEO of Northeast Supermarkets—the CEO!—encouraged you to apply for the contract."

He could see where her anger was coming from. He could even understand it, to some degree, anyway. And because he had a good example to follow in his father about how to treat the woman he loved—his dad always cleared up misunderstandings with his mother before things got out of hand, even when she was being unreasonable—Gerry tried again. "Aimee, I honestly didn't know you were my major contender for the contract. I will pull out."

"I'm not a charity case!"

"It has nothing to do with charity, you stubborn woman!" He raked his hand through his hair. Had he ever felt more frustrated? "But even if it did, who cares? I love you. I'd do anything for you."

"Anything?"

"Anything." He would.

She grabbed her purse, threw her jacket over her shoulders and went to the door. "Then leave me alone, Gerry Mitchell." She opened the door. It was cold and biting and unrelenting outside, just like their argument…

Pausing for a moment, she dragged in a breath before running pell-mell out into the storm.

Gerry pounded over the parquet floor to the coffee table and grabbed his car keys. "Aimee!" He ran outside, Cynthia beside him, keeping pace. "Let me give you a ride home!" he shouted after her. The wind and the freezing rain lashed against his bare arms. But he hardly felt it. He splashed through the icy puddles and quickly caught up with her. As gently as he could, he reached for her hand. "Aimee! Don't leave like this!" he begged. He hated pleading with her again, but he loved her despite his disappointment, so begging could be forgiven. It was a misunderstanding, and misunderstandings had to be worked out. He had to make things right with her. Just like his dad always did with his mother and his mother with his dad. It wasn't about who was right and who was wrong. It was about love; real, true, everlasting love. And that meant working through the problem. And not giving up.

She flung his hand away and turned to him. The fury in her face made the ice storm screaming around them seem like a light summer shower. "You are a *thief*, Gerry Mitchell," she spat out. "And I hate how your being here in Stoneybridge has affected my life. I wish you'd never moved here. Just…go away!" she shouted and turning, she ran down the walkway and through the gate of his white-picket fence. Shock kept him motionless as he watched her disappear into the dark of the stormy night.

When his shirt was soaked through and his arms as numb from the cold as his soul was from Aimee's words, Cynthia's whimpering finally got through to him. He turned, and taking mechanical steps, let his dog shepherd him back to the house.

He stepped through the door and as Cynthia went directly to the fireplace, he slammed the door so hard that the golden-bronze American eagle ornament hanging above the door fell, breaking in half.

Just like his heart.

18—Goodness and Mercy

Four days later, Gerry dropped off the cupcakes at Pattie's school. After watching a whole class of fifth-graders shout and jump around in delight about the treats, he and Sabrina made their escape. Coffee in hand, they went to sit in the warmth of her car for a few minutes before they continued with their busy days. Gerry had called his sister on Monday and told her what had happened.

"So, any progress with Aimee?" she asked, and with the joy of a busy mother, took a deep, long and grateful sip of the cappuccino Gerry had bought her.

"No. Haven't seen her since Sunday night. Very early Monday morning—" *before their usual 6:00 a.m. tryst, which, of course, Aimee didn't keep* "—she nailed a sign on the door of the Patisserie saying 'After seventy years, due to financial reasons, the Patisserie will be permanently closing its doors on Monday, November 25. We have loved being part of Main Street and your lives.'" He waved his hand. "She left the store in Becky's hands until then and disappeared."

"She's not living in her apartment upstairs?"

"Oh, yeah. That's where she is. All the time. She doesn't come out. Doesn't talk to anyone."

Sabrina's eyes flashed over at him. "I can't believe you aren't trying to convince her she's wrong about you."

"What else can I do? I don't want to be accused of stalking. She's already accused me of being a thief."

"Is that what you think love is, Gerry? As soon as things get a little hard—a few stupid and hurtful things are said—you pull out?" Her voice was rising louder with each word she spoke. "That's what Logan did, too! Besides, you *did* steal the contract from her! You are a thief," she said and punched his arm. Hard.

He shrugged his arm away and, as if they were five-and eight-year-olds again, shouted back. "She never told me about it!" *Were all women so illogical? Even his sister?* "How can I steal something I didn't know about?" He was totally frustrated by this catch-22.

"I need to fill you in on a few facts, Gerry," Sabrina returned heatedly as their angry breath fogged the windows of the car. "My friend Bonnie told me that Aimee *would* have won the contract if you hadn't been in the picture. They liked the fact that the Patisserie is so old, so established and came complete with ancient family recipes in the art of French patisserie baking. But Bonnie's brother-in-law, the head honcho, liked your concept better and, even more, the fact that *he* found you." She paused, taking a deep breath, and he could see that she was forcing herself to speak more quietly. "James Monroe's ego was involved. He wanted *his* person in, not his colleague's choice."

That would be Lizzy Edwards, Aimee's contact with the chain. "If this is supposed to make me feel worse, sis," he moaned, "you've succeeded." Throwing his head back against the headrest, he closed his eyes and let out a frustrated groan. Confirmation that by moving to Connecticut he *had* stolen the contract from Aimee made him feel miserable; it made his guilt level increase astronomically. He'd ruined the life of the last person in the world he wanted to hurt.

"Do you still love her?" Sabrina asked.

His eyes popped open. "What a dumb question, Sabrina!" he exploded in that universal way only siblings can and still remain close. "Of course, I do! You can't turn love on and off!"

"Good answer." Sabrina was completely calm again, her normal state of mind. All their lives she'd get him to face issues, then be as calm as a cat relaxing in the sun.

The funny thing was how her attitude always helped calm him down. Just as it did now. He could feel his pulse slowing, his breathing too.

"Next question," Sabrina said, her voice soft. "Why? What is it about Aimee that makes you love her?" She grimaced. "And please don't be totally male and only mention the obvious physical reasons." She held up her hand as he started to speak. "No. Don't tell me. Think about it for a moment. Your own private thoughts. Between you and God," she qualified with a smile, and leaning her head back, she closed her eyes.

Gerry smiled at his sister. She was good at recognizing the main point and coming up with the simplest, clearest analysis of a situation. With his elbow, he rubbed the side window clear and looked out. The fall colors, in the form of leaves from the profusion of deciduous Connecticut trees, were dancing to the ground with each gust of wind—gold, red and crimson bits of foliage floating through the sky. It was fall magic, and with that as a backdrop, he did as his sister asked. He thought.

Why did he love Aimee? Despite her saying such terrible things...such destructive things...

The image of her gently placing Louis in his treehouse and giving Cynthia a treat every day came immediately to mind. Then he recalled how little Tommy Floyd drank his milk at her café and nowhere else; how loyal Becky was to her; Miss Maggie's love for her; and how all the townspeople adored her.

Did he love her? Dear Lord, yes. For better or worse, he did. Totally, with all his heart.

Okay, that established, what else did he love about her?

How she loved the Patisserie and kept her grand-mère's memory so alive that even he, a man who had never met the founder of the pastry store, felt as if he knew her. He loved how Aimee arranged the trays at the Patisserie with perfect Parisian charm, everything just so.

And how fiercely protective she was of Stoneybridge, its history and its people. Her strong sense of right and wrong. Her people skills, and her determination.

He grimaced. *Determination.* That was the very character trait he was up against now. He actually loved it? Was he crazy?

Okay. Moving on. What else?

He loved how she treated the people around her; who she was on the inside, the soul and spirit of her, her firm belief in God. She had told him one evening at her door that her favorite Psalm was number 23. He sent up a prayer then and there that she might apply it to her life at this difficult and unsure time, and let the God-breathed words of peace and comfort heal her, heal her anger. He silently spoke verses 1, 2 and 6 to himself. *"The Lord is my shepherd; I shall not want. He maketh me to lie down in green pastures: he leadeth me beside the still waters... Surely goodness and mercy shall follow me all the days of my life: and I will dwell in the house of the Lord forever."*

He smiled. Those blessed words definitely made him feel better. *Green pastures*...like the one where they'd played with the Frisbee by the Old Stone Bridge. Beautiful, calming, rejuvenating words. *Still waters*... He took another deep breath and let it out slowly. *Still waters*... He felt his own emotions calming as he meditated on the words. He wanted Aimee to experience the same peace of mind, that "life in pink" feeling the Édith Piaf song described. He understood that it wasn't his place to try to heal her; it was his place to love her and pray for her, pray for her to experience calm and to find a way out of this seemingly impossible situation. He would give up the supermarket contract in a heartbeat. But he knew now that wasn't the answer to the problem; it would be like putting a Band-Aid over a cut that needed surgery.

What else did he love about her?

How easily she'd befriended his niece and nephew, his sister, his parents.

Sabrina was right. Her lovely outer package was a bonus—her ponytail, her bright brown eyes that usually shone with welcome and intelligence, the dimple that flashed to the left of her mouth when she was happy and on both sides when she was doubly happy.

In truth, was there anything about Aimee that he *didn't* love?

Yes, two things—when she'd jumped to the conclusion that he'd somehow masterminded stealing the contract from her, and the fact that she'd called him a thief.

A thief. Him! He might be many things but, by the grace of God, he had never knowingly stolen from another.

But did that mean he never had? According to his sister, apparently it didn't.

It appeared that, just by moving to Stoneybridge's Main Street—Aimee's territory—he'd stolen the contract out from under her.

He glanced over at Sabrina. As she had so succinctly pointed out, lack of knowledge didn't necessarily place him in either the right or the wrong, rather, in a gray area. He certainly hadn't intended to hurt Aimee or her business. But he had.

Sabrina, sensing his gaze on her, suddenly opened her eyes, making him jump just as she'd done when they were kids. "So, did you figure out what you love about Aimee?"

"Everything *except* her jumping to conclusions and calling me a thief. She hurt me, sis."

The seat leather creaked as Sabrina sat up. "You're a big guy, Gerry. Get over it. Please. Believe me, she didn't mean it."

He saw his sister then in a way he realized he'd never seen her before, as a woman trying to deal with her own romantic heartache. "Is this personal experience talking? That sure sounded like an apology. Maybe one you want to be making to Logan," he gently suggested.

Sabrina nodded. "It is. If I could only take back the things I said to him. Mean things, much worse than being a thief. Things a woman should never say to her husband of eleven years." She forced a wobbly smile and punched his shoulder, but it was friendly this time. "Maybe Aimee's wishing she could take back some of her words, too."

"You think?"

Sabrina nodded. "She was in shock. And tired." She guffawed and rolled her eyes. "She'd just spent the afternoon with my two, don't forget! They're enough to sap the energy out of a prairie dog on steroids!"

"Don't I know it," he agreed.

"There must be *something* you can do to show her how much you really love her, and how sorry you are for your part in her losing the Patisserie."

The words "losing the Patisserie" rang in his head.

Losing the Patisserie?

Wait... Aimee *hadn't* lost the Patisserie. Not yet.

The actual loss was still in the future. At this moment, on this day, and for the next six days, the Patisserie was still hers.

Did that mean the future had to remain the way it seemed to be shaping up? Did she have to walk into the upcoming week as it now stood and say a final good-bye to the Patisserie? Because of something as simple as needing the funds to repay the loan she'd taken from her uncle?

They lived in Connecticut. It was one of the wealthiest areas of the country. And it wasn't just about *Aimee,* but about the people of Stoneybridge—the *community*—having to go on without that special store and café.

That was it! They were still almost a week away from that terrible occurrence. Aimee didn't have to lose the Patisserie and neither did Stoneybridge nor Main Street. Not if he—not if the *town*—could help. He was propelled into motion as a thought, the germ of an idea, started forming in his brain.

"Ha! Ha!" He leaned over and kissed his sister's cheek. "You're brilliant, sis! Brilliant!"

"Tell that to my kids," she groaned.

"I think I know what I can do..." He opened the door. He had to get back to Stoneybridge. He had to go see Mayor Brown. "And I think it'll work!"

"Go for it, Gerry." Sabrina sent him off with a huge smile. "As long as it doesn't get you arrested!"

***

It was the day before Thanksgiving. Wednesday, November 27th. Aimee's favorite day of the year.

But not this year.

The clock in the tower chimed nine, and she cringed. She hated hearing it. But soon she'd hate the toll of five even more. When it rang five times this afternoon, the Patisserie would be no more.

Uncle Cain and Grasping Gertrude would finally have the prize they'd been after since Grand-mère died. The coveted storefront property on Main Street would be theirs. In just eight hours, Aimee would never again have the right to come in here as the owner.

It wasn't so much the property as it was the Patisserie itself, the magic of the store and its history in her family.

"*Meow…*" Louis called to her as he rubbed his sleek body against her leg.

Reaching down, she patted his upturned head. A purr was bubbling out of him. "Well, the only good thing about closing the store last Monday was that I've been able to bring you here with me every day, little friend. No county health restrictions to worry about, now that our Patisserie isn't open for business."

"*Meow…*" he replied, walking over to the door and looking up at the handle. Aimee knew he wanted to go out to his treehouse. He was a cat who could count. With the chiming of the clock, he knew that was where she should be putting him now. But she hadn't put him there in a week and two days.

Had it really been over a week since that Sunday evening when the course of her life had changed so drastically? When she'd done everything she could to kill her dreams?

Over a week since that stormy night when she'd spat out those mean and unforgivable words to Gerry…

How could she ever meet him again?

She'd claimed to love him, and yet she'd failed the very first test of their love.

Failed it miserably.

She felt close to tears as she remembered accusing him of things she wouldn't charge her worst enemy with. But she'd had no problem throwing them at the man she loved. Still loved. With all her heart.

"What is wrong with me? Maybe my heart just isn't big enough to let me love, *really* love." She lowered her head and resting her face in her hands, exhaled resignedly into her palms. She gently shook her head; it was something she'd done a lot this past week. She was so embarrassed. How had she said those things to Gerry, said those awful words of accusation?

Added to how she'd treated him was her mortification over losing Stoneybridge's Patisserie to Uncle Cain.

How could she ever face her friends and neighbors again? Knowing that, unlike Grand-mère, she'd let them all down, lost the seventy-year-old, beloved Patisserie, after only two years of running it. Grand-mère had run it successfully for nearly seven decades.

She was a failure; in love, to her community and to her grand-mère's memory.

Talk about being the town fool. She didn't need any assistance from Timothy this time. She'd managed it all on her own.

She knew they were talking about her. She'd watched from behind the lace curtains upstairs as people whispered together and cast furtive glances in the direction of her apartment. But she also knew she deserved it. She owed them all an explanation.

She should have listened to Becky. She should've told the townspeople about how the lockdown, coming on top of storm damage, had placed her in a dire financial position. She should've trusted her neighbors and friends to help her.

She should have trusted Gerry.

It was only during this last week of thinking and praying, and for the first time in her adult life just being still, totally still, for hours on end, that she'd realized the townspeople hadn't been talking about her in a bad manner after Timothy's defection. What she'd thought of as being nosy and uncaring had actually been, as Becky tried to tell her, concern and love. They'd been *sympathizing* with her, not gossiping about her. They'd all loved her just as a family should love one of its own. Grand-mère had raised her with the idea that their Main Street neighbors were family.

She'd finally came to understand, after days of not having anything to do but just *be,* that it was time to treat them as family. To trust them as a person has to trust family members over and over again, no matter what.

She recognized now that was what she'd actually done with Uncle Cain when she'd asked him for the loan. She'd been hoping that for once he'd be the relative she so yearned him to be—an uncle who acted the way Gerry did with his niece and nephew. She'd held a deep, hidden hope that needing him for his mother's Patisserie might finally draw them together. Never mind that it hadn't and that he wasn't anything like Gerry was with his sister's kids. The fact that she'd *tried,* even at the cost of the Patisserie, was the important thing. She knew her grand-mère would agree. Hadn't she made an effort to connect with her son when, at the age of ninety, she'd travelled into New York City to see him? It didn't matter that she hadn't seen him. She'd tried.

Aimee might not be able to keep the Patisserie, or have the good relationship with her uncle she'd always wished for, but she had a plan where her association with her Main Street family was concerned.

She was going to take a few beloved things from the Patisserie today—she'd already collected all of Grand-mère's recipe books, and Bob had transferred the matching *fauteuils* to her apartment at four that morning. At five this afternoon, she was going to hand the keys over to Uncle Cain. After Thanksgiving weekend she'd spend the week going from store to store on *her* Main Street, because it would always be hers—to apologize for not trusting her neighbors enough to tell them the truth about her financial problems.

But that was next week.

Tonight, she was going to the store next door.

Tonight, she would apologize to Gerry.

Once again, she exhaled a shallow breath into her hands.

She was going to ask for his forgiveness over and over again until he accepted.

Whenever she thought about calling that wonderful and caring man a thief, she was mortified. She knew he'd had no idea that she was trying for the same contract. She also knew that had he known, he would've pulled out. For her. He'd already offered to do so.

Twice.

She had to make things right with him, she had to—

The sound of hammering and banging outside the Patisserie's front door broke through her thoughts. She lowered her hands and tilted her head to the side just as Cynthia might.

"Meow, meow, meow." Louis heard the noise, too. He wanted out. Now. He rubbed his body against the door. When that

didn't get Aimee to open it, he jumped up on the window display case, which used to be covered with an assortment of her specialty pastries, and maneuvered his head under the drawn blinds to see what was going on.

The sound of people, lots of people, could now be heard.

Aimee wanted to see what was going on, too.

When she reached the window, she twisted the blind, just enough to peek out.

A very strange sight greeted her eyes.

19—Thanksgiving Eve

Main Street was setting up for a street fair!

Even the traffic had been rerouted. She could see Bob down at one end redirecting vehicles and his deputies at the other. All the shops were setting up stands outside their stores, while Stoneybridge East High School's marching band had gathered in the little park on the other side of Hale's Hardware.

What's going on?

There'd never been a street fair on the day before Thanksgiving. Normally, the weather was too cold. But after a week of bitter weather, one of Grand-mère's "Postcards from Florida" days had arrived in Stoneybridge.

"*Meow*!" Louis scooted out from behind the blind and leaped over to the door.

"You want to go out, little fella?"

"*Meow*," he answered with a blink.

Aimee decided then and there that the fair was providential. Rather than waiting until next week to apologize and explain things to her neighbors and friends, she would do so now. "Me, too," she told her feline friend. After all, the Patisserie might be lost to her, but she still lived on Main Street. She didn't like the idea of Uncle Cain's sports bar being below her, in what should be the Patisserie. But moving wasn't an option. The apartment was her home. She loved living on Stoneybridge's Main Street too much to be driven away from both the Patisserie and her home. Thankfully, her apartment wasn't legally or financially connected to the Patisserie. It was hers. She wouldn't lose it to Uncle Cain.

Reaching down, she scooped Louis into her arms, unlocked the door and opened it. She walked out into the bright sunny day.

The people on Main Street stopped what they were doing and turned to her. Miss Maggie, Mrs. Fonteyn, Pam, Hale, Lucy, Valery, Bob, Becky, the four pastors…everyone.

Her eyes locked with Becky's.

Becky skipped over to her. "Hey, girl! So glad you finally decided to join us. We've been out here setting up for the last hour."

Hour? "Becky?" She spoke under her breath as she let Louis crawl up into his tree house. "What's going on?"

Becky didn't follow her lead in speaking softly. Loudly, so everyone could hear, she told Aimee, "Everybody knows about the loan that has to be repaid to your uncle today, Aimee. And," she quickly continued, obviously so Aimee wouldn't have time to object to her personal business being made public. Aimee smiled. Becky didn't know about her decision to explain everything to everyone. "The town's decided to do something about it."

Aimee shook her head. *What? The town… Do something about… What? Her loan?*

"The town doesn't want to lose the Patisserie, Aimee," Mrs. Fonteyn explained, walking up to her. "Or it's lovely proprietress."

"That's right." Miss Maggie said. "The Patisserie's been part of Stoneybridge for as long as most of us can remember—"

"Yeah," Bob shouted above everybody's heads from about thirty feet away. "It's almost as old as the bridge." People laughed.

"Except," Miss Maggie went on, "we all knew and loved your dear grand-mère who first opened it—"

"—but some of us only know—and very much *love*—her granddaughter," Gerry said as he walked out of the store next door, *his* store next door.

Aimee's gaze flew to his.

Love? He still loved her? He loved her even after the terrible things she'd accused him of? Aimee squinted as she tried to penetrate the shade cast by the brim of his cowboy hat, which sat low on his forehead, hiding his eyes. He tilted his head upward, removing the shadow. Was that love she saw in his expressive eyes? Yes, it was! He'd never looked better to Aimee, not even on that wonderful first Monday when she'd thought he was just a cowboy…just passing through town. Feelings that were strong yet fiercely tender surged through her.

"Gerry," she whispered. She felt tears forming and blinked. *I'm so sorry,* her gaze said to him.

I know, his eyes returned, and he smiled that giving smile she loved so much. Aimee thought she'd collapse from sheer relief. Thinking she'd lost Gerry was even worse than losing the Patisserie. Out-of-the-solar-system worse. Did she dare believe that he'd actually found it in his big heart to forgive her? And that maybe, just maybe, they could…together…find that elusive "life in pink"? As she considered the possibility, she felt her knees almost give out.

Becky wrapped her arm around Aimee's shoulder, such an intuitive friend that she always seemed to know when Aimee needed support. "The people of this town have decided to do something about saving the Patisserie," she said again and motioned to Mayor Brown.

The mayor was a recent widower, so he knew a thing or two about sorrow. It was one of the qualities that made him such a good mayor. Everyone understood that when difficult situations could be fixed through human effort, he was the man to get it done.

He hopped up onto the wooden crate Otis quickly supplied. After clearing his throat, he spoke in a deep voice that easily carried down the length of Main Street. He'd lived in town for the past six years, five of them married to one of Stoneybridge's own, so almost no one had trouble with his strong Southern accent anymore. "Gerry Mitchell—" he nodded over at Gerry "—came to me last Thursday and told me about a loan you had to repay today, Aimee." He looked at her and, stretching out his hand, asking for hers, pulled her up to stand next to him on the crate. "He said that otherwise the Patisserie would become just one more footnote in Stoneybridge's very long history. So, a town meetin' was immediately called. It was unanimously decided by all your friends and neighbors here on Main Street—" he waved his arm to include them all "—that today would be Save the Patisserie Day."

"Save the Patisserie Day," Aimee repeated. After spending the last week coming to grips with the idea of losing the Patisserie, it was almost too much to comprehend that she might *not* lose it after all...

"Today everyone's selling the best of the merchandise in their stores," the mayor explained. "Fifty percent of all proceeds will be given to the Patisserie, so that when your uncle arrives at five o'clock this afternoon, you will have the funds—or at least a good chunk of them—to repay him."

Aimee knew her mouth had to be hanging open, but she couldn't help it.

So this is how it feels to be flabbergasted!

She was speechless, astonished, happier than she could ever remember being. She looked out over Main Street and saw a sea of smiling faces and encouraging nods. The good feelings coming from every corner of the street warmed her heart. "I…don't know what to say…"

But the mayor, never at a loss for words, did. "Your friends and neighbors realized, Aimee, that since the Patisserie is one of the oldest stores on Main Street, if we let it go without at least tryin' to save it, next thing you know, the rest of the stores will be gobbled up by so-called progress, not to mention storms and other circumstances beyond our control—such as the pandemic that has forced shops to close down for several extended periods of time. Our historical Main Street would join many others in towns across America that have lost their character to big-city architects, franchises, malls and…greedy people. By being friendly and neighborly and helping the Patisserie today—" the mayor turned to speak to the people "—everyone knows that they're actually helpin' themselves, too. It's all part of keepin' Stoneybridge's Main Street alive, well and in the hands of individuals, not corporations."

As all the townspeople nodded at the mayor and at one another, and murmured their agreement, Aimee's eyes found Gerry's. He'd said something similar to her the day of the Halloween bake-off. She smiled at him. *Were those the words you used to convince the town to help the Patisserie?* she asked with a tilt of her head. He nodded slightly. She knew they were.

Turning back to Aimee, Mayor Brown continued, "This fair has been advertised far and wide as a one-stop place to get everything needed for Thanksgivin' dinner." The Mayor gestured toward the food stands. "Even fully-prepared, homemade Thanksgivin' dinners contributed by Joe's Diner and the Maple Tree B&B."

"And also, as a good place to do Christmas shopping," Miss Maggie, never one to miss an opportunity, shouted to the delight of all.

"That's right," the mayor agreed. "But most importantly, it's a time for our community to come together and to give thanks to God above that we're in a position to help one of our own." He motioned at Aimee, and she knew it was her turn to speak.

Once again tears prickled Aimee's eyes as she glanced at the mayor, at Gerry—who had made this happen—and then out over all the people who were sharing their talent and their time for her and the Patisserie on this, her favorite day of the year. Opening her arms wide, she spoke the words that her grand-mère, paragon of charm and decorum, might have said. "Thank you all very much. With my heart full and feeling as if it might burst with joy, I accept your help, your wonderful offer, with much gratitude and…thanksgiving."

Everyone cheered and when Bob, using his megaphone, shouted, "The train's just pulling in. It's full of people! And cars are filling the parking lots. Back to your booths!"

Everyone scurried to the stands outside their stores, while residents of Stoneybridge started buying. The holiday atmosphere was contagious. The marching band even started playing a medley of Christmas songs, the first people heard this year.

Aimee searched out Gerry again.

He wasn't there!

Panic rose inside her.

She looked all around.

He wasn't anywhere.

Just when she was ready to run to his store and start searching for him there, the door swung wide open.

Gerry, along with his sister, niece and nephew, and several of his employees were bringing out the biggest cake Aimee had ever seen. A replica of the Mayflower!

After thanking Mayor Brown, she jumped down from the crate and ran over to Gerry.

She didn't care that she had an audience. The whole wide world could know her business now. She just had to speak to Gerry and hear with her own ears that all of this meant he was willing to give her another try, give their love another chance. She believed it did, but she had to know for sure before one more moment passed. She tentatively reached out and touched his arm. As he was turning toward her, she didn't wait for him to face her when she asked, "Gerry…does this mean you forgive me?" For a split second, she held her breath. It seemed to her that everyone around them did, too.

He didn't keep her—or any of them—waiting. His smile began in his eyes. They crinkled at the corners—while his irises shone like stars—then the smile encompassed his lips. She felt a rush of pleasure, felt the sensation of coming home. Without taking his gaze from hers, he spoke to Sabrina. "Sis, take care of things here, okay? We'll be back in a bit." Not waiting for a reply, he took hold of Aimee's hand and guided her into the relative privacy of Uncle Gerry's Cakerie.

Just as the door closed, Gerry tossed his hat onto the counter and, wrapping his arms around her, pulled her close.

Her entire body quivered with happiness at being held in his welcoming embrace again.

"Gerry, I'm so sorry..." she whispered against his ear. "I said terrible things...accused you of unfounded—"

"Shh," he said soothingly into the hollow of her neck. "It's in the past. It was an unfortunate misunderstanding."

"But Gerry, I called you a thief. How can you forgive me?"

"Easy. I love you." His husky voice was a caress. Moving a quarter-step back and placing his forehead against hers, he continued. "And what is love if not forgiving over and over again, especially when forgiveness is requested? We humans aren't perfect, are we?"

"I'm so sorry," she whispered again.

"And your being sorry, and telling me so, makes forgiving you—" he chuckled, the sound coming from low in his throat, as he motioned to all the confections in the display cases around them "—a piece of cake."

She laughed, delighted by the way he had a knack for turning sour situations into sweet ones. "But Gerry, about the supermarket contract—"

"I really didn't know you were in the running for it. I'm sorry about that, about moving to Stoneybridge and taking it away from you. James Monroe is gone this week for the Thanksgiving holiday but I have an appointment with him next Monday. I plan to tell him I don't want it, that it should go to you."

"Gerry, no! I want you to have it."

"But—"

She hushed him with a kiss. "Gerry, the only reason I wanted that contract was to save the Patisserie, to pay back Uncle Cain. That reason no longer exists."

"But—"

She cut him off again. "I've had a lot of time to think this last week. The Cakerie's product really is perfect for Northeast Supermarket's Main Street Bakery. Please, don't let this opportunity go. Not for me when all I really want is to keep the Patisserie running in exactly the same manner it has for the last seventy years." She motioned outside at the fair. "And with this beautiful gift, this fair you organized, I have a chance to do it."

For a moment he didn't say a thing. His eyes searched hers and she knew he was endeavoring to see if she was telling the truth. "Yes, Gerry. Honest. I want you to have the contract. I really don't want to change the Patisserie. I never did."

"We can talk about this later after—"

"—No, Gerry. It needs to be finished now. Nothing in this world is more important to me than you. Certainly not a *business* contract," she said and grimaced. "I still can't believe that I accused you of such terrible things."

"Just promise me one thing," he said, with a meaningful twinkle in his gaze. "When I do something for which you will have to forgive me—because I'm certain that sometime within the next seventy or so years I will—I'm asking you in advance to please forgive me."

A smile trembled on her lips. *Seventy or so years?* "What are you saying?"

"Not saying, Aimee. Asking. Will you marry me and help me find 'life in pink'?"

"Even after I was so mean to you, after I called you—"

He silenced her lips with his own and whispered against them, "Will…you…marry…me?"

"Yes, Gerry," she returned without pause. "If you don't mind my coming to you with an injured heart and an imperfect soul, marrying you is exactly what I'd like to do."

"You're wrong about one thing," he said. "You have a *giving* heart and a *loving* soul." He lightly ran his fingertips over her forehead. "My dear, dearest Aimee."

She cupped his face with her hands. "Well, then, finding 'life in pink' with you, Gerry, is exactly what I'd like to do during the next seventy or so years." She stood on her tiptoes and pulling him down to her, just before their lips met again she said, "But for now—"

And until the marching band came by and played "City Sidewalks" loudly right outside Uncle Gerry's Cakerie door, they didn't leave each other's arms.

"I think—" Gerry nodded toward the bustling street.

"Yeah. We'd better get out there and lend a hand. It's in honor of the Patisserie, after all. And in less than seven hours," she said with a grimace, "Uncle Cain will be here to collect." Not even that thought or the one that followed—that Uncle Cain should be the *first* person she told about being engaged to Gerry rather than the one she dreaded seeing—could dampen Aimee's spirits.

They walked out onto Main Street to the best Thanksgiving holiday mood anyone could ever remember in Stoneybridge. Gerry sold all his cakes, plus big chunks of the Mayflower cake, while Aimee went up and down the road helping where needed and just loving the time she spent with her friends and neighbors who were determined to keep the Patisserie for her…and for them.

***

Shortly before five o'clock that afternoon, Uncle Cain and Grasping Gertrude arrived.

The sidewalk outside the Patisserie became a stage. All the townspeople hushed as Uncle Cain walked toward the store.

"Hello, Ebenezer," Miss Maggie greeted him. She'd known him all his life. She always used the name his mother and father had given him.

He sent her a hesitant nod, and as he and Gertrude came to stand in front of Aimee, he asked, "Aimee, what's going on?"

"The people of Main Street, Uncle, don't want to see the Patisserie closed down. Without my knowing it, my friends and neighbors—" she swept her right arm out toward everyone there "—organized a 'Save the Patisserie' fair." Reaching behind her, she picked up a large pink Patisserie pastry box—the biggest the Patisserie had—and handed it to her uncle.

"What's this?"

"Are you trying to buy us off with sweets?" Gertrude asked and shook her head in disdain.

Aimee ignored her. To her uncle, she said, "Open it."

He did. He gasped. So did Gertrude. It was packed with cash and checks already made out to him, Cain Bell.

"It's short by $449," Aimee went on to explain. "But if you can give me and the good people of Main Street another quarter of an hour, we should have that money raised, too." Aimee had already added a check of her own for all the money she'd saved to repay her uncle.

For a moment, one that became too long to even be called a moment, Uncle Cain stood there, silently holding the box.

Aimee was bracing herself for a sarcastic remark. All the people on Main Street were.

But when the silence continued, Grasping Gertrude spoke up. "Absolutely not, Aimee," she answered for her husband, ever true to Aimee's nickname for her. "The contract clearly states that the *full* amount has to be paid by 5:00 p.m. today." She glanced at her gold Rolex. "That's in three minutes. If it's not, the Patisserie becomes my husband's to do with whatever he wishes."

Not even the murmur of disbelief that rose from the crowd and traveled to the very top and bottom of the street affected Grasping Gertrude's stance.

Aimee glanced at Gerry. *Do you see what I've been putting up with for all these years?*

Gerry nodded and reaching into his chef coat's pocket pulled out a blank check. He held it up.

She could tell that he'd been prepared for precisely this occurrence. He was going to give her the final amount. She shook her head. She couldn't let him do that, too.

"Aimee." She heard Lottie speak from behind her. "I would like to add the necessary amount. I can't imagine not having your fresh *macarons* in my house every day to enjoy and serve to guests." She already had her checkbook out and was writing the check.

"Let's split the difference," Mrs. Fonteyn quickly suggested to Lottie. She had cash in hand.

"Yes!" Miss Maggie agreed. "I will add to the amount too."

That started a Main Street murmur with everyone offering to add ten or twenty dollars to reach the $449. Feelings of being flabbergasted once again overtook Aimee. The love this town felt for her and the Patisserie was overwhelming.

"No." Uncle Cain's voice suddenly boomed, silencing all and drawing everyone's attention back to him. The clock in the town hall tower began striking the hour of five.

Aimee felt a sinking sensation in her stomach. She groaned. Had he been quiet in order to pass the minutes? So that she'd miss the deadline? Disgust filled her. It was just Uncle Cain's style…

But when he gave a respectful nod to Gerry, then to Lottie, then to Mrs. Fonteyn, and smiled at Miss Maggie—a real smile, not a sardonic one—hope began to work its way through Aimee's mind.

Before the bell finished the toll of five, he reached into his pocket and pulled out a wad of cash. With everyone staring at him in astonishment—including his overbearing wife who was momentarily rendered speechless—he removed five crisp hundred-dollar bills and put them in the box as the bell finished tolling.

His gaze met Aimee's. He had a look in his eyes that reminded Aimee of Grand-mère—a slight mischievous gleam coupled with affection. People always said he resembled his mother, but until this very moment, Aimee had never seen it. As he took the box from her, there was no mockery in his eyes, only peace.

He spoke loudly, so that everyone could easily hear. "In front of all these good people, Aimee Hart, I hereby declare, so there is no doubt in anyone's mind—" he glanced pointedly at his wife "—that your debt, dear niece, is paid in full. The Patisserie is yours and will always be yours." Murmurs of astonishment rose from the street. It was an organic sound of joy mixed with disbelief, and it slowly bloomed like an exquisite flower opening beneath the rays of the sun.

But when Uncle Cain returned the box to Aimee, everyone, including Aimee, gasped. No one knew what to make of it. She tentatively took the box. *What was this about? What did it mean?* When the Main Street audience had quieted down, her uncle spoke again, "Please take this money, Aimee, and use it as the seed money to set up a special trust fund, in my mother's name, for the stores and churches and other buildings here on Main Street."

Shocked silence reigned on Main Street.

"I will add a considerable amount to it each December, starting next month. That way," he said, turning to the crowd and speaking even louder, "if any Main Street proprietors ever find themselves in the position you did, Aimee—" he turned back to her "—they won't have to go to uncaring people, such as I was, to ask for a loan that might result in losing their stores."

Aimee was still speechless. The whole town was. It was like the ending of *A Christmas Carol* with Ebenezer Scrooge becoming a fine and generous gentleman.

The bandleader seemed to think that, too. The band struck up, "Thank You Very Much," from the 1970s musical, *Scrooge,* and just like in that movie, everyone started dancing in the street.

The Patisserie was saved!

But more than that, all the establishments along Main Street had a fighting chance to survive, even with malls, pestilence, storms, franchises and internet buying making life hard for private owners. They'd been working to save the Patisserie today but, with her uncle's unexpected kind gesture, had actually taken a big step toward saving the very future of

Stoneybridge's historical commercial center, the heart of their town.

Uncle Cain smiled out at the crowd.

"You've made everyone very happy, Uncle Cain." Aimee paused. "Especially me."

With the look of Grand-mère still in his eyes, he leaned toward her and said, "If you don't mind, Aimee, I'd like to come here again next week, sit back in one of those wonderful *fauteuils* my mother transported all the way from France, and taste some of the lovely *macarons* I know you bake just like she did."

With tears in her eyes, Aimee reached out and pulled her uncle into a quick hug. "You are always welcome, Uncle Cain."

He stepped back and almost as if she could see it, years of hard scales seemed to fall from him. Softly he requested, "Please call me Uncle *Ebenezer* from now on."

Aimee could only nod. He was finally that "rock," that "stone of help" his father had wanted him to become when he gave him that beautiful and meaningful Biblical name. Her throat was constricting. When she finally got the words out, they were barely more than a whisper. "Uncle *Ebenezer*. Thank you." She was so grateful for the miraculous change in her relative.

Gerry came to stand beside her. He placed his arm around Aimee's shoulder as if it were the most natural thing in the world. It was.

"Uncle Ebenezer." She smiled at Gerry who lifted his brows at the use of the different name. "I'd like to introduce you to Gerry Mitchell." She paused. "My fiancé." *She got her wish—unlikely though it had seemed that morning—that her uncle would be the first person she told!*

"It's a pleasure to meet you, son," Uncle Ebenezer said.

"The pleasure is mine, sir."

Uncle Ebenezer looked back at Aimee. He smiled wryly. "Might I expect an invitation to your wedding?"

Aimee didn't just feel tears now. This time they overflowed. She leaned close to her uncle and while whispering in his ear, glanced at Gerry for confirmation. "Only if you promise to give me away?"

The older man looked as if the best gift in the world had been handed to him. At Gerry's encouraging nod, he said, "It will be my greatest joy."

"Cain!" Gertrude finally found her voice. She was livid. "What do you mean by handing all that money back? And losing the Patisserie?"

He sighed and Aimee realized, as he turned from her to his wife, that unlike Ebenezer Scrooge in the storybook, her Uncle Ebenezer had a battle-axe wife he had to mollify. "Gerty dear, it's mine to do with whatever I want. It's time to have fun—*and* start giving away some of the money I've accumulated through the years. You can help me do that, my dear. From now on, instead of making money, we'll become philanthropists. After all," he said, winking at Aimee before guiding his complaining wife away from Main Street, "as my mother always said, if the wealthy people of the world shared what they've made with their fellow humans, there would be no poverty. God gave us a way to combat poverty. But people are often greedy. *We've* been greedy, my dear. But no longer. To improve the lives of those around us—that's how our money will be spent from now on."

Gertrude was quiet for a moment, as she seemed to assimilate the change in her husband's attitude. Suddenly, she nodded. "Well, I guess we can take any giving we do off our taxes."

Ebenezer threw back his head and laughed. "Not quite the spirit I had in mind, my dear, but it's a start."

Aimee and Gerry stood arm in arm and watched them go.

"Your uncle's got his work cut out, trying to reform his wife."

Aimee nodded. "Yes, but he's just as determined as she is." She turned to Gerry. "And after today, I think I saw that enough of Grand-mère lives in him for Uncle Ebenezer—that's his real name by the way, not Cain," she explained, "to become the person he wants to be. The person he should be."

"Today was definitely a good beginning."

Aimee nodded but as she watched her uncle's retreating back, her gaze was caught by the rays filling the sky around the setting sun. "Gerry, look!"

The world above Main Street was bathed in every imaginable shade of pink—cherry blossom, coral, florescent and French... The sky was a palette of deep, light, bold and pale pinks.

"Life in pink..." Gerry whispered.

Aimee stood on tiptoes and just before her lips touched his, she whispered, "...is where I want us to always be."

A Letter to Our Readers

Dear Reader,

"Life in pink…" describes the wonderful happy way I feel when everything is going well in the lives of my family and friends. And to be able to sit back and step into the lives of characters in a romance novel that is guaranteed to have a happily-ever-after ending is something that always puts me in that good place. It's my hope that this book has done this for you.

This past year and a half was hard for the entire world when everything looked more gray than pink. On a personal level, there were tremendous highs and lows in the ebb and flow of my family; the highest points being getting this book ready for publication, and, by the grace of God, the complete healing of three family members from very serious illnesses.

Sara and I hope that the reading of this American tale gave you joy and left you with a very good feeling!

If so, would you please take a few moments of your valuable time and leave a review on our Amazon detail page (where you bought the book). Reviews are very important to us; we read every one and appreciate them all greatly.

Just go to Amazon, type in the ASIN (B096HPZLZ7) or the name of this book, click on the image, and it will take you directly to the correct page. Scroll down more than half way to where on the left side you see, "**Review this product.**" Click in the box just below it where it says "Write a customer review" and it will take you to the "Create Review" page. A few steps to be sure… But know that it will make Sara and me smile to see a comment from you! We treasure each and every one!

Many thanks!

All the best to you and yours,

Melanie
MelanieAnnAuthor@gmail.com

About the Authors

Melanie Ann:

From a very young age, Melanie travelled throughout the USA. She has visited almost every state and lived in several of them. From California to Maine, from Florida to Washington and all the lovely states in between, she has stopped off at USA Main Streets, visited their cafés, hotels, stores, civic centers, parks, diners, talked with the townsfolk, and dreamed of the day when she would write a story set in a town that would be the culmination of all these lovely locations. When, as a teen, she moved to Madison, New Jersey, it felt to her as if she'd moved to Disneyland's Main Street USA, and so the stage was set for Stoneybridge, the fictional town in the "Saving Main Street" series. *The Store Next Door* is the first in this series.

Melanie has two children, Sara, who co-authored *The Store Next Door*, and James (PJKabos.com).

Melanie has published many books with a major American publishing house, but she is now very excited to branch out and go the independent route with her daughter and beloved brother to publish books using Amazon's great tools.

Email: MelanieAnnAuthor@gmail.com

Sara B. Bentley:

Sara became a writer the unconventional way—by studying fashion design in Manhattan, New York City and Florence, Italy. The two might not seem readily related however for Sara it's always been about the story. For her, there's really no difference whether she's telling stories through illustrations and garments, or through computer and keyboard. Sara has sold romantic comedy screenplays to production companies in the U.K. and has completed fiction novels for adults as well as a number of children's stories.

Sara likes writing, drawing, yoga, tennis, cats, dogs, good food, Greek islands, New York City, painting and taking long hikes. The steeper the hills, the better!

Website: sarabiancabentley.com

Books by the Authors

Melanie Ann and Sara B. Bentley have joined up again to write another book, but this time…a time and space travel novel for children. **The Skeleton Key Keepers:** ***Clues to the Chalice*** is a fun, fast-moving, mystery adventure novel for kids ages seven and up.

Both print and ebook versions are sold exclusively on Amazon. Go to Amazon, type in the ASIN (below) or name, click on the image and it will take you directly to the correct page!

Kindle ASIN: B098215G73
Paperback ASIN: B0982YTC71

PJ Kabos Vanilla Olive Oil Cake

Gerry Mitchell used this recipe—except for the measurements!— for his Mayflower cake.

Ingredients

For Cake Batter:
1 cup PJ Kabos Extra Virgin Olive Oil
1¼ cups sugar (or to taste)
4 eggs
1 cups milk
2 cups all-purpose flour
1 teaspoon baking soda
2 teaspoons baking powder
1 teaspoon vanilla extract

For Chocolate Topping:
3 chocolate bars—large (at least 100 g), dark (at least 70%), and of a fine quality

Putting it together!

Preheat the oven to 200°C (400°F). Oil and flour 3 baking loaf pans—approximately 8.5 x 3.5 inches (22 x 8.5 cm). Note: Any size or type of baking pan may be used in place of the 3 loaf pans…just make sure to adjust for the rising of the cake; i.e the batter should not be too much above the middle of the side of the pan.

For the Batter: In a large bowl, pour in PJ Kabos Extra Virgin Olive Oil. Add the sugar and beat—either with an electric mixer or by hand—for 2 minutes. Add the eggs one by one, mixing the batter well with each addition. Add the vanilla and milk. Mix. In a second bowl mix together the flour, baking soda and baking powder. Slowly add the dry ingredients to the large bowl. Beat on high for 1 to 2 minutes.

Pour evenly into the prepared loaf pans.

Bake in the lower rack of the oven for approximately 40 minutes. Test for doneness with a toothpick—when the toothpick is stabbed in the middle of a cake and comes out clean, it's done.

Set the cakes aside to cool.

For Chocolate Topping (optional):

Ten minutes before serving, heat the chocolate bars in a double broiler (a smaller pot—which has the chocolate—inside a larger pot—which holds boiling water—works just as well) to melt the chocolate. Using a teaspoon spread a thin layer of melted chocolate over the cooled cakes. It may be served while the chocolate is still warm or after it has cooled.

Enjoy!

See pjkabos.com for more recipes using olive oil as well as great information about extra virgin olive oil.

Made in United States
North Haven, CT
20 May 2023

36770132R00166